Under the Tamarind Tree

Under the Tamarind Tree

NIGAR ALAM

G. P. PUTNAM'S SONS
NEW YORK

PUTNAM
— EST. 1838 —

G. P. PUTNAM'S SONS
Publishers Since 1838
An imprint of Penguin Random House LLC
penguinrandomhouse.com

Library of Congress Control Number:
2023018679

Hardcover ISBN: 9780593544075
Ebook ISBN: 9780593544099
Proprietary ISBN: 9780593717707

Printed in the United States of America
1st Printing

Book design by Laura K. Corless

Interior art: Tamarind leaves © Nublee bin Shamsu Bahar / shutterstock.com.

For my parents, whose stories live inside me

Under
the
Tamarind
Tree

Prologue

Nine-year-old Rozeena stared ahead, squinting in the dark at the hordes of shouting people racing toward her family. Were those sticks and spears raised above their heads? Why were they so angry?

Her mother grabbed Rozeena's wrist and pulled her off the tonga. She landed hard on her knees, but her father didn't stop to check the bleeding skin below her frock's hem. Her mother only yanked harder, pulling and dragging until Rozeena got up running. She had to run so fast she had no breath left to ask why they couldn't go home. Wouldn't they be safe if they just went back? It wasn't even far.

The house in front of Rozeena exploded into flames.

Fire leapt into the night sky, and dense smoke entered her nose, scorching her insides. September's humidity already dripped streams of sweat down her face and back. Now it all bubbled to a boil.

Rozeena spun to her mother. Light from the flames swirled on her face. She stood frozen in place, confusion and fear contorting her mouth into pained twists. Swiveling on her feet, Rozeena searched for her father and Faysal. But they weren't there. Bodies with bundles of clothing, and suitcases, and children in their arms ran around haphazardly, their screaming faces blurred by darkness.

She turned back to her mother. "Ammi, I can't find . . ."

But a mass of people was racing toward them now, from the direction of the fire. Every second, the men grew closer and louder as did their thunderous, angry yelling. Why? Her mother didn't wait to find out. She turned and ran, her hold like an iron cuff on Rozeena's wrist.

Crowds pushed against them from the front and back, until they ripped right through her mother's tight grip.

Rozeena was pitched away.

Bodies shoved against her, colliding from all sides as she scrambled to her feet trying to keep her head up, eyes searching. Two women ran toward her, mouths open, arms waving overhead. Were they neighbors? Would they take her to her mother? But instead of stopping, the women charged into Rozeena, throwing her flat on her back. Gasping to catch her breath, she tried to stand up against the wave of bigger, stronger bodies, but her already bleeding knees fell hard on the ground, over and over.

"Rozee? Rozee!"

Her head shot up. "Here! Here!"

She spun around, searching, and saw Faysal. His face grew in size running toward her, the whites of his eyes reflecting the light from the burning house behind her.

"Rozee!" he screamed again. "Run, Rozee, run!"

Where to? Behind her was the raging fire and the approaching mob, and in front, from a lane across the street, a bigger, even louder group of men emerged.

Faysal pushed her toward the fire, pointing at the house next to it, a safe house where their parents were headed. It would lead to another house, behind it.

"Another house? A safe house?"

He shook her by the shoulders and aimed her toward it. "That way! Just run, Rozee, run!"

Without looking back, she ran like she'd never run before.

That was the last time Rozeena saw her brother.

1

NOW, 2019

Rozeena tightens her fingers around the mobile phone, but it slips down her damp palm. Her other hand flies up to meet it, pushing the phone back to her ear.

"Your voice," she says, a bit breathless. "It's the same." She leans forward in her veranda chair, as if it'll bring her closer to him.

Haaris laughs softly. "Well, I suppose it's the one thing that remains the same, Rozee."

Her throat constricts at the nickname. Only elders or close friends call her Rozee. At eighty-one, she doesn't have many left.

"Is everything all right? Are you all right?" She frowns at the black-and-white tiles under her slippered feet.

"Yes, yes. I'm well," he says. "Just finished breakfast. Around nine o'clock in the morning here."

In Minnesota. She's gotten a little news of him from friends of friends over the years and now detects the slight change in his accent, from the British English Rozeena still speaks, to the harder "r" of the Americans in *morning here*.

Her shoulders relax somewhat at hearing he's not calling from his deathbed, and she sits back in her polished rosewood chair. She hadn't recognized the number flashing on her screen when she'd answered the phone. A call with a US country code could've been any one of her old colleagues or distant relatives.

But it'd been Haaris.

She realizes the extent of her surprise as she wipes her hands one by one on her kameez. The soft cotton of her long, blue tunic absorbs the moisture of her palms, but her heart still races, heating her from within. Reaching down, she plucks away the fabric of her shalwar from the backs of her knees. Her face feels damp as well, though Karachi's evening breeze is cool as always, even in July.

She hasn't heard from Haaris in fifty-four years.

Gusts from the Arabian Sea rush toward her, setting the giant palm branches into a powerful spin in the far corner of her garden. She lifts her face to the evening, calming herself to regain control. Silver strands of hair whip in the breeze and she tries to shove them back into her low bun with one hand, but they resist. Let it go, she tells herself, and leaves them to dance on her cheeks.

"I can hear the wind," Haaris says, incredulous. "I can actually hear the Karachi wind."

She smiles. "Yes, it's as loud as ever, but only here closer to the sea. The old neighborhood is congested now, tall buildings and complexes of flats all built up where there were spacious houses." Our houses, she wants to say, but instead says, "I'll be going inside soon. It's past seven o'clock in the evening here." She hopes her statement hurries him into explaining why he's called.

The sun has already dropped low behind the line of tall, pencil-like ashok trees on the right side of her garden. Soon, the call to prayer will burst from loudspeakers at mosques near and far. Five times a day, the azaan thankfully drowns out the continuous buzzing of her neighbors' air conditioners. Beyond her boundary walls all the new houses are giant two-story, sand-colored concrete boxes made wider and noisier by air-conditioning units clinging to every side. Rozeena's single-story home, one of the older ones in this newer neighborhood, is well-balanced. The house that lies behind the veranda is equal in size to the garden that lies in front.

"It's raining here today," Haaris says finally and quietly. "It's not a rainy state, Minnesota. But these days it's raining inside and out."

"Inside and out?"

He exhales audibly. "Three months ago, my grandson died."

A soft gasp escapes her lips. "Oh, Haaris, how . . . I can't . . . I'm so sorry," she flounders. The death of a child—but not death in general—still shocks her. She remembers that dreadful saying, *The smallest coffins are the heaviest.*

After a few moments of silence Haaris speaks, his voice conversational again even though Rozeena heard it catch a second ago. Men of his time are masters at bottling up their emotions.

"Has it rained there yet?" he says. "Or is it waiting for the fifteenth?"

She smiles. He remembers the unpredictable arrival of the monsoon season, unpredictable in its intensity too, sometimes flooding the streets and other times only muddying the dust clinging to leaves. Up north they get the majority of the rains—in the fertile valleys of the Indus River and even further north over the massive Himalayas. But when Karachi does get showers, it somehow rarely happens before July 15. Families can confidently plan all sorts of outdoor events before then, including elaborate weddings.

"You remember," she says.

"I remember everything, Rozee."

She searches his words, his tone, his diction. What is he really saying? Does he want her to apologize, or is he going to?

"But right now, I have a favor to ask," he continues.

"Oh?" Her guard is up instantly.

"I have a granddaughter, his sister. Her name is Zara. She's fifteen years old and in Karachi these days visiting with her parents, my son and his wife. They visit every summer." He pauses. "Zara says she wants to do something by herself in Karachi, some 'good' while she's there. Her parents of course are scared to let her out of their sight, after her brother."

"Yes, of course."

"So, we're trying to find something very safe for Zara to do." He takes a deep breath. "You remember my oldest sister, Apa, who still lives in Karachi? Well, she mentioned you need a temporary maali."

"A maali? How does she know?" Confused, Rozeena wonders why her servant situation is being discussed.

"I think Apa heard through a mutual friend," Haaris says. "You know how news travels." Rozeena and Apa don't socialize directly, but it's a small world, this city of over fifteen million.

And Haaris's information is correct. Rozeena does need someone to tend to her garden now that Kareem, who's worked for her for more than fifteen years, has fractured his tibia. A speeding rickshaw crashed into his bicycle last Wednesday when he was on his way to his fifth house for gardening work. The following morning, the eldest of his six sons arrived at Rozeena's house, ready to fulfill his father's duties. Of course she sent the eleven-year-old away, straight to the school in which she'd enrolled him, and with a stern warning not to miss a single day.

How will they be anything but maalis if they don't go to school? she wanted to say to Kareem that evening in the hospital. But Kareem knew this well and was grateful for Rozeena's help over the years. Rozeena just hoped that Kareem's other employers would also continue to pay his wages and keep his family afloat.

"Since you need a maali," Haaris says, "I was thinking it would be wonderful if Zara could do the work and be your temporary maali."

The phone feels hotter against her cheek. Her breath comes faster. Haaris has gone from staying away and silent for more than fifty years to suddenly injecting himself into her life by depositing his granddaughter at her doorstep.

Why?

It's too close, too dangerous, for herself and for her son.

Haaris explains how Zara would do the maali's work, and her parents would worry less if she worked in a home like her own grandfather's. Rozeena stops herself from saying that their homes, like their lives, were never alike.

"And Apa knows this?" she says instead, doubting his older sister has agreed. Apa would never sully the family reputation by allowing her grandniece to be a maali, even if just for the summer.

"Apa will tell herself a comfortable and acceptable version of Zara's time at your house." He pauses, before almost pleading. "Will you do it, Rozee?"

She's too surprised by both his telephone call and his odd request to answer immediately.

"It would help," he continues.

"I'm certain Apa can find something else for Zara to do."

"Yes, maybe. But I don't know if Zara would agree. I'm not saying she's being difficult. No, no. Of course I don't mean that." He sighs. "But what she's gone through . . . Well, you can imagine, can't you, Rozee?"

She nods into the phone, and Haaris continues as if he can see her.

"That's why I want Zara to be with you, under your care. There's no one else who can help her like you can."

Rozeena nods again. She has always taken care of people. It's who she is, even before she was a trained doctor, and even now, years after retirement. But the risk is too high.

"Most of the people I knew in Karachi have moved out, or moved on," Haaris says. "Of course you don't have to agree to this, especially after all the . . . the quiet of these past years."

The past is exactly what she fears. It's what can destroy her little family, crush her son.

"I can't do this, Haaris."

"Please, Rozee. Please, just think about it. For Zara. For her sake."

For her sake. For his sake. It's the past all over again. She pushes it away to focus on practical matters.

"How long is she in Karachi?"

"Well, her parents have already taken so much leave from their work this year. Most likely they'll have to come back to Minnesota before Zara's summer vacation is over. But then I'll go to Karachi to travel back with her."

Rozeena's breath catches and simultaneously the azaan erupts in the air. Another call to prayer starts within seconds, from a farther mosque. Then another from the opposite direction. Echoes surround Rozeena like old memories rolling toward her.

Haaris is coming back.

She swallows hard, but her mouth remains dry.

He doesn't speak until the loudest azaan has ended. "That was beautiful," he says then, and she imagines his eyes closed, his dark lashes long and resting on his cheeks as he listens to the azaan from the other side of the world.

After an entirely sleepless night, Rozeena gives her answer the next morning.

Starting today, Zara will be Rozeena's maali.

Haaris is grateful, and Rozeena is scared. There will have to be strict rules and schedules, so her son and Zara never meet, so the past has no chance of entering her dear son's life.

In reply to Haaris's thank-you, Rozeena types out:

It's for the child.

She repeats the statement to herself over and over again. Perhaps by bearing the risk to help young Zara, Rozeena will finally be able to atone for what happened fifty-four years ago.

Later that day, after proper introductions are shared, Zara's parents wave through the rear window of a white BMW as it slowly pulls away from Rozeena's house. Initially Zara's parents had been apprehensive, but by the end of the visit, they'd approved of Rozeena, her lone existence in a house with a staff of servants, her past life as a pediatrician, her location so close to theirs, and of course her friendship with Haaris. Zara had nodded at everything her parents said, including how interested she was in gardening, a new but true passion. They're staying with family only two streets down, but Rozeena notices before they leave that Zara's parents' anxious faces and shaky palms seem as if they're leaving something precious far, far behind.

Rozeena isn't surprised, of course. They've suffered the worst kind of loss already. Their son was in a friend's car when it happened. All the other boys survived the crash.

She glances up at Zara now, tall like her father, and like Haaris. She wears black leggings under a light pink kameez like girls do in Karachi these days, and her straight dark hair falls well below her shoulders. She looks quite grown up with it parted down the center and framing her oval face. But she waves back at her parents like a child, smiling and swinging her raised arm side to side so it's visible even from a distance. As soon as the car turns the corner though, her smile fades as her hand falls.

"Should we go back inside now?" Rozeena says.

Zara's eyes are big and brown, also strikingly like Haaris. "You can't even tell it's a desert here." She looks up and down the road. "My friends always ask me if Karachi is just, like, sand dunes and camels and stuff."

They stand in a bubble of abundant sweet jasmine from the thick rows of bushes growing outside all the homes' boundary walls. Tall coconut palms, ashok trees, and giant neem trees stand inside the walls, some looming over sparkling swimming pools. The street is otherwise empty as it is in the evenings, with only a hint of diesel from the main road where buses honk and rickshaws sputter in the distance.

"Well, I'm sure you've ridden camels on the beach at Sea View." Rozeena turns to lead Zara back inside. "And it's certainly a desert here. If I don't take care, a lot of care, all of this will shrivel up and die," she says, stopping inside the gate to gesture at her garden. Her maali does all the hard work, of course, but Rozeena manages it.

Zara joins her at the bottom of the driveway, and Rozeena's driver, Pervez, pulls the black metal gate shut behind them. Other than the long driveway leading up to the car porch on the right side of the property, the rest of the land is neatly cut in half, with a large rectangular garden in front of the house. A wide wooden pergola juts out from its center above the tiled veranda.

Rozeena cuts across the grass on her way to the veranda and points out plants and bushes that are in immediate need.

"The organic fertilizer is coming on Wednesday, but before then the water tanker best arrive, otherwise—"

"They'll all shrivel up and die," Zara interjects, and quickly bites her lip.

Rozeena says nothing until she's settled in a veranda chair. The change underfoot from grass to tile always requires extra attention. She knows full well the dangers of broken hips at her age. As she smooths her peach-colored cotton kameez over her lap, she pulls the matching chiffon dopatta down to form a V on her chest. The breeze cools her throat as she considers how Haaris's granddaughter is not really the silent, agreeable girl she was in front of her parents.

As Zara leans back on the other wooden chair now, Rozeena says, "What did your grandfather tell you about me?"

Zara shrugs. "Nothing," and then adds, "What did he tell you about me?"

Straight to the point, like Rozeena herself. "He told me your brother died. I'm so sorry."

"Well, that's me." Zara raises her hand like someone called her name in school.

Rozeena imitates the gesture, not unkindly. "Me too."

Zara's mouth is open, as if unsure of what to say.

Rozeena shifts in her chair. Even after all this time, it's difficult to talk about. "I lost my brother too, long ago."

"Oh, I'm sorry." Zara bows her head.

"Thank you. No one's ever said that to me before," and to answer Zara's puzzled look, adds, "Those were different times."

She doesn't say that in those days, loss wasn't spoken of, perhaps because there was too much all around, and for too many families. Instead of remembering the pain and releasing the anguish, they used that energy to protect whatever was left behind.

2

THEN, 1964

Ten Days Before

Rozeena woke thinking of Haaris. In one more day he'd be back from Liverpool, and then she'd know, or at least begin to discover, what he'd meant by his last goodbye.

The four of them had gathered in Zohair's garden that night—Aalya from upstairs, Rozeena from next door, and Haaris from across the street—neighborhood friends who might never have met. Three of them had crossed the border seventeen years ago with their families, refugees of Partition who by chance landed here, on short Prince Road. Only Haaris's family had firm roots in Karachi. Seven generations of amassing wealth had established the Shahs among the powerful elite, their branches spreading past their import/export business and into local government as well.

But as always, that night in Zohair's garden Haaris was simply the friend they'd grown up with. As he told them he'd be back in only six months this time, his eyes lingered on Rozeena's. She'd held his gaze, and her breath, until he turned away, slowly.

Now, at the end of the day, Rozeena set the thought aside for the hundredth time. There were more important things. She pulled off her stethoscope and looped it around her neck.

"Your lungs are clear," she said to Gul, Aalya's maid from next door. "There's no wheeze at all. Are you in any pain?"

They sat facing each other on the only two chairs in Rozeena's free clinic, the tiny storeroom tucked in the corner of the boundary wall at the back of her house. Gul looked as she always did in her clean shalwar kameez, with her hair in a neat, tight braid down her back.

Aalya's mother did most of the housework herself and only called upon Gul once in a while for cleaning or washing. It was a convenient arrangement for both since young Gul had no other work. She'd only recently married and arrived from the village to join her husband, Abdul, who was Zohair's cook in the downstairs portion of the house. Abdul and Gul lived in the servants' quarters behind the house.

Rozeena's gaze fell to Gul's leg which wouldn't stop bouncing as her eyes flicked around the room. When they hovered on the single window again, Rozeena turned to check it. But there was nothing outside except the night made darker by the tamarind tree, so overgrown it shrouded most of the sandy lot at the back of the house. Even the old wooden swing hanging from the branches was hidden in the shadows.

"You were having dinner. I shouldn't have come and—"

"It's all right," Rozeena said. "But tell me, what's bothering you?" She planted an encouraging smile on her face, trying to erase the exhaustion Gul must've noticed and assumed was from a busy day.

Gul didn't know that Rozeena had seen only one patient in her new pediatric clinic downtown. She hadn't told her mother, of course, because one patient meant nothing when every day brought more expenses to the household, the latest being her father's old car that had started knocking at every left turn. But the blue Morris was still running, so Rozeena avoided discussing the ominous sound with her mother. After the sewage pipe burst last month, Rozeena had noticed a shift in her mother. Uncharacteristic panic had spread across her face as they stood behind the house that day, foul-smelling waste rising from the earth and bubbling up at their feet.

"We'll have it repaired," Rozeena had said quickly, waiting for her mother's veneer of strength to return.

Instead, her mother's spine had curved as if weighted down. "How much more can we fix? Soon it'll be just this, and no house." She shook her head at the rising rot. "And then Sweetie will have her way."

It was the first time in years that Rozeena witnessed her mother's apprehension, and that her mother mentioned the future they'd been trying to avoid since Rozeena's father died of a sudden heart attack eleven years ago. But now, every new expense could be the final blow, the one that would bring her mother's brother, Shehzad, but mostly his wife, Sweetie, to their front gate ready to snatch away their life and independence in Karachi.

Because what would people say if Shehzad's own sister was living in such conditions, with the house crumbling around her?

Shehzad and Sweetie were bent on avoiding any missteps that could cause disfavor among their new crowd. They'd risen in society over the years and had managed to secure a place in the top tier, for themselves and their children. Shehzad ran the Lahore office of Sweetie's family business, but Sweetie ran Shehzad and their family life, determined to shine worthy of their status in society.

Rozeena and her mother's downward slide would definitely be a blemish. The only respectable solution would be to swoop in and take them to Lahore.

Until now Rozeena's mother had refused her brother's help in order to stay free of the strict expectations that would certainly come with it. For one, Sweetie would've arranged Rozeena's marriage in her late teens or early twenties, like she had for her own daughters. It was the way things were done, she'd say. Girls didn't need careers. They needed to get married at the right time.

And if Sweetie had her way now, would Rozeena be allowed to work, earn her own money, make her own decisions?

Facing her mother over the rising heat of sewage, Rozeena had insisted she'd have the pipe repaired in no time. Her mother had finally pushed back her slight shoulders and lifted her chin. But after that day, Rozeena noticed her mother's shoulders curving in whenever she thought she was alone.

"I took datura," Gul blurted now. "That's why you don't hear anything here." She thumped her chest. "They say if you light a match to the dried leaves and breathe in just a little bit of the smoke, it helps with the breathing disease." Her voice dipped as Rozeena frowned.

"I've told you to stay away from datura." Rozeena released a breath to lessen the frustration and fatigue in her tone. "It's not safe. You can even . . ." How many times before had she warned Gul?

Whether people called it datura, thorn apple, or jimsonweed, the folklore medicinal plant was a poisonous analgesic and hallucinogenic. Yes, a paste of its crushed leaves could soothe and heal burns. Inhaling the smoke of burning leaves did relax muscles and could rid Gul of an asthmatic spasm. Rozeena didn't deny the medicinal properties of natural remedies. Many medicines came from plants after all, even aspirin. But regulation was needed, and formulas and dosages had to be monitored.

"Where did you get the datura?"

Gul bit her lip and shrugged.

"It came from some hakim, didn't it? I saw the new store sign in the market. You know, just because a person calls himself a hakim doesn't mean he studied in a college to learn medicine. Most hakims just cook something up in their kitchens and sell it to you."

Gul nodded, but Rozeena knew the girl didn't really believe that these hakims, the doctors of traditional remedies, preyed on the poor and illiterate. To add to the confusion, there were some hakims who had studied homeopathy and pharmacology. People like Gul, however, were bound by access to the closest, cheapest care, which was also the most suspect. That's why Rozeena offered this free clinic, if only Gul would listen.

But now Gul's attention was back at the window.

Rozeena jumped up this time and marched over. "What's out there, Gul? What do you see?"

Leaning into the pane, Rozeena squinted in the dark. The loose fabric of her pale blue sari brushed against her back, tickling the inch of bare skin between blouse and petticoat. Cool November air swept over her face, and a prickly shiver ran through her. Something out there was bothering Gul, but there was only the side boundary wall in the distance and beyond that the back of Aalya's house, rising tall.

Gul leaned right and left trying to get a glimpse out the window, but Rozeena positioned herself directly in front. Folding her arms across her chest, she waited for an answer.

"I saw something," Gul said finally, her voice dropping to a whisper. "I saw Zohair Sahib. He was at the bottom of the stairs." She motioned toward the spiral concrete staircase clinging to the back of Aalya's house. "I was near my quarters when Aalya Bibi came out of her door, alone, and came downstairs." She paused. "There are guests visiting for dinner. If they see Aalya Bibi with Zohair Sahib in the garden . . ." She didn't need to complete her sentence.

Log kya kahenge?

What would people say? What would they think?

What was Aalya thinking? Mere gossip could ruin her reputation and her family's social standing in a second. Rozeena clenched her jaw. Recently, she felt distant from Aalya. She used to know everything about Aalya, as if they were the same person, but now Rozeena felt more and more in the dark with each passing day. Why was Aalya meeting Zohair?

This was Gul's real reason for banging at the back gate tonight. Confessing about using datura was a filler while she gathered courage to inform on her employer's daughter. Rozeena was utterly grateful for the information but also had no time to spare. She ushered Gul out of the storeroom, and they exited the back gate together.

"And remember, no datura. You don't have any more in your room, do you?"

Gul insisted she was well now and didn't need any more cures. They reached Aalya's house in quick, long strides, and as they entered the back gate, shrill laughter sprang into the night. Gul went into her quarters behind the house, and Rozeena hurried along the side of Aalya's house toward the front garden.

Glancing up at the windows, Rozeena curled her fingers into a fist, bracing herself for the faces that might appear in search of the laughter. She'd curled her fingers the same way holding Aalya's small hand that first day when they stood waiting for the school bus.

"Take care of her," Aalya's mother, Neelum, had said, placing her daughter's hand in nine-year-old Rozeena's. "Aalya doesn't know these things. How to be in school, how to sit and listen."

Aalya didn't even know English yet, Rozeena thought. What would the nuns think? She nodded at Neelum but wondered how many words she could teach six-year-old Aalya on the bus.

"Promise me," Neelum insisted, squeezing the girls' hands as if she could meld them into one. "Promise me you'll make her just like you, so much like you that people will think she's your little sister."

Rozeena's family had arrived from Delhi a few weeks before. She didn't know where Aalya's family had come from, but migrants and refugees were pouring into Karachi from all over, and Rozeena's father had told her to simply accept and be grateful, and not to pry. The past was painful for many, and Rozeena knew that well.

This was her chance to start afresh too.

So when the bus arrived, and Neelum released her, Rozeena's grip had remained tight around Aalya's hand, vowing to do it right this time.

Now, Rozeena came to a sudden halt. Before her, the garden lay bathed in extra lights to impress the dinner guests tonight. Everything glistened—the water trickling down the three-tiered fountain in the center, the thick grass outlined by pearl-dotted jasmine bushes, the bougainvillea bursting with bright pink flowers climbing up the front boundary wall and arching over the gate like a fairy tale.

And there, in the corner farthest from Rozeena, Aalya stood under the full, dense canopy of the giant tamarind tree, her back turned to everything except Zohair.

3

W hat're you doing here?" Rozeena hurried toward them, switching from Urdu to the convent school English of her friends.

Aalya's thick, blue-black waves slid across her back as she spun around. The lights shone on her fingers slipping out of Zohair's hands. Rozeena froze, shocked silent at this meeting, this relationship she'd never known existed. The way Zohair twisted in place and Aalya wrung her hands, sliding farther away from him, it was clear they'd been keeping it a secret—the first-ever secret Aalya kept from Rozeena.

Looking away to hide the pain and confusion, Rozeena's eyes fell on the stack of magazines under Zohair's arm. *National Geographic*, *Time*, and *Reader's Digest*. She moved closer to read the dates. They looked like the latest issues.

Zohair fidgeted and rolled the magazines into a cylinder, fingers tense around them.

"Picked them up from TitBit, in Bohri Bazaar," he said, his eyes nearly hidden under his brown, floppy curls.

Rozeena waited, but he gave no further explanation. Of course they were from TitBit bookstore. But Rozeena had always been the one who bought them to share with Aalya—Archie Comics when they were younger, and then these magazines as they grew older. Zohair had never been interested, until now.

How often was Aalya meeting him here, holding hands, accepting gifts?

A rustle from above startled them, and all three heads turned up to the balcony—where Aalya's mother and the dinner guests stood staring down at them. Rozeena immediately checked Aalya's position, but she was thankfully far from the tree. Only Rozeena was close enough to Zohair to hear his rapid breathing. She planted an innocent smile on her face and smoothed her loose hair back into the low bun.

Neelum's face remained rigid with surprise at seeing her daughter downstairs. "I wanted to show our guests the garden from up here." Her voice wavered.

"Of course," Rozeena called out cheerfully. "It's the most beautiful one in the neighborhood."

But the guests still had matching frowns and suspicious squints. Aalya and her family's future depended on what these two—the bald husband and rotund wife—believed about tonight, and what they shared with everyone tomorrow.

"I asked Aalya to meet me here," Rozeena explained, "because I needed my magazines from Zohair." She grabbed the magazines from his hands and held them to her chest. "He's so helpful and . . ." She pursed her lips. It was best not to prolong this awkward meeting.

Hurrying over to Aalya, she hooked an arm around hers and nodded at the guests before quickly walking toward the side of the house. They ducked under the balcony and waited while Zohair bounded across the garden and into his own house. Above them, Neelum was saying something about all the wonderful people who lived on Prince Road, including Dr. Rozeena from next door.

When Neelum and the guests finally went inside, Aalya smiled gratefully. Her cheeks flushed, she swiped at the perspiration dotting her forehead, despite the cool night. Neelum was right about her daughter's beauty, and about her possible future prospects. Aalya could get the crème de la crème of Karachi bachelors, but now she was jeopardizing it all.

"Where's Ibrahim Uncle?" Rozeena asked. Aalya's father had missed the entire spectacle.

"Probably out in the back. He's planted some mint there too, in a shady spot. You know how he likes plants better than people." She smiled.

Rozeena nodded. Technically, it was Zohair's garden since his father owned the downstairs, but it was Ibrahim's hobby.

"Now, about Zohair—"

"It's nothing, really." Aalya stepped out from under the balcony and crossed the garden.

"But does Zohair know that?" Rozeena said, catching up. "We all know how he is."

Aalya's cheeks turned the deep pink shade of her shalwar kameez, and her large, dark irises reflected light from the sconces flanking Zohair's front door.

"You mean, Zohair-with-the-hair?"

They giggled softly, like they were young girls again, and for a moment the air turned sweet, tinged with jasmine from the bushes surrounding them.

"You know what always surprised me the most about his hair drama?" Aalya reached down for a skinny stem of leaves that had broken off one of the newly potted mint plants near the tamarind tree.

"Was it that he got punished over and over again for the same thing?" Rozeena shook her head. "Unbelievable, but he knew what he wanted."

Every three months Zohair's school barber would sit him down in the middle of the courtyard, in front of the whole school, and place an actual upside-down bowl on Zohair's head. The hair below the rim would be chopped off in accordance with hair-length rules at the all-boys school.

"And we could never convince him to change, to stop caring, to spare himself that humiliating punishment," Rozeena said.

She'd tried once when all of them—Aalya, Rozeena, and Haaris—had gathered here in Zohair's garden to commiserate yet another fresh bowl cut.

"Get it cut even shorter," twelve-year-old Rozeena had told him, feeling wise being two years older than him. "Don't you want to look like a boy? Don't you want to look like Haaris?"

With tears streaming down his cheeks, Zohair had spun around to her and yelled, "I don't want to look like Haaris. I want to look like me!"

And although Haaris, at fourteen, had seemed much older than Zohair then, he'd nodded somberly in agreement with the sobbing boy.

"Yes, Zohair knew what he wanted," Aalya said now, staring behind Rozeena, at his front door. "But what always surprised me the most was that he cried so openly, freely. He was so angry at losing those shiny curls that he just spilled it all out in front of us." She shook her head. "He's always himself, even if that person is someone who cries loudly, blubbering like a baby over something that'll grow back anyway. Isn't that something?" Aalya said. "There are no hidden parts of him."

"We were children then," Rozeena said. "What did we have to hide?"

Aalya fidgeted with the small, ridged leaves still in her hand.

"What is it?" Rozeena said.

She shook her head slowly. "I should go. The guests." She glanced up at her balcony.

Rozeena wondered if Aalya wasn't admitting her feelings for Zohair because she was uncertain herself, or because she was afraid of disappointing her mother.

Because Rozeena knew all about expectations and duties.

"I applied for the National Hospital position," she said. "The salary isn't much, but it'll be regular, and I'll get some referrals for my new clinic." Swallowing, she added, "Ammi needs the money."

Aalya frowned. "She does? Why didn't you tell me?"

"I'm telling you now."

Rozeena waited, but Aalya offered no secret of her own, not a word about Zohair.

"Dawood told me about the position," Rozeena continued. "Seems like doctors at the hospital hear about these things first. And Dawood is obviously much nicer than his mother."

They both laughed. No one could deny his mother's sour temperament.

Rozeena called Dawood's mother Khala, or aunt, because she was distantly related though there wasn't much resemblance, in physique or personality, to Rozeena's mother. But the two women had become close because they had little other family in Karachi. During Partition, their relatives had scattered, settling in Lahore, Hyderabad, and other cities. It was their newfound friendship that had allowed Khala and her perpetual scowl to move into their house soon after Rozeena's father died. Only in retrospect could they all appreciate the timing of their tragedies. At the time, Khala had needed a home and someone to live with after her divorce, and Rozeena's mother had suddenly become a widow in need of financial help and companionship.

Rozeena remembers being frightened all the time when her father died, when only half her family was left in the world. She didn't want to sleep or wake or go to school or stay at home. Fear of another loss had settled in her every cell. Khala's arrival had somehow slowly shaken that feeling. Or maybe it was the passage of time that had done it. Either way, the new arrangement had suited everyone—two single women, one child to raise, and some money coming into the household from Khala.

"I know you'll get the position, Rozee." Aalya reached for her hand and squeezed it. "Don't worry. It'll be all right."

"And you? Will you be all right?"

Aalya looked up at the balcony again and spoke quietly. "Do you always do what you're supposed to?"

"What? Well, yes." She frowned. "I mean, why not? I think." She wrapped her arm tight around the magazines, and her heart thudded against them as doubt crept into her words.

Aalya nodded, unsurprised. She handed Rozeena the mint leaves on their tiny stem, and circled around the other side of the fountain farthest from Zohair's front door, before disappearing down the side of the house.

4

NOW, 2019

When Zara arrives for her next evening as temporary maali, she's dressed in jeans and a white T-shirt. Rozeena notices Zara's thick strapped sandals, the kind her grandchildren used to wear when they'd race to Rozeena from the gate, practically knocking her off her feet with the force of their hugs. But they're grown up now and much too busy for regular visits.

Zara should be busy too.

Her hair is tied up in a high ponytail, as if she's ready for work, but she's been settled on the veranda sipping her lemonade for a while now. Maybe the taste of home has made her too comfortable. Rozeena was careful to use the Country Time mix common in America instead of the usual fresh lemon juice and sugar, because even though she worries about this growing connection to Haaris, she wants Zara to feel comfortable in this new place.

"I had my driver, Pervez, bring out the hosepipe and attach it in front over there." Rozeena points to the coiled pile of lime-green rubber beside the gate.

Early evening is the best time for watering to prevent immediate evaporation, but Zara probably knows that. Apparently, she's become very fond of gardening.

Zara finishes her lemonade and stares at the grass in front of them. "Is this, like, your passion?"

"Passion?" Rozeena smothers a chuckle. These young ones speak in such extremes. For now, Rozeena's new hobby simply fills some hours of the day, a made-up purpose when there's no real one left. "Is it *your* passion, Zara?"

Her voice is barely audible. "Maybe? I don't know, but it was his."

"Fez's?"

Zara nods and reaches for her phone lying on the rosewood table between them.

It's all she's brought with her today, no hat, no long-sleeved covering, no gloves. Rozeena has seen enough well-outfitted ladies in the gardening club she's recently joined to know how women dress for this work, not that she herself is one of them. She only attends the meetings to learn about plants, so she can instruct Kareem, her maali, better. But after a few gardening club meetings, she surmised that those ladies don't touch the soil either. They simply enjoy having the proper gear and looking the part so they too can better instruct their maalis.

"Maybe we can both just enjoy looking at it for now, without worrying about making it a passion?"

Zara looks up tentatively. "Really? Yeah, I can do that. Like maybe just take some pics today, for *Landscoping*?" She explains how Fez's blog is not land*scaping* but *scoping*, like scoping the land. Her thumbs hover above her phone screen. "But it's not like a real blog. All he did was post pics, and he wasn't really good at taking them." Her voice dips talking of him.

"Well then, perhaps you can take new photographs, replace the bad ones."

Zara whips her head around so fast her ponytail almost slaps her face. "What? I can't do that."

"Oh? I suppose I don't know much about blogs and photographs." But of course Rozeena knows enough. These days youngsters are much the same across the globe with respect to their phone activities.

Zara stands up, fingers tight around her shocking pink iPhone case. "No. I don't mean it's not possible, but I can't change all his work." Her voice rises. "What would everyone think if I did that? What would they say?"

"Who?"

"My parents, my school, everyone who knew him. I'm supposed to keep his blog alive, not just . . ." Her voice trails off, and frowning, she steps off the tile and onto the grass.

Poor child. What a burden she's living with. Rozeena follows her into the garden, and Zara stops in the center to peer at her phone raised to the sky, bright blue and cloudless as usual. When she holds the phone out to Rozeena, it's a photograph, and it's breathtaking. Zara has captured Rozeena's twin coconut palms on one side of the screen, just down to their necks, dark green and full, fanning like spiky giant heads. But the photograph gives the impression of space as well, two lone heads against the vast blue sky stretching all the way to the other side.

Zara smiles shyly at the reaction on Rozeena's face. The girl knows she's good, and it's not just photography for her. It looks like pure joy.

"Can you write down the name of where all these pictures are? I'd like to see more of your photography. You really are quite talented."

Zara nods and takes some quick photographs of the bougainvillea covering the front boundary wall before stuffing the phone into her back pocket.

"I guess I should do the watering now?"

Rozeena would let her skip all the work since Zara isn't showing much interest, but she seems to need it now, like an unpleasant but necessary chore. A duty, but for whom?

Zara turns on the water and aims the hosepipe at the bougainvillea first. But given the water pressure, the stream is limp, so Rozeena shows her how to cover half the mouth of the hose with her thumb to force a stronger spray. Zara giggles, wincing at random sprays misdirected by her inexperienced thumb.

"Is it okay to water the flowers?" she says, once the spray is under control. "I don't want to, like, blow them all off the bush."

"Blow them off the bush?"

Zara points to the pink bougainvillea flowers covering the top of the hedge, high on the boundary wall.

"Oh, those aren't as flimsy as they look," Rozeena says. In fact, they always remind her of her mother, paper-thin and delicate like she'd be swept away by Karachi's gusts from the sea, but deceptively unwavering.

Zara starts watering the flowers directly, high up above their heads, while the roots of the vine lie at their feet grounded in the bed. Rozeena reaches up to lower Zara's arm.

"Let's focus on the roots today," Rozeena says. "If there's dust on the flowers it'll get washed away when it rains in a couple of weeks."

Zara's ears turn red, and Rozeena moves away as if to examine the kangi palm in the corner. She steals a glance, hoping the girl isn't too embarrassed, but water really is too scarce to waste. As it is, Rozeena pays for weekly tankers to supplement what comes through the city pipes.

Water hits dry dirt and the earthy scent reaches Rozeena as she runs her fingers along the kangi palm's giant leaves, like rigid, spiky feathers sprouting from the short, shaggy trunk. The leaves fan out to nearly four feet in diameter now, majestic in their perfection, though the slow-growing plant is only thigh high. She planned on telling Zara the story of this beloved kangi palm, and how Haaris had known its ancestor, a memory Rozeena had pushed aside for decades.

But now she admonishes herself for reaching to the past. So much of it needs to stay there. So much of it can jeopardize her present, the life she's built without Haaris by her side, a good life, a precious one.

After Zara finishes up with the beds around the perimeter, Rozeena says Pervez will water the grass and sends her inside to wash up. Back on the veranda for hot samosas—potato filling is the best kind, Zara says, especially with this tamarind chutney—Rozeena begins to dig for information.

"Maybe next time you should wear your gardening shoes." She points at Zara's black leather straps and silver buckles. "Birkenstocks are quite expensive to ruin in the dirt."

Her eyes widen. "You know about Birkenstocks?"

"I have grandchildren." Rozeena smiles. "And they don't shy away from asking for gifts."

She doesn't add that they're not children anymore, and don't spend long afternoons at Rozeena's house munching on samosas, watching movies, and eating as much ice cream as they want. In fact, she hasn't seen her three grandchildren in months. Adults get busy with their own lives.

"Have another samosa, Zara." Her crunchy bites are comforting.

When Zara finally wipes her mouth with a napkin, Rozeena reminds her to write down the name of the blog.

"You're really into everything," Zara says, jotting it down on Rozeena's writing pad. "I mean, for being Haaris Daada's friend."

Rozeena winces at the word *friend*. Yes, along with Aalya and Zohair, they'd all been friends once. But Rozeena had lost Haaris along the way.

Zara leans back on the wooden slats, and her ponytail hangs low over the back of her chair as she squints up at the sky. Brimming with questions, Rozeena opens her mouth to speak, but Zara's eyes close. The breeze has blown her hair across her face, and she twitches her nose under the dark brown wisps. A small smile appears as if she's ticklish. This serenity seems too precious to disturb, so Rozeena leaves her questions for another day.

That night, before Rozeena can decide whether or not to call Haaris and give him an update on Zara's visit, her phone rings.

"I disturbed your dinner," Haaris says, eerily aware of her every move.

"No, no. I'm done anyway," she lies, pushing her plate away and leaning back in her chair at the head of the table. Later, she'll ask her cook, Basheer, to reheat her plate of rice and daal in the microwave.

"Well, I wanted to say thank you, Rozee. I received a text message from Zara. These children don't use their phones for actual telephone calls, you know." He chuckles like he's made this joke many times before.

"You're sounding like an old man, Haaris." Her words are clipped, more critical than she intends but she can't help herself. She's feeling manipulated. "I mean, there's value in all this technology, and you're complaining."

"And you're still telling me what to do."

She's silenced. It's as if they've picked up from where they left off over half a century ago.

"I shouldn't have said that, Rozee. What I wanted to say was that Zara was very happy at your house today. She said she can't wait to go back and that you're cool even though you're my friend."

"Really?" She sits up straight, eager to understand the true situation. "I'm glad I can help, but tell me, Haaris, why does she want to do this gardening work?" She doesn't add that Zara clearly has no passion for it.

"It's just something to do to get her mind off—"

"Fez? But it's for him, for his blog that she's doing it, right? All those photographs she takes."

"Photographs?"

"She said she's taking them to keep *Landscoping* alive."

"Oh, I didn't know that. She told her parents she's interested in the work now, like Fez was, but I didn't know she was doing it for *Landscoping.*"

Rozeena hears the scraping of a chair on tiles, or is it wood, and then the slow, deliberate clicking of a computer keyboard for quite some time while Haaris checks *Landscoping.* She wishes she could picture him there, in his room with the Minnesota view outside his window.

"I see them now. Zara has put up some pictures of coconut palms. Yours? Yes, she's got quite an eye." He exhales. "It's a piece of my Karachi, and it's still the same. How I miss it."

"Just the sky is the same, trust me. The city is unrecognizable now with all the overhead bridges and underpasses and tall buildings and malls. And, Haaris"—she softens her tone, so she's not accused of trying to tell him what to do—"no one stopped you from visiting all these years. You can see your Karachi and your old friends too, if you want."

She knows about his life, though, even without his visiting. He married, had children and grandchildren. His oldest sister, Apa, and some of his extended family still live in Karachi, expanding their import/export business over the years. Rozeena doesn't meet them often socially, only at very large weddings, or funerals, where their circles overlap. But one hears about people all the time, especially those who've lived in the same city for decades, since the birth of the country and even before. Rozeena has heard that Haaris is well settled in Minnesota, taking care of their business interests on that side of the world.

"It was easier to stay away, Rozee. I'm sure you can understand."

Easier for whom, she thinks.

She wonders if he knows of her life as it is now, of how the days that never used to have enough hours now have the longest minutes she's ever lived. Even after her dear husband left the world, she'd had her work to get lost in. But now that's gone too.

Of course she's grateful for what she has. So many of her friends are no longer here or suffer from illness. Rozeena still manages to visit the club library regularly, and she walks on the track in the park at least three times a week. Yet, she can't shed the feeling of outlived utility, and lately her empty life is driving her mind to the past.

Maybe she should be praying more, asking for forgiveness.

Haaris's voice startles her into the present. "When I suggested this maali work, Zara agreed so quickly. I suppose photographing the plants is not exactly gardening, but we try not to question too much. I hope it's all right for her to continue? Her parents just want to see Zara smile again, genuinely. We can all see her pretend to be happy, like everything is okay. She goes out of her way to please her parents, but they just want to have their old Zara back, like she used to be, before."

Rozeena realizes then that the smile she saw on Zara's face when her hair tickled her nose was probably the genuine one her family has been searching for so desperately. And it had appeared at Rozeena's house.

"Of course she can continue, Haaris. But tell me, did you send her to me because you think I'll be a good example?" After all, Rozeena survived the loss of her brother, stepped into vacant shoes, managed responsibilities. But her jaw tightens at another possibility. "Or do you think I'll be a warning?"

He's silent for so long, she wonders if his cheek has touched the red button on the phone by mistake. But then she hears him take a breath, a long one.

"No, Rozee. Of course not that."

Even from across the world, she detects the affectation in his denial. She wants to say she'd been trying to do the right thing all those years ago. But her excuses are pointless, because for decades now she's felt only regret for what happened at Haaris's Welcome Home Ball, for what happened to Aalya because Rozeena left her alone when Aalya needed her the most.

5

THEN, 1964

Nine Days Before

Zohair burst through Rozeena's front gate the next morning as if there were an emergency, but no one even rose from their veranda chairs. Zohair always exuded this heightened level of energy.

"Why is this boy banging the gate so early? Is Haaris back?" Khala squinted at him from her seat.

Rozeena wondered too, especially after the incident with Aalya last night. Khala was unaware of what had happened obviously, but she needed no reason to be critical. Her stout body jiggled as she shook her head at the figure approaching from the other end of the garden.

To Rozeena's left, her mother wrapped tense, lean fingers around her wooden armrests before pushing herself up. "I need to check on Shareef."

They all knew there was no need to check on their cook. Shareef knew their routine well, and breakfast would be on the dining table at eight a.m., as always. But Zohair was headed their way, and Rozeena's mother would make sure she wasn't here when he climbed the stairs to the black-and-white tiles.

Rozeena hurried to meet him midway to prevent any chance of their interaction. "Won't you be late for the railway station?"

He shrugged with a smile. "I don't do anything too important. They won't miss me."

Glancing over her shoulder, Rozeena watched her mother disappear inside. Zohair didn't ask where or why Rozeena's mother had gone suddenly. No one spoke of it anymore. The last time Rozeena had mentioned it to anyone was when Khala moved into the house, but the complaint had been futile.

"What do you know about the pain your mother suffers?" Khala had said. "You know nothing. Every day she has to see that boy bouncing around." She'd tutted at Rozeena for the rest of the day.

"If you're here to tell me about Haaris, I know he's arriving tonight," Rozeena said now. "You didn't have to come and—"

"I came to thank you." Zohair bowed his head toward the polished shoes below his trousers. "If you hadn't been there when the guests stepped out . . ." His eyes flicked up over the boundary wall to Aalya's balcony.

Rozeena gave him a curt nod. At least he knew Aalya's reputation would've been ruined if she'd been seen alone with him. She'd be labeled entirely unmarriageable and of loose character.

Following his gaze now, Rozeena was struck by the peeling paint and weathered window frames next door. She hadn't noticed before, but the neglect set the house apart in the neighborhood. Her own home was fresh, its façade a clean white. No one knew the bedrooms inside were in need of paint. But Aalya's outside had only been painted once from top to bottom, when it was transformed from the original gray-white to the palest of blues. Now the whole building was tired and worn with streaks of dirty gray emerging from underneath like flowing tears.

"I need some time." Zohair's voice was small, childlike. "I need Aalya to wait for me. I must have something to offer her before I can say anything formally. Neelum Aunty has great plans for her daughter, greater than I can be right now."

Zohair was like a son to Neelum, but she definitely wanted more for her daughter. Other than wealth, though, Rozeena saw nothing lacking in loud and impulsive Zohair-with-the-hair. She'd known him longer than she'd known her own brother, and never once had she seen Zohair cheat or lie or even quietly criticize a team member who'd made a glaring mistake during a precious street cricket match.

And as Aalya had said herself, Zohair hid nothing of himself.

But Rozeena couldn't encourage or discourage him, not knowing what Aalya truly wanted. There'd been so many silences between them lately, and worse.

The other day, Rozeena had suggested Aalya consider teaching as a profession. It was such respectable work for women, and perfect for Aalya given her gentle demeanor and intelligence. Aalya had lit up at the idea, but within seconds, she'd dropped onto the foot of her bed, shaking her head.

"I can't, Rozee. Just let it go."

"But why not?"

"I don't have the time, all right?"

"What else are you doing, waiting to get married?"

Aalya had turned stone cold, a mix of anger and extreme hurt in her pulsing, moist eyes. All Rozeena could do was mumble sorry and leave.

"It's as if I don't know her anymore," she said to Zohair now.

"What do you mean?"

"She's different, keeping things to herself. Don't you think?"

He looked away, tugging at his cuff, and stomping invisible dust off his shoes. "I should get to the railway station before someone misses me."

Flashing a smile, he stepped through her gate, taking with him whatever he was aware of and Rozeena wasn't. Her shoulders tensed as she replayed Aalya's question.

Do you always do what you're supposed to?

Haaris will be a good example for Aalya and Zohair," Khala was saying as Rozeena stepped through the tall teak double doors and crossed the drawing room into the dining room.

Khala's toast already had a thick layer of butter on it. No one had waited for Rozeena to start breakfast, another example of her mother trying to keep their lives orderly, safe, and in control. Right now, her erect posture was probably contending with Zohair's visit.

Rozeena slid into the chair across from Khala. "How is Haaris a good example? Haven't his parents been calling him back for two years now? He comes to Karachi for a few weeks and then runs back to Liverpool."

Stirring milk and sugar into her tea, she let her mind wander to his face and the last memory of them together. That night, after Haaris announced he'd be back from Liverpool in six months, he was the first to leave Zohair's garden. But when Rozeena stepped out the front gate ten minutes later, Haaris was still there waiting for her on the dark, empty street.

"I thought I'd walk you to your gate," he said.

Rozeena laughed. "Why? Do you think I'll get lost on the way?" She'd been walking to her house next door since they were children.

Without joining in the laughter, he reached for her hand but stopped short of touching her. "Of course not. But I'd like to walk with you from now on, if you'd let me."

She had no words, unsure of his true meaning. But when she nodded, and he fell in step with her, she recognized a new connection blossoming between them.

Khala grunted, her mouth filled with half the glistening toast, while Rozeena waited for her mother to say something from the head of the table. She sat wrapped like a cocoon in her cream-colored sari with its perfect folds, not about to spill random words or thoughts like Khala. The chair to Rozeena's right was empty, Faysal's chair, she called it, only in her mind though. If her brother were here, they'd exchange a glance while they waited for their mother to speak. They'd giggle, trying to guess how long it would take this time, how much of their breakfast they could gobble down before their mother's first word. Rozeena cocked her head with a frown. Would Faysal giggle now, at this age? She didn't know. But she imagined he would, like she imagined he'd care for them, being the oldest child, the son to a widowed mother.

"Haaris knows what he needs to do," her mother said, setting down her cup on its saucer without a clink or clatter. Her eyes scanned the white-on-white embroidered tablecloth and landed on a faded stain the dhobi hadn't been able to wash out. "He'll do the right thing, ultimately." She nodded and not a single strand of dark hair moved in her tight, smooth bun. Reaching over to pat Rozeena's arm, she smiled. "Like you're doing. Your father would be so proud to see his Rozee—"

Shareef burst into the dining room, nearly tripping over his own feet. He shot out an arm to brace himself against the wall, the other hand still holding his cooking spoon, yellowed with turmeric and matching the splatters on his beige kameez.

"You must come quickly," he said, panting. "It's Gul. Something is happening to her. Something is not right."

Rozeena got up and ran after Shareef.

The back gate stood wide open. Abdul, Gul's husband, was struggling to hold her up. She had no balance, no control. He held her from behind, his arms tight around her waist, as Gul's head lolled back and forth, arms flailing by her sides and legs wobbly underneath. Aalya was on the street behind them, waving down a rickshaw.

"Gul said she felt sick, like she would vomit, but then she was so thirsty also," Abdul said to Rozeena. He twisted his head from side to side away from Gul's tossing and turning. "She kept on saying her mouth was dry, too dry, and then she started screaming about seeing snakes and other things. But there weren't any in our quarters. I looked under the bed and behind the door, everywhere." His eyes widened in panic. "Do you think it's a snake bite?"

Gul's face was darker than normal, flushed. Rozeena cupped her face to hold her still. Her cheeks radiated heat and her pupils were dilated.

"Did she eat anything, Abdul? Or did she take any medicine? Tablets?"

He shook his head.

She checked Gul's wrist and registered an elevated pulse. It struck her then. Datura. Could Gul have gone back to her quarters and inhaled the burning leaves again, too much this time? Her symptoms—dry mouth, confusion, hallucinations, dilated pupils, a very fast heart rate—pointed to the plant's natural atropine. Or it could be something else.

Rozeena yelled for the rickshaw to come closer. There was no time for more questions. If Gul had taken too much datura, they had to reach the hospital before convulsions began. Rozeena and Abdul sandwiched her between them on the seat behind the driver. Aalya and her mother would have to follow in a second rickshaw. If it had been an hour later, Rozeena's driver could've taken them all in the Morris, but they couldn't wait even a second longer.

National Hospital was the closest and best equipped but even that felt too far. Gul's head fell back and forth with every bump and brake of the rickshaw. Her forehead burned.

She pulled phantom objects from the tips of her fingers saying, "What's this, what's this?" Her speech slurred.

Rozeena begged the rickshaw-walla to drive faster.

Finally at the hospital, Gul disappeared behind the emergency room doors. Abdul and Rozeena, breathless, stood in the center of the waiting room, too panicked to sit down even though empty chairs lined the walls.

Convulsions hadn't started yet, so perhaps Gul would be all right. Rozeena turned to Abdul. "When did she take the datura?"

"What? Datura?" But the realization hit him too. "Yes, yes, she did take it. At Fajar, I think." He bowed his head, swiping at tears with his palms. "I sleep too much, but Gul always wakes at Fajar. Never misses the first prayer of the day."

Sunrise was a couple hours ago, and Fajar was even earlier. Enough time had passed for the full range of overdose effects.

"Did she burn the dried leaves, Abdul? Maybe you woke up and saw? Try to remember if she took the seeds instead."

He shook his head and dug palms into his temples. He couldn't remember. He'd slept through whatever she'd done, he said, and couldn't forgive himself for it.

But Rozeena knew it wasn't his fault. It was hers.

She knew Gul had been taking datura for her asthma. Last night, she'd warned Gul about the dangers before running to Aalya to save her from being seen with Zohair. But Rozeena hadn't done enough for Gul. She should've walked Gul back to her quarters and demanded she hand over all her datura, the stalks, seeds, leaves, whatever she had, everything. She knew Gul listened to hakims and needed more persuasion, more action on Rozeena's part. Now the result was before them. A racing heart, delirium, loss of motor coordination which could lead to—

"Rozee?"

She spun around. "Dawood?" She switched to English. "What

are you doing here?" Khala's son was a pulmonologist and should've been in the outpatient ward at this time.

"They called me for the emergency patient," he said with a quick nod toward Abdul but continued in English to keep the conversation between the two of them. "The patient was struggling with respiratory failure." He pushed back the sleeve of his white coat to check his watch.

"And?" Rozeena kept her eyes averted from Abdul whose head swung back and forth between the doctors.

"We tried everything we could. Ultimately respiratory paralysis . . ."

She blinked a second too long and heard Abdul groan. He covered his face with both hands and sank into the closest chair. Dawood gave his gray trousers a quick tug, took the seat beside Abdul, and repeated his words in Urdu. After the requisite minute and with a gentle pat on the grieving husband's shoulder, Dawood stood back up.

"It was datura poisoning, wasn't it?" Rozeena said as they stepped away from Abdul. She held her breath and squeezed her insides tight to brace herself for the news, desperately wanting to be wrong.

"Most probably, yes," Dawood said.

Her mouth opened wide, but she could only release her breath in short spurts. She shut it, nodding for him to continue.

"The symptoms indicated datura poisoning, and there have been other cases coming in but nothing fatal until now." He paused. "The patient asked for Abdul and for you also. She was coherent sporadically, but then before we could send someone to get both of you, she"—his voice dipped lower—"she said you were her doctor. Everyone in the room heard her say you knew about the datura. Something about leaves being safer than seeds for asthma?" His frown deepened and his eyes darted left and right. "Were you treating her with datura, Rozee?"

She jerked her head back. "Of course not. You know I'd never do that."

"She said she went to Dr. Rozeena for her asthma and that you knew she'd taken datura before."

Her legs went weak. She stammered, shaking her head, "No. I mean yes, I knew, but I warned Gul about using it. I never prescribed it."

"She didn't say that you prescribed it, but—"

"Dawood, you know I'd never tell anyone to use it. I—"

He stopped her with a raised palm. "Not here. Not in the hospital. I'll call on you."

"Why not here? What is it?"

He pursed his lips but then spoke, probably because he'd known her for over a decade, and even as a teenager she'd always insisted on answers, insisted on understanding.

He lowered his voice even more. "The others in the room, doctors and nurses, asked her where she got the datura, but her speech was slurred. Your name, as her doctor, was clear though. And now I have to return to the OPD so we'll talk later. I'll visit tonight." His firm nod ended the conversation.

Rozeena nodded too, trying to push away her questions for later. She trusted Dawood to be honest and complete in his explanation. Right now, Abdul was her concern. Sitting down next to his quivering shoulders, she held her arms across her stomach and listened to the grown man cry softly.

"My Gul," he whispered between sighs and gentle moaning. His hands trembled as he picked up the edge of his beige kameez and wiped his eyes, shaking his head over and over again.

As she sat there in the stillness of the quiet room, her own silent tears salty on her lips, Rozeena's senses slowly sharpened. The antiseptic Dettol clean of the hospital invaded her nose. Grains of sand rubbed between her toes as they twitched in her house slippers. She'd run to the back gate and dug her feet into the sand to brace herself against Gul's agitation, helping her into the rickshaw with Abdul. The sputtering of the rickshaw had been loud, so loud, as they'd driven full speed to the hospital.

But it had been for nothing.

Rozeena's chest twisted. Gul was gone because Rozeena hadn't done enough.

6

The day went by in a blur of activity, perhaps the best way to combat Rozeena's mounting pain.

They gathered at Aalya's in the evening to pray for Gul and meet Abdul before he left with her body on the train the next morning. Gul would be buried in their village up north as per custom. Rozeena's mother gave Abdul a thick envelope of rupees for the expenses. Rozeena would've given him anything, everything if it could fix what had happened. Giving money was the least they could do—and the most too.

Dawood was waiting for them in the drawing room when Rozeena, her mother, and Khala returned from next door. He joined them at the dining table as they toyed with their dinner, and Rozeena waited for additional bad news.

After a while, Dawood cleared his throat and spoke gently but without pause. "Your application for employment at National Hospital won't be considered, Rozee. No one is accusing you of giving datura to Gul, but everyone heard her ask for her doctor, for Dr. Rozeena. Her words were clear enough to know that you were aware

Gul was burning datura leaves and inhaling the smoke." He paused. "Everyone heard Gul say that, and everyone talks, and the hospital has many qualified applicants."

Rozeena couldn't speak.

"Try to understand." He softened his tone even more. "What would people say if the hospital hired you immediately after this tragedy?"

Log kya kahenge?

She did understand, perfectly. She understood that she deserved at least this for what her neglect had caused, for running away instead of investigating Gul's datura use further.

Rozeena kept her head down for the rest of the meal and didn't question the hospital's decision, telling herself she didn't even care for the position. She'd only always wanted to build her own private clinic, her father's dream for her independence, the dream her brother hadn't been able to fulfill. But her father hadn't foreseen how short his own life would be. Now, eleven years later, even with Khala's help, there was little money left, and the life Rozeena's mother had so carefully orchestrated and maintained was in jeopardy.

And they'd lost so much already. Too much.

Rozeena glanced at the empty dining chair to her right, imagining Faysal there next to her. He should've grown up. He should've been in her seat, the lead seat to the right of her mother, and her father before. But how could they have known Faysal would never take that role?

She released a heavy sigh in the deathly silence around her.

After a while, Dawood pushed his chair back to leave. She blinked up at him and nodded a thank-you. She knew he must've tried hard to convince the hospital to consider her application.

When he left, Rozeena's mother finally spoke. "Gul's death was an accident, Rozee. You must accept that it was Gul's mistake, not yours."

Rozeena clenched her jaw but kept silent.

"Sometimes, many times, it is the unexpected, the tragic, that determines the direction of our lives."

"No, don't." Khala's short, thick arm shot out as if to halt the passing of a sentence.

Confused, Rozeena swung her head from one to the other.

Her mother continued without even a glance at Khala. "It's time to sell the house and move to Lahore."

"What?" Rozeena shook her head. "No, no, no."

Her mother's fingers tensed on the armrests, like she'd surprised herself with the decision and she too was afraid of moving twelve hundred kilometers away.

"But why, Ammi?" Rozeena said, her voice rising. "We didn't move to Lahore when Abba died, even when everyone said we should. Why should we live with Shehzad Uncle now?"

"Shehzad isn't a bad man, not a bad brother at all," her mother said, releasing a breath. "He and Sweetie have different ideas, that's all. Different from us, from your father, but not from most other people." She gave a small smile. "He'll take care of us, Rozee."

"I can take care of us. You know what they'll do, have me married off like they did with their daughters." Rozeena's mind flashed to Haaris and their increasing closeness. She couldn't leave Karachi. She couldn't give up the possibilities between them.

"And what's wrong in that?" Her mother tilted her head and waited for her response.

Rozeena shrugged. "Nothing. But they didn't even send them to college. You and Abba wanted me to study, have a career, earn a living."

"And you've done it, haven't you? I made sure we stayed here until you were done. I used everything I had to keep us here. We made our own decisions until your education was complete." She paused. "What happened today is a sign that it's time to go."

Rozeena swallowed, flattening her palms on the table for support. She blinked down at them to keep her eyes from filling. "And this house. Our house, where we came after . . ." She couldn't say it out loud. They never spoke of Faysal. "We could keep it and—"

"No," her mother said. "We can't. We have no choice but to sell it, Rozee. Don't you see?"

Of course she did. They needed money to fix it and run it if they were to keep it.

"I can work, and slowly we can take care of things here. I just need some time." Rozeena's voice cracked. "It's our house." Where her father had built his dreams for their future.

Khala's eyes lit up at this idea, but Rozeena's mother shook her head firmly.

"Shehzad will be here in four weeks, and this time he'll see the state of the house and car and whatever else crumbles by then. He'll also see my inability to take care of it all. Before he can say anything, I'll tell him what I've decided."

Her mother released a long sigh, like she was actually relieved at the thought of leaving, of letting go of the house and the responsibility, like she was all done. Rozeena winced as her eyes landed on the single gold bangle on her mother's wrist. *I used everything I had to keep us here,* she'd said. There used to be twelve, six on each wrist, clinking gently with every movement. Now, when her mother got up from her chair and walked away, there was no sound at all.

Khala frowned at the empty seat and spoke slowly, as if trying to comprehend the reasoning.

"Your mother wants it to be her decision. She doesn't want to be forced to leave when everything falls apart around her, when everyone can see she can't stay. She wants to leave before she has no choice *but* to leave." Khala nodded and before Rozeena could ask, added, "No, I don't have enough money. Don't you think I'd give it

49

to her if I did?" Even Khala's generosity sounded like a scolding. "My allowance is barely enough for the day-to-day running of the house."

"But you want to stay here too, don't you?"

"Want to?" Khala pushed her weight off the chair. "Of course I want to, Rozee. But I have no choice. Dawood and his wife will have to take me in when your mother sells the house and leaves."

Rozeena sat up straight and leaned forward, trying to stop all these decisions, or slow them down at least. "But what if you didn't have to? What if we could stay?"

Khala cocked her head. "Yes. What if we could?"

Rozeena had no answer.

"I found a way to get what I wanted before," Khala said, one hand holding on to her chair. "It wasn't easy. No one else did things like I did."

Rozeena nodded. Most women would've quietly accepted the existence of their husband's mistress. Instead, Khala had insisted on a divorce, choosing to retain her dignity and self-worth rather than her marriage. She'd bought half this house with the money her husband gave her at the time of the divorce, apart from the allowance. Khala had solved her own problem and simultaneously helped Rozeena's mother financially, just months after she'd become a widow.

"Leaving him was easy," Khala said now of her husband. "But leaving my children with him?" She shook her head and pressed the heel of her palm to her chest. "I had to do it, for their sake, so they wouldn't be touched by even a shadow of their divorcée mother."

"They love you. They really do." Rozeena knew it was true of both Dawood and his sister, who lived in London now with her husband.

Taking a deep breath, Khala lifted her chin, her fleeting weakness tossed to the side. "Of course they do. But it doesn't mean it was easy. Just like it wasn't easy for your mother to get this far."

Rozeena remained there long after Khala left the room and

Shareef cleared the dishes from the table. Even when he turned off the kitchen light to retire to his quarters for the night, Rozeena sat heavy in her chair, in her home.

She remembered that day in September 1947, when her father brought them to this house. It had been just weeks after crossing the border, and her young mind still couldn't comprehend what was happening. They had celebrated the creation of Pakistan, had desperately wanted a homeland where they would have a say in the government. But they hadn't been prepared for the way in which it happened.

The people's struggle against the British had finally come to an end. After two hundred years of rule, the British were leaving the subcontinent. Her father had explained to both her and Faysal how the British Empire had started crumbling after the Second World War. It had cost His Majesty too much money, and this hastened the decision to pull out of the colony.

Rozeena's father would always shake his head before and after speaking about Mountbatten, the man sent to British India as the last viceroy and given the task of leaving the colony for good. First, Mountbatten quickly moved up the date of departure by nearly a year. And then, he summoned Cyril Radcliffe, a barrister who'd never before set foot in British India. Radcliffe was given outdated maps and old census figures and was instructed to divide the colony into the two independent nations of Pakistan and India.

And Mountbatten gave Radcliffe about five weeks to do it.

Radcliffe never even left his offices. He was never shown anything of the land. He knew nothing about the different cultures, ethnicities, and often-violent tensions between people of different religions, those who wanted one country after independence, and those who wanted a separate nation for the Muslim minority, a nation where they'd have representation in governance. Without any of this knowledge, Radcliffe did as he was told and scribbled lines across the map.

The scribbles became known as the Radcliffe Line, a brand-new border along religious lines that created two new nations.

And they kept this line secret.

Rozeena dropped her head to her lap, still unable to comprehend how that had been done, how it had been decided and executed.

Pakistan's Independence Day was August 14, 1947. India's Independence Day was August 15, 1947. And the British announced the Radcliffe Line on August 17, two days after they'd officially exited from all areas of governance, including overseeing an orderly transition and acting as the neutral party. Withdrawal of their troops had begun immediately, and they'd already started dividing the colonial army along religious lines. Essentially, there was no one left to ensure a peaceful transition.

Some say they acted cruelly negligent. Others say it was done intentionally to cause mass panic and chaos that would lead to violence. How could it not? The British knew of the religious tensions in the region. For years, they'd exploited and deepened the differences, using the policy of divide and rule to colonize and control— pitting Muslims, Hindus, and Sikhs against one another. By the time Partition neared, tensions and communal riots were only rising.

When the Radcliffe Line was announced, everything exploded.

People woke up that day, August 17, and discovered that a new international border cut right through their villages and sliced up neighborhoods and even houses. They didn't know where they belonged or if they were safe. It was as if suddenly they were on opposite sides, and no one knew who to trust. Violence erupted.

Rozeena's family had never thought they'd have to run for their lives. But Muslim neighborhoods were being set on fire by mobs in Delhi, and there was no warning, no time.

Thousands of Muslims had lain rotting in the streets of Delhi, and fear had led to a mass exodus. More than a hundred thousand joined other Muslims from different cities who trekked across the border into Pakistan. Refugees traveled by train and bullock carts too. But most traveled on foot, in convoys miles and miles long, carrying very few possessions, suffering from exhaustion, dysentery, cholera, starvation.

Now Rozeena knew, like everyone else, that over the next many months at least fifteen million people—Muslims, Hindus, and Sikhs—were displaced. People fled their homes and crossed the border in both directions. Muslims ran to Pakistan for safety, and Hindus and Sikhs ran to India for safety. This movement and exchange of population, one of the largest mass migrations in human history, hadn't been part of the plan, but it had been necessary for survival.

Up to a million people died.

Rozeena's family became refugees of Partition like millions of others. They'd planned on migrating, moving peacefully with all their belongings. Instead, they'd had to run. When they reached Karachi and arrived at this house in September 1947, they were finally safe, but they were not intact.

Rozeena's father had stepped inside the front gate and said, "Look at our new house, Rozee. Aren't we lucky?"

Her mother sucked in a breath loudly and whispered, "Lucky?"

In an instant, her father lost his smile, standing there in his coat and tie, holding the gate open for them to cross the threshold.

"What I mean is that many people don't get their claim so soon after arriving," he said softly. "In that sense, we're . . ." But he didn't say the word again.

Nine-year-old Rozeena doubted they could even pretend to feel lucky, but she took a step forward. Her mother, however, stood frozen, like she'd taken such a weighty breath it shoved her soles into the paved road. She couldn't dislodge herself. So Rozeena waited, standing there in her green cotton frock and puffy short sleeves. She surveyed the empty street to her right and left, squinting against the strong breeze that swept through the fanning palms visible over the boundary walls. All the houses stood taller than the walls and extended far back, perhaps all the way to the street behind, she thought. It was early, so the koels were coo coo-ooing, just like they would be doing in Delhi. Were these refugee birds?

Her father had explained earlier that most families had to stay in refugee camps, but because he had a distant cousin already living in Karachi, in a place called Jacob Lines, they were spared those camps and could stay with him. Her father had given Rozeena a small lesson on their new city, in their new country. Karachi was a port city with a long coastline and the crashing waves of the Arabian Sea. That's why it was always breezy in Karachi, even though it was a desert, and it was cool at night even in the summer.

Rozeena had never lived by the sea before, or in a desert.

After a while, her mother's shoulders relaxed a bit, and they stepped inside. The white house was set far back on the wide plot. Twin staircases led up to a deep veranda, which ran the width of the house. Thick stone pillars held up the roof over the center portion of the veranda, and on either side, symmetrical balconies jutted out from the tall, flat roof.

But Rozeena's eyes lingered on the concrete courtyard that lay between them and the house. All she could think of was how much cricket Faysal would've played here with his friends. Her throat constricted and face crumpled before she could swing around and bury it in the folds of her mother's sari.

Her mother said nothing, only tightened her grip until Rozeena's muscles lost their tension, and even then she hadn't let go.

Now her mother was letting go.

Rozeena knew that trying to delay Shehzad's visit was pointless. Her uncle arrived like clockwork every December, his winter escape from Lahore's freezing temperatures. So Rozeena had four weeks to show her mother and Shehzad proof of their stable and respectable future in this house. Rozeena had to make everyone believe that betterment was simply around the corner.

She was the caretaker now. It was her turn to find a solution to their problems, like her mother had done before, and like Khala had too.

And like her brother would have, had he lived.

7

NOW, 2019

Rozeena would run if she could, but the stairs are slowing her down. With each careful step from bedroom to the foyer below, her frown deepens. Asr prayers took her ten minutes at the most. What could Zara have done to make Basheer, the cook, rush upstairs in a panic?

The front door bangs behind Rozeena as she steps outside. Zara jumps up with a shy smile. She's by the champa tree on the farthest side of the veranda. Pervez, the driver, stands next to the same tree and is practically in tears.

"What is it, Zara?" Rozeena calls. "Did something happen?"

She's come better prepared today, with a pair of brand-new gardening gloves, but not only are they already covered in dirt, there's too much green stuck on them.

"I finished with the onions, so I moved on." Zara pulls off the gloves and tosses them at her feet.

Rozeena reaches the end of the veranda, and when Pervez moves to the side, she lets out a small gasp.

"Oh, I just got rid of some of the weeds in the beds," Zara explains. "There's, like, a whole bunch of pics of weeds on *Landscoping*. He hated them." She quickly returns to her chair and to her Country Time lemonade.

Rozeena and Pervez stand before the destroyed ground cover at their feet. She notices that he was trying to replant it, but it's clearly beyond repair. Six months of care and water and labor ends like this, a cloud of earthiness rising from Zara's excavation.

"I told her this has to stay," Pervez says. "But she looked at her phone and said, 'No. It has to go.'"

Rozeena nods. "I'm sorry. We'll try again later." Pervez has such love for the garden, and he's good at caring for it too.

"Did I do something wrong?"

Rozeena jumps at the voice by her ear. Zara's abandoned her lemonade and returned to the champa tree. She bites her lip, eyes hopping from Pervez's mournful face to the dirt at their feet and back up.

Rozeena speaks gently. "They weren't weeds, Zara."

Her mouth falls open. She pulls out her phone before bending down to examine the torn leaves scattered below.

"Oh no. I didn't look close enough." Zara stands up, shaking her head, and says to Pervez, "I'm so so sorry. I should have listened to you when you told me they needed to stay." Turning to Rozeena, she adds, "I was so sure they were the same weeds. I can't believe I killed your plants. I'm really sorry."

Quickly, Rozeena pats her arm. "Thank you for saying sorry, Zara. I know it was a mistake, and we all make mistakes."

"No, I have to fix it. I have to," Zara says. "Please, tell me what to do."

Her panic doesn't subside even with Rozeena's comforting smiles and insistence that it's not a problem. Rozeena realizes Zara needs this for herself more than for the garden.

After some discussion with Pervez, it's decided that at least the bare spot next to the tree and along the boundary wall can be filled right away. There's a small jasmine bush waiting to be planted, and though Rozeena wanted it near the gate so guests would be greeted by its sweet scent as they entered, this new place would do as well.

Rozeena and Zara squat in the flower bed, heads practically touching, as they remove the foot-tall shrub from its clay pot and drop the plant into the freshly dug hole. Together they fill in the soil, patting it smooth around the base. The activity makes Zara's forehead slick, but she seems engrossed in the work and only stands up to join Rozeena when there's nothing left to do.

"You think it'll grow all right here?" Zara squints up at the sky to determine how much sun the spot gets.

"It's a good place for jasmine," Rozeena says. Fat, pearl-like buds dot the new shrub. Some have already opened into creamy, white layers of tiny petals. "We call it jasmine, but it's mostly double jasmine here, fuller than the regular kind."

Zara inhales deeply, smiling at the fragrant sweetness, before reaching for the hose to water as per Pervez's instructions.

When they're finally settled back into their veranda chairs, Rozeena wonders what it is that Zara wants from this internship as she calls it. Is it for school? There's so much competition these days for the good colleges. Do they prefer such international and unique internships, or is Zara doing it for some other reason?

"I don't think I mentioned before," Rozeena says gently, "we were also just the two of us, my brother and I." It's been decades since she's spoken of him. She sighs at how she's lived a whole long life, and he barely had a childhood. "I learned something from losing him." She nods at Zara's raised eyebrows. "I learned that we can't wait for the difficult times to go away. We have to decide to be happy even when things are hard."

"Decide to be happy?"

"Yes. Decide and take action, even if it's something small." She doesn't add how she's trying to do the same today, in her old age. But so far, the gardening club hasn't brought much joy. The plants don't need her like her patients did, nor like her son and grandchildren used to.

"You mean like how coming here makes me happy?" Zara says.

Rozeena can't hide her surprise. "Coming here makes you happy? I didn't know."

Zara looks away, her lips quivering and eyes pooling fast. Blinking rapidly, she examines her lap, then the sky, and finally the grass.

"I guess it's just that I'm happier here than at home right now."

"Of course. It must be hard to see your parents so—"

"Sad? Yeah. I try to, like, do stuff that makes them feel better, but . . ." She shrugs.

"That sounds difficult."

Zara's nose twitches, and she nods.

So this is why she's here, pretending to embrace her brother's passion. She's doing it to please her parents, but from a distance, so she can escape the constant pressure to keep their sadness away.

"You're welcome to come here whenever you want, Zara. In fact, you make my evenings so much better."

It's the truth. Rozeena hasn't felt so energized in months, maybe years. She even managed to squat while planting the jasmine bush. Tomorrow, she'll suffer the consequences with aches and pains, but today was invigorating. Even scrubbing her hands and digging out the lines of dirt from her nails made her feel more alive, more necessary.

Zara looks at her skeptically, her mouth slightly open, but before she can speak, Basheer steps through the front door with a tray of hot potato samosas for Zara and cardamom tea for Rozeena. With each crunch of the crispy samosa, Zara sinks further back into her chair, and a sea breeze adds to the restoring calm. The twin palm trees in the corner rustle in applause of the July evening.

"Well, then," Rozeena says after Zara reaches for another samosa and spoons a dollop of tamarind chutney on top. "Have you already taken your photographs for today?"

She nods. "But now I'm thinking maybe I can write a longer caption, make it more like a blog?" She screws up her face, unsure. "I mean, I like writing and stuff. Maybe gardening tips for Karachi? That could be cool, right?"

"Yes, that certainly could be." Rozeena nods encouragingly.

Zara grabs a second paper napkin to wipe her hands—children these days dispose of things so quickly—and bends over her phone, thumbs flying over the screen.

"Okay," she says, looking up. "I started a whole new segment on *Landscoping*. I call it 'When in Pakistan, Tips and Tricks.'" She holds out her phone to Rozeena. "See? It looks more like a real blog now, right?"

Without her glasses, Rozeena sees only a blur.

"A common way to expel ants from your lawn in Karachi," Zara reads. *"It's cheap, and it works. And no, you don't have to peel the onions first!"*

"Sounds perfect. And I do hope it works after all this effort." Burying three onions around each anthill is a gardening club tip that may end up doing nothing but wasting vegetables.

Zara smiles at her phone before setting it on the table. As she drops back into her chair, her arm falls to her side, fingers caressing the leather satchel sitting on the tiles below. She arrived with it hanging across her T-shirt today, but this is the first time she's even touched it.

"It's a lovely bag." Rozeena takes a sip of her tea.

"Oh this?" She shrugs. "It's fancy, right?" She laughs a little self-consciously. "No one in my school has anything like this, you know? But Haaris Daada gave it to me for my birthday before I left for Karachi, so I brought it with me. I didn't want to, like, hurt his feelings."

Every mention of Haaris makes Rozeena's heart thud in her ears, like she must prepare herself for some unknown. There must be some reason he's reconnected with her after all these years. Helping Zara cannot be the sole objective, but the girl is the link, and links can work both ways.

"The bag is quite fancy, like the Haaris I remember." Rozeena nods, imagining he still shaves daily, even after retirement, and never wears unpolished shoes. "I thought maybe he'd become more casual living in America. Perhaps he wears shorts in the summers now?"

Zara laughs out loud this time, pulls off her black scrunchie, and runs her fingers through her hair before tossing it all over the chair back.

"No way," she says, reaching for a third samosa. "Haaris Daada only wears shorts at the beach."

"You have beaches in Minnesota? Isn't it landlocked?"

"Yeah. Landlocked. But it's called the land of ten thousand lakes, you know? So, we have lakeshores."

"And you call them beaches?"

Zara nods slowly. "Yeah. It must sound super weird to you, especially since you have a real beach here." She pauses. "But you know what sounds super weird to me? How people in Karachi run to the beach on cloudy days. Everyone says it's the best time to go. And if it starts raining a little, it's even better." She blinks, with a little shake of the head.

"You are so observant, Zara." Rozeena means it too. "Maybe it's because we don't need a tan, don't like one either."

Zara nods. "Or maybe we all just want what we don't get easily."

Rozeena sets her cup down slowly, thoughtfully. The girl is quite perceptive, in areas other than gardening. "Another very smart thing to notice."

Zara's eyelids are heavy but not closed. With her head tilted back, she stares at the cloudless sky.

"If you let your mind wander, it can surprise you, you know?" she says. "You've heard of Isaac Newton and Archimedes, right? Well, one was chilling under a tree, and the other was soaking in the tub when they made their discoveries that changed the world." A small smile appears.

She says nothing more, and though it seems as if Zara's mind is as blank as the sky she stares at, Rozeena senses thoughts darting around inside that head. Zara ponders, observes, evaluates, but are her discoveries correct—about her place in her family, about her duty to her parents?

Rozeena won't push her more today. Questions about Haaris can be left for later as well.

Sipping her tea, Rozeena remembers how she'd waited for his return the last time, waited to see what would happen between them. Her heart had fluttered like a silly young girl's then. But now, her memories of that time are overshadowed by the single night that ended everything, for all of them.

8

THEN, 1964

Eight Days Before

Rozeena stood on Prince Road the next morning, her hand pressed against the cool metal of her front gate as she tried to calm her heart before entering. Her hurried visit next door had been futile. There'd been nothing to say to Abdul before he left for the railway station. No words of hers could help him or bring Gul back.

"Rozee?"

Her hand tensed against the gate. She recognized the deep voice behind her, coming from across the road. As she turned around, her smile grew.

Haaris grew too, walking toward her. He hadn't actually grown taller in these past months, but his shoulders seemed to take up more space. His gray suit coat fell just right, and he strode comfortably in his impeccably pressed trousers and polished black shoes.

She smoothed down her kameez, hoping the shalwar wasn't too crumpled already, and admonished herself for not taming her randomly wavy, shoulder-length hair into a clinic-appropriate bun.

"Rozee." He grinned as he neared. "What are you doing out here with your hair like that? What would Khala say?"

She folded her arms across her chest and inspected him in mock appraisal. "And is this how you tumble out of bed now? Is this what Liverpool has done to you, always the proper gentleman?"

They slipped into comfortable banter until he paused and looked up at Aalya's house. "I heard about Gul. I'm so sorry."

Air left her lungs, seeped out in jagged, scraping breaths. She dropped back against her gate with a heavy thud.

"You shouldn't feel responsible."

He knew her well. Possibly better than anyone.

She nodded, staring at the road beneath her slippers. He'd known what to say when her father died too. Everyone else at the funeral prayers had murmured facts, and pity.

It's so tragic, so sad.

What a wonderful husband he was, such a caring father.

What will happen to the family now?

Haaris had been only seventeen then. He'd sat down next to her, and in his low, deep voice said, "You'll be all right. I know you will."

She wanted the same now. She wanted to tell him everything that had happened—the datura and Dawood's visit, the National Hospital position and her mother's decision to leave Karachi and their house. And then she wanted Haaris to tell her that everything would be all right.

But his words wouldn't be enough anymore. Rozeena needed to take action, do something that would keep her family here and making their own decisions.

Across the street, Haaris's gate opened with a clang, and his cook walked out carrying a tray laden with dishes.

Rozeena frowned. "We've already sent over today's—"

"We'll take care of it, for the whole week." Haaris nodded at his cook.

"The week?"

"Or the month. As long as they need."

Rozeena folded her lips between her teeth to keep her mouth from falling open. Meals were only sent to grieving households— Aalya's in this case, since Gul lived there—for three days, not weeks. But perhaps it made no difference to the Shahs, or their pockets. Before Rozeena could ask if he was serious, Haaris's gate opened again, all the way this time, and a brand-new white Toyota Corona pulled out. It turned in the direction of the main road and stopped.

The driver jumped out and held open the passenger door.

"Your father wants you in the office on your first day back?"

"According to my father, I'm already several years late." Haaris's smile drooped.

"Is the car a bribe for you to stay?" She teased, trying to lighten his mood, but his face became serious instead.

He turned his back to it all, the car, the driver, and the expansive family home that took more space than both Rozeena's and Aalya's plots combined. His house was also the newest, and one of many his business-savvy father owned in Karachi. Apparently, Haaris's father had seen an opportunity to knock down two smaller ones here and build his own, predicting the investment would grow rapidly in this north-of-downtown neighborhood.

That's how Haaris came to be the last of the friends to move into this small street, even though he'd always lived in Karachi. She remembered how they'd joked that the prince had finally arrived on Prince Road. But the joke hadn't lasted, because the title hadn't fit.

Haaris never did anything to set himself apart from the others, and when he did use his position, he did so unassumingly. In street cricket matches, when balls got lost in the thick bougainvillea covering boundary walls, Haaris would appear with new balls the next day, tossing them to Zohair and the other boys with no explanation, as if they'd never gotten lost in the first place. Of course the others could afford balls as well. Most fathers, like Rozeena's and Zohair's, worked in good government positions, as they'd done before Partition. And by now Rozeena's family would've become even more financially secure if her father had lived. But yet, Haaris knew how wide the gap truly was between them all, and it went well beyond the size of their homes.

"You know that I don't care about any of that," Haaris said now. "If I stay, it won't be for those things, or for my father's business."

"Then what will it be for?"

He held her gaze just as he had the day of his last goodbye. "Come with me?"

She blinked. "To Liverpool?"

He laughed. "No. I mean, right now. I want to say hello to my city, but with you. Will you come?"

In the back seat of his car, Rozeena let out a long breath to release her nervous anticipation. It didn't help. Something new raced inside her. It beat against her chest and burned her insides, even in cool November.

"McLeod Road is the other way," she said, leaning forward when Haaris's driver turned left at Metropole Hotel. "Aren't we going to see Habib Bank Plaza?" That's what she'd told her mother, after all.

"Why would we go there?" Haaris turned to face her with a confused smile.

"Because it's what everyone wants to see, even if it's still under construction."

Their faces were close. She could clearly see those impossibly long, curled eyelashes that somehow softened his jawline. But he looked older, and not because he was dressed in a suit and tie. She touched her own face, wondering if she too had a few lines around the eyes or in between the brows. At twenty-six, she was only two years younger than him.

She sat back with a smirk. "Or have you been away too long to know what we do here?"

Everyone adored seeing the new, cylindrical Habib Bank Plaza rising high into the Karachi sky. They were so proud of the building. It would be the tallest in the subcontinent. And McLeod Road had other new buildings too—the Karachi Stock Exchange, banks, news-paper offices, and insurance companies. Industrialization and a booming economy had arrived with Ayub Khan's presidency.

"People call McLeod Road the 'Wall Street of Pakistan' now," she said.

Haaris nodded but didn't turn around this time. His family's im-port/export business was probably flourishing as well, but for him, that was nothing new. Rozeena turned her focus outside, to the sprawling homes of Bath Island that appeared on her right. They must be headed to Clifton Beach. Where else? There was only sand and emptiness up ahead.

"Isn't this better than your Habib Bank Plaza?" Haaris said.

His driver parked at the base of Jehangir Kothari Parade, the grand sandstone structure on top of the hill overlooking the Ara-bian Sea.

They'd never come here alone before, never without Aalya and Zohair, at least.

While Haaris gave instructions to the driver to deliver papers to his father's office, Rozeena scanned the mostly empty road. Public buses didn't come to this part of the city, and there were only three other parked cars. For most people, it was much too early in the morning for such leisure activities.

Haaris's car shrank in the distance behind them as they climbed the yellow sandstone stairs flanked by balustrades all the way up the smooth, sloping sides of the structure. They landed on the wide, raised platform facing nothing but open sea up ahead, the shoreline extending in both directions. A waist-high balustrade continued around the platform's periphery, and in the center, a circle of columns held up a grand pink and yellow sandstone cupola. Her arms tingled with goose bumps under her lemon-colored kameez.

They were alone under the dome.

To her left, another set of stairs flowed down to the rest of the Parade. The broad promenade led to a pavilion, five arches along each length. Everything lay in a line facing the sea, except midway to the pavilion, an elevated stone pier extended out and ran all the way to the beach. The wide pier sloped past small gardens on either side and over desert bushes up ahead until it opened into a vast rectangular pavilion, the roof held up by thick, wide pillars inside and around as well. Twin staircases at the far end of the pavilion led down to Clifton Beach. From where she stood, Rozeena spotted two camels with their red-carpeted saddles sauntering along the shoreline, their owners leading them to the group of people waiting for a ride on the soft, wet sand.

"Should we walk?" Haaris's voice felt close perhaps because the wind was quieter in November. Winter tamed the blustery gusts of summer into sweeping breezes. Waves rippled instead of crashing.

She nodded and rubbed her arms again. Before her first step toward the stairs, Haaris's suit coat fell heavy onto her shoulders and pressed warm against her back, or was that Haaris himself? Reaching from behind, he brought the coat together at her front. She stiffened as his forearms brushed under her breasts.

It lasted only a few seconds, but she wanted more.

Without looking at each other, they walked onto the promenade and didn't speak until they were close to the entrance of the pier. She stopped, leaned against the balustrade facing the sea, and lifted her face to her favorite place.

"Don't you miss this when you're away?"

Soft, beige sand lay up ahead, as far as they could see in either direction. Gentle waves rippled back and forth, caressing the sand into a darker, glistening surface. Beyond that, the infinite expanse of sea reflected the cloudless blue above, turning the horizon into an indistinguishable merging of water and air. She licked the sea's misty salt on her lips.

"It's perfect, isn't it?" His hand pressed on her back.

She turned to him, squinting slightly under the early morning sun. "Then why do you stay away?"

His eyebrows arched, as if he wasn't expecting to be questioned. But she couldn't help herself. She needed to know if he'd leave again, especially now.

He cleared his throat. "Last night, as soon as I got home from the airport, I went straight to see Zohair, because it was too late to visit you." A small smile played on his lips. "He's the same as always, full of energy, all these plans and ideas." Rozeena smiled too. "But then, the first thing this morning, I went looking for you, Rozee." He tilted his head in a helpless sort of way. "You are the best part of coming back."

Her ears burned. She shook her hair to make sure they remained covered. He'd never said it in so many words. Neither one of them had. They'd been friends since childhood, yes, but each time he'd returned from Liverpool there'd been a newer, deeper attraction, like the distance had transformed their relationship into one of strangers meeting for the first time, strangers pulled to each other. She hadn't quite understood what that meant until now.

And he felt the same for her.

Just then she saw the approaching car from the corner of her eye. It shook her awake. She stepped back, creating distance.

"I . . . Haaris." She swallowed. "There's so much happening with the house, my work, and—"

"Of course. I understand. Tell me what you need." He reached for her arm, buried in his coat, and squeezed gently. "I'm here."

She blinked, unable to say that she needed everything he turned his back on, the established career, the security of knowing there was money in the bank, a safe future for herself and her family in Kara-chi, free from Shehzad and Sweetie's decisions. But no. She pursed her lips tight. She wouldn't exchange her independence for these things. Her parents hadn't sacrificed so much so that she could relin-quish it all for ease and comfort, and the wealth of a friend, or more.

"Maybe next time we can walk all the way to the end of the pier." Haaris nodded at the building they hadn't reached.

When she still didn't answer, worry crept over his face.

He took a step back. "I'm sorry if I said—"

"No, it's not that." She smiled a little. "I should get back home. Ammi and Khala are probably pacing the veranda waiting for me."

He smiled. "Of course."

She handed him his coat before heading down to where his driver waited on the street side of the Parade. With her back to the sea now, her mind crowded with problems again. The water always emp-tied her mind, vanquished all her worries, even when the wind was mild and not slapping away her thoughts. Facing the sea, she could always see what she really wanted for herself.

"What will your father say?" They were steps away from the car when she stopped to point at Haaris's feet. "Dusty shoes on your first day back."

His eyebrows arched again, amused this time. "I hadn't thought of that. Perhaps he'll throw me out of the office and solve at least one of my problems."

She joined in his laughter but had never understood his intense dislike for his father's work. Horribly dull, Haaris would say whenever asked. He'd managed to avoid it for an extra few years by continuing to work in Liverpool after completing his chartered accountancy qualifications. Now he was back in his father's world.

The idea came to her suddenly, as she slipped into the back seat of the car. His father's world was one of connections and power, not just wealth. She remembered the day years ago when Zohair had stumbled across a copy of *The Star*, the evening newspaper that hawkers waved at cars waiting at traffic signals. Its society pages were always filled with photographs of celebrities, politicians, and top businessmen. That day, staring up at them was a photograph of Haaris's parents at a terribly posh party. Haaris had shrugged it off and refused to even talk about it, so the friends never brought it up again. In fact, they learned to mostly gloss over their differences as children. But now it was becoming more and more difficult to ignore how their careers and futures were moving in opposite directions.

She took a deep breath to stop the twist in her gut. It was nothing more than a verbal suggestion, a recommendation.

For a fleeting moment she'd considered asking Sweetie for help. Sweetie had grown up in Karachi too, like Haaris's parents, and knew many people. She could easily recommend Rozeena's pediatric clinic to her friends and family. But Rozeena had rejected the idea quickly, afraid Sweetie would contact Rozeena's mother about the request, and what if that pushed her mother to share her decision about leaving Karachi even sooner than planned? Rozeena needed time.

She told herself there was nothing wrong in asking Haaris for help. It wouldn't take away her independence. After all, he'd just asked her what she needed, and she was certain he'd do the same for any one of them, Zohair or Aalya, if they asked.

When the driver turned onto Prince Road and stopped at Rozeena's gate, Haaris got out of the car too.

Rozeena placed a hand on the cool, black metal of her gate for support. "Can you do something for me, Haaris? Tell your friends about me, about my clinic. Only those with children of course. And only if you want to. I mean—"

He raised a hand for her to stop, nodding. But his lips drooped.

"What is it?"

He gave a little shake of the head. "Nothing. Of course I'll tell them about you. But you don't need it."

"I know," she lied, not wanting his pity. "But what's the harm in a recommendation?"

"You asked me earlier why I stayed away."

"Yes?"

"Well . . ." His pause turned into a sigh. "I'd better get to the office. Don't want to be too late on my first day, do I?" He gave a wry smile.

Rozeena didn't ask more questions. Right now, she needed his referrals and connections, even if he resented everything he had. She'd never before felt so separate from Haaris, and yet she'd never felt so close either.

9

THEN, 1964

Five Days Before

Like an invisible and powerful force, Haaris's connections reached Rozeena within days. She'd be seeing a new patient later in the afternoon, but before going to the clinic, Rozeena had a task.

Opening the door slowly, she stepped into her father's study.

She'd spent hours here over the years, preparing for medical college exams and fulfilling the plan originally meant for her brother. It was where she came to read the morning newspaper too, completely uninterrupted as no one else entered this room of the house. For her mother, it was too painful to come face-to-face with the ghost of her husband, but Rozeena welcomed it. It motivated her and brought her peace at the same time. She'd sit reading at her father's wide teak desk facing two wooden chairs and the wall of windows overlooking the veranda and garden. When early morning sunlight filtered through the windows, she'd watch the room turn golden, rays bouncing off the mustard floor tiles and filling the space with a glow. She'd bask in the radiance, believing her father was there with her, watching over her, proud of her.

Then some months ago she stopped coming, when each new household expense began illuminating her inability to care for her family and shamed her into hiding from her father's memories. Now Rozeena had an additional goal, one he could never have imagined. Today she'd be taking the first step to keep her mother's plan from materializing and preventing their move to Lahore. Rozeena would be taking the first step to preserve their home.

The scent of newsprint hit her even before she reached the stack of old *Dawn* newspapers, and others, piled high on her father's desk. Her eye caught a headline from some months ago, when she'd stopped saving them for imaginary conversations with her father.

TEENAGERS SWARM AIRPORT BAR;
BEATLE MCCARTNEY MOBBED

She couldn't help but smile, imagining the dinner table discussion this would've brought.

Every day, her father would insist she choose a favorite news item, and in the evening, she'd wave the newspaper at him as his blue Morris turned in to the back gate. Over dinner, he'd listen to her with complete attention, enthralled by her analysis, and respond with his entire being, his eyes round with surprise or narrowed with suspicion or glistening above a wide, proud smile. Sometimes he'd thump the dining table with his fist, eyes tearing with laughter.

Rozeena nodded at the stack of newspapers now, ran a gentle hand over them as she straightened the pile. Today, once again, she could face her father. She could stand tall, push back her shoulders, and feel confident that yes, before Shehzad's arrival, she'd be able to grow her clinic.

She had a plan.

An hour later, Rozeena unlocked her clinic door on the third floor of MPS Chambers.

She'd chosen this building two months ago for its popularity and central location. Even after saving her previous salary from the small city hospital where she'd worked, she could only afford the tiniest room in this building. But she had enough floor space for two patient chairs and an examination bed along one wall. There was an attached bathroom too, and the large window behind her skinny desk brought in ample sunlight in the late afternoon.

With a quick nod to her door plaque, DR. ROZEENA MASOOD, MBBS, PEDIATRICIAN, she crossed her room to scan busy Victoria Road below, filled with double-decker buses, bicycles, cars, camel-carts. She sent down a wish for more and more of those cars to come straight to her.

There was a double knock on the door.

"Your first is here," Jamal said in his quiet but brisk tone. He reached her desk in two long strides, placed the file in the center, and was halfway out the door before Rozeena could thank him. Jamal wasn't unfriendly, just efficient, and she liked being treated the same as the other two doctors who shared the waiting hall. Both were men, older and with more established clinics.

She slid on her white coat, and her patient was being ushered in as Rozeena stepped out of the bathroom with freshly scrubbed hands.

"Rozeena!" Saima planted a kiss on both her cheeks before Rozeena could step back. "I find it so unbelievable, and wonderful of course, that you're a pediatrician. Our pediatrician now." Saima beamed.

Her former convent school classmate floated in on a cloud of perfume so strong that Rozeena had to hold her breath to keep from coughing it out. She hadn't recognized the married name in the file and wasn't expecting *this* Saima. Haaris must've had to remind her about the girl called Rozeena in her class, because they'd certainly never been friends.

Saima settled herself on one of the chairs with a flourish, shaking the pleats of her sky-blue sari so they cascaded flawlessly from her knees to the floor. The ayah walked in behind Saima carrying the actual patient, peaceful in the nanny's arms, and sat gingerly on the other chair.

"How are you, Saima? And look at little Daniyal. Let's give you a checkup, shall we?" Rozeena spoke fast to keep random conversation from filling in the gaps. She needed to maintain a professional clinic, and they would have nothing to chitchat about anyway.

She remembered Saima vividly. The strict uniform—white shalwar kameez, white canvas Bata shoes, and white socks—had kept most differences at bay within the school gates. But girls like Saima had enough well-placed accessories to set them apart. She'd refer to her hair ribbons as ruby red and emerald green and would casually mention how she'd picked up the pure silk from Paris during her family holiday in Europe. It had sounded like something you'd see in films or read in novels.

Saima took Daniyal from the ayah and held him on her lap. Mother and son were in matching colors, down to the shade.

"Isn't he the most perfect baby you've ever seen?" Saima laughed, but Rozeena knew it wasn't said lightly. Having perfect offspring would be the natural expectation for Saima.

After checking his weight at the scale, Rozeena scanned the file Saima had brought from her previous pediatrician. "There'll be one vaccination today."

"Yes, of course, but why the rush?" Saima handed her child back to the ayah. "I hardly ever see you anymore."

Anymore?

"I want to hear everything." Saima stretched her arm across the desk reaching for Rozeena's hand. "What have you been up to all these years?"

Rozeena stared at the smooth, blemish-free arm, looking especially long in the sleeveless blouse. Tightening her grip on the pen in one hand and the file in the other, she tried to avoid meeting Saima's hand. The appointment was devolving into some sort of tea party, but without the tea.

"I wish I could offer you chai and talk about everything," Rozeena said. "But you know how full the waiting hall gets." It wasn't a complete lie. The hall was full already, but with the other doctors' patients.

Saima's eyebrows arched high into her smooth bouffant as she pulled back her arm. If she was offended, she hid it well.

"Well, of course this isn't the right place." She waved a hand around the room with an easy smile. Her pink Cutex nail polish flashed, and thick gold bangles clanged. "I'll come and visit you at your house. And you don't have to tell me where you live. Haaris said you're right across the street from him. Did you know my oldest sister was in school with one of the Shah sisters? The oldest one. Everyone calls her Apa. And my brother, Waleed, was with Haaris in school. Such a small world."

Rozeena nodded, surprised that her address would be the subject of any of Saima's conversations, but not surprised that she knew Haaris's entire family so well.

"That would be nice. Excuse me while I prepare for the vaccination."

Thankfully, the smallpox vaccine kept Saima silent. Rozeena dipped the bifurcated needle into the tiny bottle and brought it to Daniyal's soft arm where he sat in Saima's lap once again. With each jab—the vaccination required several—Daniyal's wailing became louder. Rozeena functioned in a bubble, focused on the needle, the patch of upper arm in her line of sight, and the angle of her wrist allowing for precise punctures to the skin.

After cooing to calm little Daniyal, Rozeena looked up and saw Saima's eyes glistening. The tip of her nose had turned pink.

"There's nothing like it." Saima dabbed her nose as Rozeena

returned to her desk to add notes to the file. "Having children, you know. It's heartache but utter joy too. Can you believe anything could be both? I know you work with babies all day, but there's nothing like having your own."

Rozeena braced herself for the onslaught of pity. Marriage was necessary for motherhood, and at twenty-six she was practically a spinster.

"I hope to be Daniyal's pediatrician for a long, long time," Rozeena said. "I hope to watch him grow up."

Saima laughed. "Well, yes. That would be wonderful for us too." She paused. "Haaris told me about your father. I didn't know, and of course this makes sense now." She gestured at the stethoscope on the desk.

Rozeena's jaw clenched.

"I understand how sometimes things happen to us, things that aren't our fault. At all," Saima emphasized. "The strong ones overcome, don't they? And you're one of them." She nodded. "I am definitely going to recommend the brilliant Dr. Rozeena, our own Rozeena, to all my friends. In fact, I'll arrange a little cinema outing so my friends can meet you. If that's all right with you?"

Rozeena's lips quivered, unsure of the correct answer. She wanted to yell, *Yes! Yes!* but didn't want to sound too desperate.

Taking a deep breath to steady herself, she said, "Yes, of course. I'd appreciate whatever you can do. And please drop by for chai whenever you'd like. You know where I live."

Saima's attention was most certainly welcome.

10

NOW, 2019

Haaris is in Rozeena's house, in front of her face. At least that's what it feels like to her. Blood swishes loudly in her ears, competing with the pounding of her heart. She hasn't moved, or even taken a deep breath, since opening his email.

She's at her desk in the study, where she goes straight after breakfast every day. Three large windows behind her open to the back of the house, and Basheer's shadow falls over everything on the desk— her laptop, the electricity bill, and today's *Dawn*—as he walks back and forth to the kitchen from his quarters. Daal is simmering on the stove for lunch, and he must keep an eye on it.

But even Basheer's comforting and reliable presence cannot calm Rozeena's heart today.

Her son, her precious Mansur, has contacted Haaris.

Rozeena reads Haaris's email for the fifth time that morning.

I have not replied to a single email, but your son has sent eight of these since the beginning of the year. I'm sending you the latest one here.

Now that we are in touch, I thought you should know.

He found my email from Apa. I don't know why he would do that. Did you say something to him, Rozee?

Of course not. And Haaris too must remain silent.

But he'll be in Karachi soon. What if they meet? What will Haaris say to Mansur then?

She turns to the old four-by-six color photograph that sits on her desk in its smooth wood frame. Lately her Mansur has been asking too many questions about the past, and this photograph is always where he begins, his only point of reference.

Rozeena remembers the day Mansur found it, the photograph of herself, Aalya, Zohair, and Haaris. Even at six, Mansur loved visiting Rozeena's clinic, especially near the end of the day when he could stuff his ears with her stethoscope and pretend to be the doctor. That day he was searching Rozeena's desk for a pen and paper to scribble a list of medications for make-believe patients, when he stumbled upon the framed photo.

"Are these your friends?" Mansur held it in his two little hands and peered down at the faces.

Rozeena stared from where she stood by the filing cabinet across the room. How could she have forgotten to tuck the frame back under the pile of papers? She'd taken it out today, like she did sometimes, but the sharp pangs of sorrow and regret had made her quickly drop it back inside the drawer.

She tried to make light of her son's discovery. "That old photograph?" She shrugged. "Yes, it's the four of us."

Mansur knew about her friends, of course. They were part of Rozeena's childhood, and he always wanted to hear about how the friends would walk to the general store to buy toffees, and how the boys played cricket on the street and balls always got lost in the thick bougainvillea. But in this photograph the friends and Rozeena were all adults. She'd never recounted stories of that time because it was a part of the past she wanted to keep from Mansur.

"Can we take it home?" he said, holding on tightly to the frame.

They did take it home that day, because denying Mansur would've only made him more curious. But as Rozeena dreaded, having the photograph in the house made it a topic of conversation. She found herself having to skirt around Mansur's questions until the day she finally formulated a story that left no room for further inquiries.

Until now.

Rozeena realizes that the story she told Mansur all his life is no longer enough for him. He's taken matters into his own hands, contacted Apa through their mutual acquaintances, and is sending emails to Haaris behind Rozeena's back. She should've known that her fabricated story would lead Mansur to seek out Haaris, of all the friends.

Rozeena picks up the photograph and carefully lays it on the papers in her bottom drawer. If only it were this easy to erase the lies she's been telling Mansur all his life. She pushes the drawer shut and clicks out of her email with a trembling hand.

Later that evening, Rozeena makes sure to keep a smile on her face so her worry stays hidden. Even though it scares her to know Mansur has found Haaris, she must keep calm and pretend she knows nothing. This lying, she's always told herself, is necessary to protect Mansur, and for that reason alone she'll happily maintain a façade.

"What's making you smile like that?" Mansur asks from the other veranda chair.

She beams genuinely now. Mansur's attention and care are always exemplary, even before she realizes she needs something, like these visits.

He started them quietly two decades ago after somehow recognizing her desire to have him to herself at times. Off and on he began visiting alone, dropping in after work on a weekday for chai before heading home. All they do is sit quietly on the veranda and let Karachi's cool sea breeze blow at their faces. Mother and son are similar in that they're not chatterboxes, unlike Mansur's wife who feels compelled to fill all the peaceful moments of quiet. But Rozeena keeps her mouth shut and nods at her daughter-in-law. The woman is not a bad person, and Rozeena has learned that the best mother-in-law is the one who's least intrusive and who gives excellent gifts.

Of course they visit as a family too, over dinner when their schedules allow. Mansur's three children, all in their twenties now, are an injection of youthful vigor for Rozeena. Their stories, their ways, the new trends of the world she hears from them, it all keeps her mind churning and heart beating.

"I was smiling at the thought that he's in the wrong profession." She gestures at Pervez who's watering the other ground cover he planted himself some weeks ago, under the twin coconut palms. "He has an invisible green thumb."

Her driver smiles to himself while he works, probably relieved Zara won't be gardening today. Each day last week, Pervez waited anxiously in the kitchen, sipping cups of chai with Basheer, until Zara left. Then he emerged and spent the next hour inspecting the plants, the soil, and the grass to make sure not a single spot had been missed.

Many had been.

That's how Zara's latest mistake had been discovered, for which she apologized profusely. She'd buried the onions around the anthills, but she'd placed the root side down. If Pervez hadn't checked and dug them all up to aim the roots toward the sky, Rozeena's entire garden would be sprouting onions in no time. Zara definitely hasn't been up to standard—though Rozeena enjoys Zara's company and sees a slow change in her toward what, Rozeena suspects, is her true self.

"Yes, well thank God for Pervez's green thumb," Mansur says. "Kareem will be out recuperating for another three weeks at least."

He frowns as if he's back at his clinic, flipping through a patient's file. Rozeena wants to reach over and rub away the folds of skin above his nose. He takes off his dark-rimmed glasses, pinches the bridge of his nose to massage it himself before dropping his head back with a sigh. The curved slats of the rosewood chair cradle his spine as they do Zara's each time she visits. Rozeena was surprised the first time Zara relaxed so fully and easily. Then she remembered that youngsters these days aren't as reserved and restricted by formalities.

Relaxed now, Mansur looks younger than his fifty-four years. His jaw turns as soft as an angular one can get. His full head of hair, though graying, is tousled by the breeze like a child's. But the grooves on his forehead remain. Her child is truly grown, a responsible adult.

"Thank you for all that you've done for Kareem." Rozeena knows how hard Mansur works for all his patients, how full his days are. "I wasn't sure if he'd ever walk again. He has seven children, and—"

"No need to thank me. It's my job." He turns to her with a smile before letting his eyelids droop again.

The steamy chai and thick slice of pound cake comfort him like a baby after a feeding. He's always been that easy, that good.

Rozeena wonders if the choice of name makes the man. Mansur means victorious, and he has certainly excelled in all areas. He says he's just doing his job by treating Kareem, but she knows Mansur has been checking on him at his home between appointments at the hospital and clinic. And when she telephoned Kareem's wife, suggesting she buy them a new bicycle since the old one was useless after the accident, she was told Dr. Mansur had already done so. Her heart bursts with gratitude to Allah for being given such a perfect child.

"You are my responsibility too," he says now, straightening himself from his brief recline. He leans toward her. "Don't you think it's time to wrap up here and move in with us?" He looks down, pretending to flick off imaginary lint from his khakis. He knows full well Rozeena resists this discussion. "I mean, I've heard the transition is easier before it becomes a necessity."

"And who says it will become a necessity? Perhaps I'll just drop dead one day, with no prolonged illness or debilitation."

She smiles to make light of it before he accuses her of being morbid, though he's the one being morbid by insisting she give up her independence. Leaving her house will mean taking up even less space in this world, less reason to be. Before he can continue his gentle, oft-repeated argument, a car honks at the gate. They watch as Pervez drops the hose, turns off the water, and pulls open the gate. Rozeena is grateful for the interruption—until Zara walks in.

Rozeena's breath catches, and she blinks, hoping her mind has misidentified the person heading toward them. But no, her past is about to collide with her most precious present.

She pushes herself up and stands between Mansur and the approaching Zara. The girl's high ponytail swishes left and right behind her, and the thick strap of her brown leather satchel hangs across her pink T-shirt.

Is this why you sent her to me, Haaris, to disrupt my life with reminders of the past while you stay hidden on the other side of the world?

Rozeena trembles with anger until Mansur's hand finds her elbow and she's stilled. Nodding at him, she sits back down and waits for her breathing to calm. Zara and Mansur stand facing each other. Pervez is behind them, on the grass, waiting for instructions. Rozeena tells him to continue the gardening.

"I thought we canceled today's meeting," Rozeena says with a forced smile. She clearly typed out a WhatsApp message to that effect right after Mansur called this morning.

Zara pulls off the satchel and drops it on the tiles next to the third chair. "Oh, I'm so sorry. I didn't see your message." She quickly takes out her phone, searching for the text. "I don't really check WhatsApp that much. Is it okay that I'm here?"

Mansur jumps in and insists that it's a pleasure to meet her, though he wasn't aware she'd been visiting regularly. He glances at Rozeena, who quickly makes the introductions, and the three, all seated now, form a semicircle around the table and face the garden.

"You're Haaris Uncle's granddaughter?" Mansur says again, swinging his head from Rozeena on one side to Zara on the other, and back. "Your Haaris from the old neighborhood?"

"Yes, yes, Mansur. Why is it so surprising to you? Do you think I can't remember my old friends?" Rozeena laughs away his questions and quickly continues. "But, Zara, the work is all done now, as you can see." She points to the hosepipe neatly coiled up again. "You really should check your messages more and follow our schedule, like a real internship."

"What internship?" Mansur says, and gets a quick explanation from Zara. "So, your grandfather connected you with my mother," he says slowly.

"Zara has a particular interest in gardening, and Apa had heard I needed a maali, temporarily. That's all." Rozeena shrugs to play it down.

Mansur frowns but seems to accept it.

Zara doesn't mention any telephone calls between Haaris and Rozeena, so hopefully she's unaware they communicate directly.

"Well, I guess I'm not really that good at the gardening stuff." Zara bites her lip and flashes a look at Rozeena. "I promise to check my messages more from now on." She takes the iced lemonade from

Basheer, who now knows what this regular visitor drinks, and absently draws lines down the sides of the glass, already dripping with condensation in July's humidity. "I'm glad I didn't miss my day with you though. It's just easier to be here sometimes."

Mansur's head swings around to question Rozeena, who ignores his concern and nods at Zara, in appreciation of her honesty.

She's been escaping to Rozeena's, freeing herself of her parents' constant focus. Every day, Zara's gardening time has given way to photography, eating samosas, and simply lounging silently on the veranda. No questions, no judgments, no expectations.

She smiles back at Rozeena now and downs her lemonade before pulling the satchel up to her lap.

"I brought you a gift."

She wrinkles her nose like she's not sure if Rozeena will like it, but Zara's excitement is palpable. Taking out a folder, she opens it on her lap and holds up a single, full-page portrait of an old man.

Haaris.

"So, you're an artist," Rozeena whispers. The drawing is even more breathtaking than the girl's photography.

Zara shrugs and passes it to Mansur. "I draw portraits mainly."

Rozeena takes it from her son and lays it on her lap. Haaris has aged. She touches her own face and smiles at the wrinkles and loose skin that she knows exist on herself too.

"He's lucky he still has hair."

Zara laughs. "You'll see for yourself when he comes."

Rozeena sucks in a breath. Mansur turns to her, his eyes round, eyebrows raised, and she continues the charade of her ignorance.

"Really?" Mansur says to Zara. "When? And why, after all these years?" His second cup of tea rattles against the saucer in his hand as Zara explains the need for a companion on her flight home.

Then she scoots to the edge of her chair with urgency, eyes wide. "You know what? I want to find a really old pic of Haaris Daada, like from when he lived here, and surprise him with a sketch when he comes." She grins widely and waits.

Zara is more excited than Rozeena has ever seen her. It's like she's completely transformed, but into herself.

"The idea just came to me, like suddenly," Zara says. "But I need a photograph."

"Well, that's easy." Mansur is up in a second. "And please, I'd love to see the drawing and your grandfather too when he arrives."

Rozeena knows exactly where Mansur is going, but there's nothing she can do to stop him now. And what will happen when Haaris arrives? Will she be able to keep them from meeting? Mansur returns with the frame from her study—the last photograph taken of the four friends on Prince Road.

"It was in your desk's bottom drawer again," Mansur says with a confused smile. "Why do you keep putting it there?"

Rozeena doesn't answer that, from time to time, she still can't bear to see it, can't bear to remember.

Zara squints at the photograph. "The faces are so small." Even though it's a clear photo, from a high-quality camera for that time, it was taken from a distance. The garden and fountain take up most of the space. "How come no one's smiling?"

Ignoring the question, Rozeena says, "Haaris and I are on the ends."

"And of course the middle two are Aalya and Zohair," Mansur adds, still standing over Zara's shoulder. She looks up at him blankly. "You don't know about them?" he says. "Hasn't your grandfather told you anything of his life here?"

Zara shakes her head.

"Well, then," Mansur says. "I think both of us will have some questions for him when he arrives, won't we?"

By the time Mansur asks Zara for her father's mobile number and gives his own to keep in touch, Rozeena's worry is visible on her damp forehead. Haaris's portrait lifts with a gust, rippling on her lap, and his white mane resembles a blowing plume of smoke—or a ghost traveling from afar.

She shivers in the breeze.

The last time Haaris returned, it had started out well, so well. But within days, nothing had ever been the same again.

11

THEN, 1964

Four Days Before

Zohair thumped his grass with the shiny new cricket bat, the gift Haaris brought back each time he returned from Liverpool. Standing on the other side of Zohair's garden, Haaris swung his arm hard, fake-bowling with an invisible ball, and whoosh, a perfect swing by Zohair. They'd spend hours doing this on the street as children, but usually they had a real ball.

"Are you afraid you'll hit the ball into the fountain?" Rozeena said, shutting Zohair's front gate behind her.

Zohair shuffled his feet and shrugged in response to her question.

She was the last one to arrive at their usual gathering spot, even though she'd rushed through dinner after the clinic. A friend of Saima's came today with her infant daughter. Every new patient brought Rozeena closer to her goal, and Saima was doing as she'd promised.

Rozeena passed the fountain in the center and felt Haaris's eyes on her. She turned to smile at him, and for a beautiful, simple moment, it was just the two of them in her world.

"Did something happen, Rozee? Why are you late?" Aalya sat on the slim tiled veranda outside Zohair's front door. Her feet sank into the thick grass and her eyes jumped to Zohair with every word.

"What do you mean?" Rozeena dropped down next to her. "I'm not that late."

Aalya mindlessly cradled the tin of Mackintosh's Quality Street chocolates and toffees Haaris always brought back for each of them.

"I thought maybe you were late because of the ball." Aalya lowered her voice further. "They had one, but it went into your house, over the boundary wall. They should've switched sides and batted from the right instead of the left."

Rozeena looked up and saw both men staring at her from their respective sides, waiting.

She shook her head with a small smile. "No one even noticed. I'll throw it over as soon as I get back."

Visible relief spread over her friends, especially poor Zohair. She dropped her head low, popped open the tin on Aalya's lap, and stuck her hand deep inside, pretending to search for a toffee.

"Ammi really is better now."

"I know," Aalya said gently.

It had happened seventeen years ago, but everyone knew about it—the howl Rozeena's mother released the day she first saw Zohair, when he and his father moved into their house. It filled Rozeena's head now like it had filled the air then.

Aalya squeezed Rozeena's fingers under the layers of colorfully wrapped toffees.

"Your tin is inside," Aalya said. "If you give me all the Toffee Pennies, I'll give you all the orange ones. Go and get it."

She knew exactly how to distract Rozeena, like old friends do, with tenderness and conviction.

"Thank you."

Aalya frowned, amused. "You don't have to thank me, Rozee, like I'm some stranger."

But at times she was, wasn't she?

The growing distance between them wrung Rozeena's heart, squeezed it tight. She'd guided and protected little Aalya from that first day of school, been so proud of her when within months she'd learned to read and write. Right away, Aalya's mother had given her the task of keeping a record of the milkman's deliveries and the number of bedsheets and other items picked up each week by the dhobi for washing and ironing. Rozeena, who'd never done such grown-up work as a child, had been utterly impressed by her smart little friend.

So when Aalya quietly accepted her mother's plans some months ago, Rozeena had to speak up, and the conversation had resulted in their first rift.

"Tell your mother how miserable you feel," she'd said to Aalya. "Tell her how you feel being paraded in front of potential in-laws, serving them chai and mumbling agreeable words so they send an official proposal. You could do more with your life, be more." If her parents approved of the match, Aalya would be expected to say yes without ever even meeting the prospective groom.

But Aalya had shot back. "I can't say that to Ammi. Everyone's not you. I have a duty to—"

"I have responsibilities too," Rozeena said, shocked that Aalya couldn't see.

"Well, my duty isn't any less worthy than yours."

"I never said it was. All I'm saying is you should marry someone you can meet first, and find something else to do too, see what's out there."

"No, Rozee. You don't understand. You can't understand," she had said with a heavy sigh. "My mother, my parents, they're different."

Her anger had fizzled instantly into distress, so Rozeena hadn't persisted.

She wondered if Aalya was hurting because she knew Zohair wasn't settled enough, wealthy enough, for her mother's approval. But there seemed to be something more behind her commitment to pleasing her mother.

Rozeena handed Aalya the magazines now, the ones she'd taken from Zohair the night they'd been spotted together in the garden. Aalya showed no surprise or embarrassment and gave an easy smile and a Toffee Penny in return. But when she looked up to find Zohair, their eyes locked. Rozeena said nothing, asked nothing. She was grateful for the smile Aalya had offered her, and she wouldn't jeopardize the tenderness between them by questioning these secret gifts from Zohair.

Remembering the other gift, Rozeena jumped up to get her tin from inside.

"Hurry back," Haaris said, holding up his new Instamatic. "I need photographs."

"Of me?"

His face split into a wide smile. "Of all of us, actually."

She kept her smile in check, not too eager, and certainly not too endearing for Haaris. But Aalya's eyes darted back and forth between them. Rozeena turned away and headed to the front door. Guilt pinched inside her, but it wasn't the right time to share, not until Rozeena was certain herself.

She stepped inside Zohair's house and froze.

The drawing room was bare, unrecognizable. Two wooden armchairs sat askew with tattered cushion covers. There were no sofas or tables or lamps anymore. The mustard tiles on the floor were the same as always, but the walls needed paint and the sconces were gone. Naked bulbs lit the sad room.

She heard coughing in the back, and quickly headed to the kitchen to find the tin before Zohair's father caught her staring.

In the kitchen, she wanted to yank open cupboards and drawers to see if they too were empty. Apart from the Quality Street tin, there was only a stone mortar and pestle on the counter, next to a small bowl of green cardamoms and some tiny dried leaves. Her nose twitched at the sweet, clean scent. Mint.

"Are you looking for something, Rozee?" Rauf entered the room from behind.

She grabbed the tin and turned around with a smile. "Just this." She paused. "What are you grinding in there, Rauf Uncle?"

"Ah, that. It's my mint drink, for the ulcer." He patted his concave abdomen, his belt hardly keeping his trousers up.

"Are you seeing a hakim, because I don't think—"

"It's not harmful, Rozee." He waved away her concerns. "They're just simple everyday things we put in our food, aren't they? But it soothes my stomach, so why not?"

She couldn't disagree but was certainly surprised Rauf was using these natural cures.

"Are you getting new furniture in the drawing room?" she asked, her eyes settling on his shirt collar. She stared so long that he brought his hand up and tugged at it, before lowering his chin. The cuff of his sleeve was the same—frayed, every edge jagged and rough, the threads sticking out like short hairs.

"No, no. But we're just two in the house. We don't need much furniture."

She nodded and added gently, "I'm glad Zohair started work at the railway station."

Rauf's tone turned soft. "His mother would be so proud."

Zohair had been only seven when she died. Father and son had arrived in Karachi alone and moved in next door after buying the downstairs from Aalya's family. Perhaps it was because Zohair had no mother that Rauf was so lenient, agreeing with every whim, every desire, like that ridiculous fountain Zohair had installed in the garden some years ago.

Aalya passed her tin to Rozeena when she returned to the veranda. The four always shared one before opening another.

"Have you been inside? Did you see they don't have anything?" Rozeena unwrapped an orange foil.

Aalya nodded, unsurprised. "Zohair has a plan. He wants to do something big with the money."

"So he's sold everything? And how long will the 'something big' take?"

Aalya shrugged and took the tin back.

Rozeena filled her mouth with a second orange chocolate to keep herself from asking more questions and annoying Aalya.

Haaris sauntered over as Zohair ran past them to call his father for the photographs.

"I was telling Zohair that my parents insist I celebrate my return." Haaris winced. "A Welcome Home Ball, they're calling it. Anyway, you'll come, won't you? It's up on the roof, as always." He gestured at his house across the road.

Rozeena and Aalya exchanged glances. They'd never been invited to a party at Haaris's before.

"We must go." Aalya bolted upright. "I'll only be allowed if you're there, Rozee."

Haaris grinned, waiting for her reply.

"Well, if all your friends like Saima will be there, how can I say no?" Her smile quickly faded, though, seeing Haaris's knitted brow.

She'd planned on thanking him for sending Saima her way, but now wondered if the mention of his favor would only irritate him.

Rauf stepped out then, and the four of them posed in a line. The thick trunk of the tamarind tree rose tall behind on one side, and the three-tiered fountain on the other. The outdoor lights of the house cast a glow on their faces as Rauf fiddled with the camera.

Rozeena leaned forward.

"Why do you want these photographs anyway?" she asked Haaris, on the other end.

The camera clicked.

She pulled her head back and faced forward for the next shot.

"As a reminder of us," Haaris said. "Old friends from before."

Her heart twisted, and her forehead wrinkled to match, wondering if Haaris was planning to leave again.

The camera clicked.

"Before what?" Aalya asked from next to Rozeena and then laughed. "Before the ball?"

"Oh no. Not that." With a pensive gaze ahead, Haaris said, "I mean, before we all grow up."

Aalya nodded silently, and Rozeena too understood. Technically, they'd left childhood years ago, but now they stood on the precipice of growing up—making life-altering decisions and taking definitive steps for their future.

Zohair pulled himself up, tall and serious. "Let's hurry up and grow up then. I want to run this city like Haaris's other friends, and I'll start by meeting them all at his Welcome Home Ball."

As Aalya turned to look up at Zohair, a sadness washed over Haaris's face. He opened his mouth to reply but then caught Rozeena staring. His face relaxed into a smile before he turned back for the camera, straight-faced.

The camera clicked.

12

THEN, 1964

Three Days Before

Khala was immediately suspicious. She squinted at the early morning visitor from the veranda as Rozeena and her mother rushed down to greet Sweetie at the gate.

"Is everything all right at home?" Rozeena's mother asked. For years, doctors had been warning Shehzad about his excess weight, for the sake of his heart.

"Of course everything is all right," his wife answered. "I'm in Karachi visiting my parents. That's all." Sweetie pursed her lips at Rozeena and added, "But I'm wondering if everything is all right here."

Rozeena tensed. Sweetie never visited without Shehzad, and she certainly wasn't in Karachi visiting her parents. She'd practically moved here permanently now that her children were married and settled. Sweetie was happily expanding her role in her father's massive construction business. Shehzad meanwhile remained very much an employee, tinkering about in the smaller Lahore office.

"Do have Shareef make chai," Sweetie said to Rozeena's mother. "I want to go up to the roof first and take a look at the neighborhood.

Quite interesting how it's grown. Come with me, Rozeena." She marched ahead.

Rozeena followed her up the concrete stairs behind the house. Sweetie's back, draped in a mustard-colored sari from her broad shoulders all the way down to the heavy, wide base, rose like a massive mountain. Surprisingly though, her movements were swift and purposeful, like an animal on a hunt. With each step, Rozeena shed more and more of the confidence she'd gained by having new patients at the clinic every day, mostly referred by Saima.

Reaching the top, Rozeena shivered slightly in the cool morning.

"I didn't want to wait for Shehzad's arrival to come and see you. He's much too simple." Sweetie sighed. "He doesn't always see things like I do."

She waited for a response, so Rozeena nodded tentatively. Shehzad was a gentle man, at least that's how her mother explained the success of his marriage. Khala said it worked because he was a weak man. Rozeena herself didn't care either way, as long as Sweetie didn't consider herself the owner of Rozeena's life as well.

"Walk with me," Sweetie said.

At the front of the house, they peered over the waist-high boundary wall down to the large rectangle of grass. Small shrubs and jasmine plants filled the beds around the border.

"Now this was a good decision your mother made, to have a garden put in place of that original courtyard." She scoffed. "It certainly stopped those ragged neighborhood boys from playing cricket here."

"You know about that?"

"Of course I know. Your father was too generous to allow it. He should've . . ." Even Sweetie wouldn't speak ill of the dead. She moved to the front left corner to look down at Zohair's garden. "The one who lives here, he was the rowdiest of all."

"Zohair? No, all of them were rowdy. It's cricket." Rozeena shrugged.

Sweetie shook her head. "I heard he was the difficult one. Your parents told me themselves."

Rozeena held her breath, waiting for more, but from the silence it seemed like Sweetie didn't know the whole truth. Yes, Rozeena's mother had grass put in to stop all future cricket matches in the courtyard. But it wasn't because of Zohair's unruliness, and the general mess of smashed flowerpots and balls wedged in the bougainvillea. No. It was because of Zohair's love of cricket, and his dusty knees under khaki shorts, and his loud arguments about runs and outs. It was because of his infectious laughter.

Four years younger than Rozeena's brother, Zohair was a living, breathing reminder of Faysal in too many ways for her mother. Even their heights had been similar, because Faysal had always been much too short for his age.

"It doesn't surprise me that Zohair caused your poor mother so much grief with all his yelling and screaming over cricket," Sweetie said. "These are odd neighbors you have. Nothing like the Shahs across the street." She nodded at Haaris's house, and Rozeena sucked in her cheeks to prevent the automatic smile that spread over her face when he appeared in her thoughts these days.

"They're so established in the city, a foundation really," Sweetie continued. "Do you know they even did a good deed for these odd neighbors of yours? Yes, they suggested some relative of theirs, some third or fourth cousin, for the girl who lives upstairs." She pointed at Aalya's floor. "We all have some distant and different family members, don't we?" Sweetie shrugged. "Anyway, it could've been a good match. But do you know what the woman, the mother of the potential groom, did when she returned from meeting the girl who lives upstairs?"

Rozeena shook her head.

"She spread gossip. About you, Rozee."

"About me? But what could she—"

"I took care of it, of course, because you're family and we"—she paused for effect, with a hand on her chest—"we do not behave in such a way as that woman suggested. So, I made sure she understood she was mistaken, that she didn't see you meeting a young man in the garden, receiving gifts from him at night. Yes, there was another girl somewhere there too, but you, Rozee, were the one seen with him."

Rozeena's ears burned, and she stared at her feet, wondering how to explain away her behavior without implicating Aalya.

"I . . . I'm sorry," she whispered finally.

"This is why girls should marry at the right time." Sweetie fixed her eyes on Rozeena. "Instead of delaying it for education and whatnot." She shook her head. "But it's what your father wanted."

Anger roiled inside Rozeena hearing her father blamed and his plans attacked, but she said nothing, afraid Sweetie would change her mind about Rozeena's innocence. *Log kya kahenge?* mattered more to Sweetie than what had actually happened that night. She didn't even ask about Rozeena's version of the events. She didn't care as long as it was resolved and never mentioned or repeated, as long as Rozeena's behavior didn't reflect badly on Sweetie and her family.

Sweetie clucked again and shook her head. "And look at the house. I'll say it again. These are odd neighbors you have. Such a lush garden below, the tree dripping with tamarind pods, and even a fountain in the middle. But then this up top."

Rozeena didn't have to look up to register the general neglect that set Aalya and Zohair's house apart from the rest.

"Best to stay away from them." Sweetie waved a large, thick hand dismissively at the house. "You don't want all that spreading here." Rozeena opened her mouth to defend her friends, when Sweetie added, "And I hear you weren't offered the National Hospital position?"

Rozeena immediately shut her mouth. Her forehead grew slick with perspiration even though the sun was still low in the sky and the winter air cool and dry.

Gul was gone, and there was no denying it.

"Keep your distance from all those types of people, Rozee, the ones who go to hakims and such." Again, Sweetie didn't ask for any details about what had really happened. "The less you have to do with them, the safer you'll be. It's already cost you the hospital position, and everyone knows about it." She looked Rozeena straight in the eye. "No more mistakes."

Rozeena swallowed deeply and nodded, trying to make sense of how being seen with Zohair in the garden was being equated to Gul's death, and how both had resulted in the same lesson—do what is expected of you. Otherwise, what will people say?

With a firm nod, Sweetie turned and headed back across the length of the roof toward the stairs.

Squinting in the distance, she said, "This neighborhood is changing, isn't it?"

Mumbling agreement, Rozeena stood by, watching Sweetie rotate slowly in place for a complete view of their surroundings. Her eyes grew and shrank as she took in the new engineering university on the main road, and further in the distance, the residential areas where new markets sprouted all around. When she licked her lips and smiled, all Rozeena could think was that at least Sweetie's focus was elsewhere now, on a new construction project, a block of offices, or maybe even a university.

A rickshaw sputtered to a stop outside Aalya's back gate. Sweetie stopped her survey and leaned over the boundary wall. Ibrahim stepped out of the rickshaw in his regular attire, a beige shalwar kameez, and Rozeena hoped Sweetie wouldn't ask who this was. Such a rumpled, improper appearance would be another mark against the neighbors.

And somehow Aalya never had a good answer for her father's attire even when Rozeena asked.

"Does he go to an office?"

Aalya would shake her head. "He has some old friends he meets."

Rozeena had never seen those old friends or heard about them from anyone else, including Ibrahim himself. Soon she stopped asking. She'd heard of people like Ibrahim, men who'd never again put on a suit and tie and gone to the office after finally managing to cross the border. Whatever they'd suffered during Partition had made them incapable of returning to their old life. Sometimes Rozeena wondered what Aalya's family would eat if they hadn't sold the downstairs to Zohair's father.

By the time Sweetie and Rozeena returned downstairs, tea was laid out on the dining table. The sweet scent indicated it had been brewed with several pods of cardamom, as Sweetie preferred. She complained continuously of indigestion, and gobbled cardamom like it was some magic cure.

"My Usman is doing wonderfully with the business in Lahore. He has such excellent ideas." She beamed about her son between sips, with no mention of her husband who'd been working there since before Usman's birth. Her eyes settled on Rozeena, across the table. "That reminds me. I think you met Saima recently?"

"Yes." Rozeena spoke slowly. "Her son is my patient. How did you know?"

"It's a small city, at least for us, and everyone talks." Sweetie planted a smile on her face. "Now, you take care of Saima's son, Rozee, so that her family takes care of mine. They're close business partners, you know."

She laughed heartily at her wit, but Rozeena knew her command was not to be taken lightly. After one last gulp of tea, Sweetie told Rozeena to walk her to the gate.

"I spoke to you alone on the roof because your mother doesn't need the burden of your mistakes."

Rozeena nodded.

"And I don't want to have to talk to your uncle about them either.

He'll feel responsible. He'll feel you can't stay here on your own anymore. Do you understand?"

Rozeena understood the threat perfectly.

But Sweetie didn't know that in less than three weeks, when Shehzad arrived in Karachi, Rozeena's mother would be handing over the responsibility herself. She'd give up everything and move to Lahore, to Shehzad's house and care, unless Rozeena could convince them all that she could take care of the house and its inhabitants without making any more mistakes.

"What sort of a woman still uses the childhood name Sweetie?" Khala said when Rozeena returned to the dining room. "Does she believe that if we call her Sweetie, people will actually think she's sweet?" Khala grunted in disgust.

But yes, perhaps Sweetie did believe that. Because it mattered what people thought. *Log kya kahenge?* could change everything.

And now Rozeena would have to adhere to the rules even more closely because her recent activities had entered Sweetie's radar. From now on, she'd be scrutinizing Rozeena's every move.

13

NOW, 2019

There is some unknown reason behind Zara's every move today.

She insisted on accompanying Rozeena to the nursery this afternoon, but now that Rozeena's here to pick her up, there are at least twenty cars parked outside the gate. It's obvious Zara isn't attending a simple family lunch, as she claimed.

Before Rozeena can send in a message with the guard, Zara herself flings open the gate and quickly climbs into the back seat of the car, flushed and grinning.

"Let's go," she says, leaning back and splaying her arms wide. "That was ex-haus-ting. Felt like it would never end."

"But it hasn't ended, has it?" Rozeena peers at the cars outside before turning to Zara's embroidered kameez, intricate white on lemon, with the slim strap of a tiny black purse hanging across her front, shoulder to hip. "Seems like quite a formal, large gathering."

Zara shrugs as Pervez turns the car around to head to Rozeena's favorite nursery.

"You know how Haaris Daada's sister is," Zara says. "I have to be a certain way with her friends and answer all their questions appropriately, or just sit quietly and nod. But I have to be present at all the events, the grandchild from America and all."

"And what's so difficult about being present? I'm sure the food was good."

"It was," she agrees. "But, like, I couldn't even talk about my internship with you when they asked what I do the whole day."

Pervez parks in the empty plot on the quiet residential street. The nursery sits next door, on the corner, where the street meets a busy main road.

"And why can't you tell them about the internship?" Rozeena steps out of the car.

"Because, you know." Zara raises her hands in mock horror as she walks around to her. "What would people say if they knew I was a maali?"

Rozeena frowns at the ground, at this constant worry about other people's perceptions. Zara bristles against it much like Rozeena did in her youth. She has a sudden urge to protect Zara, ensure that she doesn't make the same mistakes Rozeena did. She never imagined she'd find even a glimpse of herself in this very young girl from the other side of the world.

Pulling her purse onto one shoulder, Rozeena lets Pervez hold her other elbow while they traverse the loose, uneven sand. "I'm sure they'd understand you're not really a maali, Zara."

"But so what, even if I was a real maali?" Zara's voice rises. "I have to be so careful about what I say around Apa. I mean, does she even like her brother?"

"Like her brother?" Rozeena stops abruptly at the entrance of the nursery. Arching leaves of areca palms, like tall feathers, create a wall on both sides of the approach. "What does this have to do with Haaris? What do you mean?"

Zara twists her lips to one side and shrugs. "Nothing. I don't know."

Rozeena feels her heart thud in her ears. The green walls sway in front of her eyes. Has Haaris said something to Apa, told her something about before, and is that why he's coming back?

"So, you said you needed a replacement tree, right?" Zara says.

Rozeena sucks in a breath. Her body trembles with her jagged exhale. She can't speak.

"Are you feeling all right?" Zara adds tenderly.

Nodding, Rozeena forces a smile and waves away the rickety chair offered by a nursery worker. "It's just this humidity, that's all." She gathers herself. "Let's go in."

Zara reaches for Rozeena's arm. "I can walk with you."

Rozeena accepts, and Pervez returns to the car.

They enter to all shades of green in every direction except straight up, where the late afternoon light spreads across a cloudless blue sky. An earthiness and the scent of foliage envelops them.

Atif's Nursery is the closest thing to a forest in Karachi, other than the dense mangroves in the creeks, of course. In the nursery, clay pots are lined up by size and type of plant. Splotches of rust, yellow, and green knee-high crotons fill an area to their left, next to rows and rows of light green ferns. Up ahead, bougainvillea grow in pots, forming a wide wall in all shades of pink. To their right, after lines of spider plants, young champa trees rise up with their perfect five-petaled ivory flowers.

Rozeena shares her new gardening club knowledge by pointing out how those types of champa trees, unlike her own, don't lose their leaves in the winter.

"Cool." Zara smiles, swinging her head left to right. "But this whole place is cool. Like so much green right in the middle of the city."

Along the perimeter, the larger trees keep the city from view. Only slices of low, sand-colored commercial buildings are visible through the tall ashoks with their downward folding branches and the foxtail and Malaysian palms growing in large cement planters.

Zara offers Rozeena the crook of her arm to follow the narrow dirt pathways that form a grid between the green. The ground is uneven, and if Zara's words shock Rozeena again, she may wobble right off her feet. She tightens her hold as they step onto the closest pathway. A few other customers linger in the expanse, but the only sound is of traffic in the distance, buses honking and engines running on the main road on the other side of this giant corner plot.

"I killed a cassia tree," Rozeena says, pausing to run a hand down a big banana leaf. "It was a young cassia, a naked twig that was growing taller and taller but with no branches or leaves or anything. So odd. And since my maali, Kareem, had the accident, I've had to make all the decisions on my own. I had the twig removed, thinking it was dead. But apparently, I was supposed to cut it, shorten its height quite a bit and it would've spread, branched out, and flowered in the winter."

"The winter?"

"It's our springtime here, temperature-wise," Rozeena says with a smile. "Not like your snowy, icy winters in Minnesota, I hear."

Zara's face goes slack, eyes blank, until she shakes her head a little and turns away, searching this way and that.

"Do they have cassia trees here?"

Before she can point them out, Rozeena's phone starts ringing loudly. She digs around in her purse, reaches in, and finds it. The screen flashes *Zara's Mom*, the name the woman entered herself the first day the family visited.

Zara's mom is frantic before Rozeena can even greet her. "Oh, thank God you answered. Is Zara with you? This is her mother. Is she there?"

"Yes, yes. Of course she's with me. Is everything all right? Should we come back?"

Zara focuses her attention on the plant closest to Rozeena, reaching for the star fruit hanging from a low branch and running a finger down the ridges of the waxy orange-yellow flesh. She stays there, repeating the movement over and over again, careful not to look in Rozeena's direction.

"What a relief." Zara's mother breathes loudly on the other end for a few seconds, inhaling, exhaling. "We looked all over. What is Zara doing there? I mean, she left in the middle of the luncheon. That's why I'm asking."

"The luncheon wasn't over yet?" Rozeena locks onto Zara, who gives a weak smile and then pulls out her phone from the tiny purse hanging at her hip. She mouths, *Landscoping* and starts taking photographs of the plants.

"No, the luncheon wasn't over at all, actually. I'm surprised Zara made a plan with you today. Anyway, the ladies wanted to meet her and congratulate her on the new gardening club prize she suggested, but we couldn't find her anywhere." An audible gulp came through the phone. "You can imagine my panic."

"Yes, of course. I'm so sorry. I didn't know. She's taking photographs here at the nursery, for *Landscoping*. Should I call her over so you can talk?" Rozeena watches Zara pause her photography to pull a rubber band off her wrist and tie a high ponytail.

Her mother's tone drops a note, calmer now. "Oh, no need if she's happily busy. She really likes spending time with you, doesn't she?"

Rozeena doesn't mind the hint of surprise in the woman's voice. They continue the conversation a bit longer, and Rozeena discovers the gardening prize has been set up in Fez's name, by Zara.

When Rozeena finally drops the phone back into her purse, Zara says, "I'm sorry for not telling you everything about the lunch and all." She bites her lip. "I was just trying to do what you told me to."

"What do you mean?"

"Didn't you say I should decide to be happy?" Zara lifts her face to the tops of the trees in the distance. "I'd rather spend time with you, talk about other stuff. I mean, I set up the prize and all, and sat through most of it." Rozeena watches a lump travel down the girl's throat. "Isn't that enough?" Zara turns to face her. "Isn't it?"

Rozeena isn't sure if running away is the best solution. But at least Zara is moving in the right direction, remembering her own needs and desires. Rozeena had taken too long to arrive at even this point. She reaches for Zara's arm, as if in need of support, but wraps her other arm around the girl, gently patting her back. Zara steps closer and rests her head on Rozeena's shoulder, perhaps to hide her watering eyes, or perhaps to allow a full embrace. They sway for a while, rocking side to side in silence. Rozeena isn't sure who is rocking who, even though she's the adult.

When Zara straightens, she's calmer.

"Should we get our work done now?" Rozeena says.

Zara nods with a growing smile. "So do you want to get something easier this time, so you don't kill it again?"

Laughing, Rozeena says, "I suppose that would be the safe choice. But when cassia trees flower, they're really quite beautiful, such bright yellow blooms with long petals. What a sight that would be." She points to a plant on the left. "But maybe this kangi palm is better for me. It's much easier to care for. Looks a bit like a crown, don't you think?"

Zara walks over, frowning. "You already have one of these in your garden. And it's so common. Apa has one in all of her houses."

"All of them?" Rozeena says, amused at how casually Zara accepts Apa's wealth.

"Uh-huh. And you know what," she says, hands on hips with sudden realization, "they're all descendants of Haaris Daada's plant!"

Rozeena freezes in place. "You know about Haaris's kangi

palm?" The girl has an unsettling mix of information. "The one from his family's Prince Road house?"

"Yes! He said the kangi palms keep growing baby plants from, like, the bottom, right? So he used to hand them out to all his friends and family and neighbors."

Rozeena nods. "And you'll be surprised to know that the one in my house is also a descendant of that original kangi palm, a grand-child or some such relation, I believe." She takes a deep breath. "Another cassia tree it is, then."

"You know, if Haaris Daada were here, you'd get your big, huge yellow flowers for sure." She offers her arm so they can walk ahead to the tree section.

"Oh, and why is that?"

"Because of his huge green thumb, of course. Why else?"

Surprised, Rozeena's fingers instinctively tighten around Zara's arm.

"It's okay. I got you." Zara pats Rozeena's rigid fingers. "I got you."

But all Rozeena can think of is, if Haaris has a huge green thumb, what other surprises are waiting for her?

"If he's really that interested in plants, you should tell him about this nursery, Zara. We didn't have such large ones in the old days."

Zara nods. "Every year I go back and tell him how it doesn't look like a desert at all here. There're so many trees all over, even on the dividers in the middle of roads." She shrugs. "He says it's probably because I stick to this part of Karachi. But where am I supposed to go? We don't know anyone on the other side."

She's not wrong. Haaris's family lives in a bubble, like Rozeena's.

But from what Zara says, it sounds like Haaris has been keeping track of his old city, of its growth and its increasing disparity. When a city's population grows from half a million to more than fifteen million in seventy years, how can there possibly be enough of anything for everyone? Even water isn't abundant anymore. Though of course too much watering is dangerous as well.

In her youth she hadn't known that excess could be a problem too. Just as a plant can drown in too much water, people can lose themselves in too much comfort, too much ease.

And the Prince Road group of friends had both too much, and too little.

14

THEN, 1964

Two Days Before

Y*our mother doesn't need the burden of your mistakes.*
      Take care of Saima's son, Rozee, so that her family
takes care of mine.

Sweetie's warnings were still ringing in Rozeena's ears when
Saima telephoned the next morning to arrange the outing she'd mentioned during the clinic visit.

"You remember my friends from school, don't you?" she said.
"They have three children each and are so eager to meet for the
cinema tonight. You'll be done with the clinic by then, won't you?
And we'll get our hair done earlier in the day. I'll pick you up in the
afternoon for the appointment."

Hair appointment for the cinema?

Rozeena had hardly mumbled yes and thank you before the
phone clicked shut. She'd do as Saima said, of course.

The owner of the beauty parlor on Tariq Road fluttered around
Saima the entire afternoon. She'd been there the day before as well,
to prepare for her Wednesday evening event. Rozeena had never seen

the inside of a parlor before. She reeled from the chemical hodge-podge smell and squinted at the mirror while a woman pulled and tugged at her hair as if it might grow in length and be better behaved.

"Just do the best you can with it," Saima said sweetly from her chair.

Rozeena clenched her jaw. She felt like a child being cleaned up to look presentable, but she played along. After some more back-combing and hair spray, the cloud overhead dispersed, revealing a bouffant in the mirror, its height and texture as fake as she predicted the evening would be.

Dressed in her pink sari with the white flowers, Rozeena stepped out of her front gate that night and froze at the sight of Haaris and another man. She peered behind them searching for the old school friends Saima had promised, and then pursed her lips as Saima rattled on about how there'd been some last-minute change of plans.

"She didn't tell you we'd be here, did she?" Haaris said quietly, holding the car door open for Rozeena, as Saima and her brother slid into the back seat from the other side.

Rozeena could've refused to join them but what a scene it would create, and the news would definitely reach Sweetie. Offending Saima and her brother would no doubt be counted as another mistake.

With a small smile, Rozeena shook her head. "No. This is all a surprise, but you're here, so it'll be all right."

Saima had been clever to include Haaris, a mutual and childhood friend, so even Rozeena's mother wouldn't object.

The drive to downtown was thankfully short. Haaris sat with his driver in front, and Saima was in between her brother, Waleed, and Rozeena in the back. At the first traffic signal, hawkers dashed for the car, bringing over thick bracelets of threaded jasmine buds and waving magazines and newspapers at car windows. Saima immediately asked for *The Star*, and before they reached Nishat Cinema, Rozeena knew exactly where Saima had been the previous night, what she'd worn, and how tall a bouffant she'd carried. A quarter-page photo of Saima and her friends stared up at Rozeena from the newspaper lying open on their laps. Apparently, Saima's crowd was photographed regularly for the society pages.

"And Waleed is often in it too, aren't you?" She nudged her brother, who grunted in response.

Inside the cinema, the four made their way to the balcony, the most expensive seats. The screen's lush burgundy curtain was at eye level here for the best view. Perhaps the evening wouldn't be too difficult after all.

Waleed hadn't said a word after their initial hellos and seemed immensely bored already. Rozeena managed to avoid sitting next to him. The lights dimmed and her shoulders relaxed, ready to enjoy the film and forget who she was with and why.

"You know he's divorced," Haaris whispered in her ear from his aisle seat.

"What? Who?"

Ashiana started off with loud, lively music as cast names flashed on the screen in both English and Urdu.

"Waleed. Recently divorced. Very short-lived marriage." He stuck to the main points, probably afraid of being overheard by Saima on Rozeena's other side.

"So what?" She frowned at the screen.

But clearly Haaris too had recognized this meeting as a matchmaking event. She burned with embarrassment. Saima had mentioned Waleed at the clinic the first day she'd come with her son. Now, within days she'd arranged a meeting between them with suitable chaperones. It was how her type of people brought couples together and arranged marriages. But Rozeena had no interest in marrying Waleed.

"You should know there were rumors," Haaris said.

"Why are you telling me this?" Rozeena checked to see that Saima was engrossed in the film before continuing. "What are you trying to say?"

"You know how these things are," he said. "Probably a competition to see who can get remarried first and come out the better person."

She tipped her head toward him. "You think I want to . . ." She shook her head.

He moved closer too. The warmth of his breath played on her temple. "I don't know what you want, Rozee. All I know is what I want."

Her breath caught, and her hand jerked toward him like a reflex, like catching something before it toppled over.

"Rozee." His voice was hoarse, deep. He pressed his palm on hers between them, knotting his fingers to hers.

Shifting in her seat, she stood her small, white purse like a wall on her lap, a barrier between Saima's eyes and the intertwined hands. Rozeena tried to pretend she was alone with Haaris like that day at Clifton Beach. The darkness of the cinema hall helped. She tilted her head toward him again, keeping her eyes on the screen. His arm pressed against her shoulder, so hard she felt it deep within. She wanted that force all over her, from head to toe.

He reached toward her with the other hand, his palm open. "I picked this up for you the other day, for your collection."

She squinted in the dark. A cream scallop shell fanned in his palm, the ridges near the wider part a deep brown while a blush of orange smudged the narrow end. She felt the heat of the blush rise inside her, gloriously. She couldn't help but smile as her heart yearned for him, for how easy it was to be with him, for being cared for and remembered by him.

With a furtive glance at Saima, who was luckily still absorbed in *Ashiana*, Rozeena covered the shell with her other hand, and the ridges against her skin brought a rush of memories.

Her father would take them to Clifton Beach, all four friends packed in the blue Morris with her mother. As soon as they parked, Zohair would dash to the nearest camel, screaming for Haaris to join him, and Rozeena would immediately shout back that Haaris couldn't go, because he'd promised to help collect more shells.

She never thought twice about protecting or lying for Haaris.

Rozeena knew how much he hated the sudden feeling of falling headfirst when the camel folded his tall, front legs to sit after the ride. And Haaris, in turn, was probably the only one who knew about Rozeena's three favorite shells, because he'd asked her, genuinely wanting to know.

"It's perfect," she said now, tucking away the memories.

When the film ended, Rozeena quickly slipped the shell into her purse, ready to leave, but Saima grabbed Rozeena's arm and gestured for the men to go ahead.

"I had such a lovely time. We'll do this again soon?" Saima raised her eyebrows all the way to her hairline.

Rozeena responded with nothing more than a brief stretch of the lips.

Saima squeezed her arm. "I know you must've heard about the divorce." She lowered her voice even though the chatting people streaming up the aisle made it unnecessary. "You know these situations are always, well, unfriendly, but we," she said, hand to chest, "we have behaved properly and haven't spread any lies." She held Rozeena's gaze. "The girl's parents are planning to send her off to the UK or even all the way to America, for further studies or something. She'll be far, far away. It'll be best for everyone, don't you think?"

Despite the air-conditioning, Rozeena was sweating under Saima's stare. "Yes, probably." She swiped her damp upper lip with the back of her hand. "Should we go?"

As they made their way out of the hall, Saima kept a hand on Rozeena's elbow, not wanting to get separated, she said. They spotted the car with Haaris and Waleed waiting beside it, but Saima pulled Rozeena to a stop. The two of them stood on Bandar Road with the bright lights of Nishat Cinema behind them and their saris, pink and red, flowing with the gentle breeze.

"We're so lucky Haaris told us of your clinic." Saima flashed a smile, perhaps for *The Star* in case the cameras were nearby, or perhaps to calm and endear Rozeena. "And it's wonderful for your work too, isn't it?"

"It certainly is. Thank you, Saima, for all your help."

Rozeena meant it too. But she was also afraid of getting too entangled with these people. They all belonged to the same web of power, Saima, Sweetie, and Haaris too. And Rozeena would not demean herself and be paraded in front of Waleed for his pleasure, or not. She needed to step back from Saima's matchmaking and whatever other plans she had. Hopefully, referrals to the clinic would continue regardless.

After dropping Saima and Waleed at their homes, the car continued on to Prince Road in silence until the driver stepped out to pull open the gate.

"Haaris, I can't go to your Welcome Home Ball."

He turned around, surprised. "Why not?"

"Because I don't really belong there."

"But I'll be there."

She gave him a small smile, a little disappointed he hadn't insisted she was mistaken, and that she did belong in his crowd.

"We can always meet in Zohair's garden," she said. "Or maybe we can go to Clifton Beach again?"

"Of course." He held her gaze and then nodded. "I understand. I do." He paused, then added, "I'm actually surprised you wanted to go in the first place. You're getting involved with these people—"

"You mean, like going to the cinema with Saima? She invited me so—"

"Oh no, not that. I'm talking about the clinic and asking for referrals. What's the rush? Why can't you build up your clinic slowly instead of needing favors? Didn't you just open it?"

She fell back in her seat, shocked. "You think I'm being greedy?" Her irritation grew. He didn't know her urgency, and she wouldn't tell him either, but why did he resent helping her? "There's no one but me now. Have you forgotten?"

He shook his head. "I haven't forgotten, of course not. But you're a doctor. You will succeed, and it'll happen for you without these favors. If you need some money right away, take it from me."

She pushed air from her nose to release her fury and keep her tone calm. "I don't need your charity. I can work. All I asked for was a little help, a word, a recommendation. How difficult was it for you to say that to your friends? Why do you mind it so much?"

He'd turned completely in his seat by now. "I don't mind it at all, Rozee. And yes, it was very easy for me to recommend you to my crowd, but that's the problem. It's too easy, and you'll have to handle whatever comes with it. All the expectations and tightening their hold."

"What are you talking about, this cinema thing with Saima's brother? I can take care of myself. From now on, I'm not meeting her anywhere but the clinic." She shrugged. "That's the real reason I don't want to go to your ball."

"All right." He sighed, nodding. "Be careful. That's all. I know these people. There are always conditions. Inviting you to the ball was Saima's idea too, you know?"

"It was?"

"I didn't think you'd be interested. I mean, we've never really done that before, have we—you and Aalya and Zohair with my family friends? But Saima said I should make sure to invite the neighborhood friends this time. She'd met you at the clinic and liked you, I suppose."

Rozeena blinked at him, wondering if she should be hurt he hadn't considered inviting his neighborhood friends to his party. But a more pressing thought came to mind.

"Is this why you keep leaving Karachi? Because of all these connections you have to maintain with these people?"

"Not just these people, my family too." He stared at Rozeena as if to say more, but then shook his head. His hand reached for her, hovering in the air between them. "I care for you, Rozee. Don't you see? I don't want you involved in whatever Saima and her friends are up to."

She let her gaze fall to her lap where she held her hands, keeping them from meeting his. When she looked back up, he hadn't moved. His eyes seemed rounder, his hand reached closer, his mouth open slightly. Her hand rose to his then, and he brought it to his lips, his cheek, where she felt a quick flutter of his thick lashes against her skin. He kissed each of her fingers, one by one, until she gently slipped away.

As she walked to her front gate, she only wanted to remember Haaris's touch. But her head ached under the bouffant. She'd wash it out right away, forget it ever adorned her head, and banish Saima's manipulation from her mind, together with the worry about Haaris's family and whatever it was he didn't want to tell her.

"Is that you, Rozee, under the hair?" The voice came from high above.

15

I recognized your sari, but not your head," Aalya called from her corner balcony. Her laughter filled the night. "Come up to your roof, Rozee. I need to see that hair closely."

Standing on the roof, across from Aalya's second-story bedroom window, Rozeena was reminded of their furtive, post-bedtime childhood meetings up here. As Aalya laughed again tilting her head this way and that, inspecting the bouffant, Rozeena's agitation from the night was replaced by relief at this old, easy connection between them.

"Did Saima do that to you?"

Rozeena touched her stiff, crunchy hair, and shuddered in the cool night. "For the cinema, *Ashiana* at Nishat."

"And Haaris was there too." Aalya had seen Rozeena step out of his car. "Who else was there?" She raised a single eyebrow and was about to continue when commotion at the back gate startled them both.

Banging and clanging reached them, and then a woman's voice called, "Doctor! Doctor!"

Rozeena headed straight back to the concrete stairs where she met Shareef running up.

"There's a woman," he said. "She says the hakim shop is shut, and her husband has pains in his stomach, and—"

"Is it an injury, bleeding?"

He shook his head. "No bleeding. He says the hakim gives him something for the burning inside."

Rozeena reached for the banister but stopped mid-motion.

"Tell them the doctor doesn't see patients here anymore." She straightened and pushed back her shoulders. "They'll have to wait till morning and take him to National Hospital, or a private clinic, or to the hakim if that's what they want." With a nod, she quickly turned away before Shareef could ask her about her sudden refusal to care.

"What are you doing?" Aalya called from her window. "Why aren't you going downstairs?"

Rozeena didn't answer until she was closer. "He's not bleeding, just indigestion most likely." Her tone was clipped. "It can wait until the morning when his hakim opens up."

"You're making the man go to the hakim?" Aalya clenched her window ledge with both hands. "And here you're telling everyone how dangerous they can be?"

"No one listens to me, Aalya. Trust me. Either way, these people will go to him as soon as he opens his shop in the morning. And if something happens then, and I've already treated him, it'll be my fault, won't it?"

Aalya dropped her gaze, shaking her head.

"What is it?"

Aalya's lips parted, but then pressed shut again. After a minute she spoke quietly. "You're a hypocrite, Rozee."

"What? No, I'm—"

"No? What do you call someone who says one thing but does the other? Telling people not to go to hakims and then turning patients away yourself?"

Aalya's glare traveled over Rozeena's bouffant, rigid and tall, like a wall between her and the ill man at the gate.

"But I can't afford to, Aalya, not after Gul."

"That was a mistake, her mistake." Aalya leaned out the window as far as possible. "But you can't just stop caring about these people who come to you. So what if they go to the hakim too? Why do you insist on pulling them to your side? Let them see you and the hakim both. There can be a balance."

Rozeena had heard these same words, or something similar, before. A memory sparked inside her, one she'd pushed far away, trying to forget.

It was a month or so before her family fled their house in Delhi. Rozeena was nine, and Faysal was about to turn eleven, and the doctors had started showing concern for him by then. Though his proportions fell in the normal range, and he was healthy and active otherwise, they said he might never grow to be of even average height.

So that morning, when Kabir, the milkman, arrived at the kitchen's back entrance on his bicycle, Rozeena said, "Pour my milk into Billee's dish today."

Kabir nodded, and as he'd been doing every day, he poured a splash of milk from his canister into the stray black-and-white cat's metal bowl. They'd named her Billee together when she'd started visiting six months ago. Others in the lane fed her regular meals of leftover roti and even some meat at times.

"But pour my milk in there too," Rozeena insisted.

"Why should I give Billee your milk today? Is it her birthday?"

"No," and then with a frown, she added, "Maybe. But it'll be Faysal's eleventh birthday soon, and what if he doesn't grow by then?"

121

Kabir shook his head and chuckled, but he poured a little extra for Billee before stepping into the kitchen to deliver the household milk to the cook. On his way out, Kabir stopped where Rozeena sat cross-legged on the ground watching Billee lap up her extra breakfast. Her pink tongue darted in and out between quick glances left and right. Ever wary, she paused when Kabir joined them. Perhaps she expected more milk. But he just tugged at the dhoti he wore under his kameez and squatted on the ground not far from Rozeena. Billee returned to lapping the milk.

"She's loud," he said, propping his elbows on his knees and settling in even though his bicycle was ready to go, the milk canisters secured on either side.

"It's because she's hungry in the morning." Rozeena looked up at the haze of July and listened for sounds. "But maybe she's loud because everyone else is quiet so early."

Pots and pans clanged in the neighbor's kitchen, but otherwise there was only a low whistle of the breeze, announcing the monsoon rains were around the corner.

Kabir's eyes disappeared in his wrinkles as he smiled, reminding her of a walnut shell.

"You're very smart, you know?" He frowned and scratched his graying head. "But tell me, how will your brother grow if Billee has your milk today?"

"Not just today," she said. "Every day."

He nodded. "As you say. But how will giving Billee your milk make your brother's legs grow longer?"

She frowned and, pulling her dress over her legs, brought her knees to her chin to concentrate.

"I haven't gone to school like you," Kabir said after a while. "So, you will have to explain to me how this will happen."

She wrapped her arms around her legs and squeezed hard. Perhaps an answer would pop out of her. But nothing came, and Kabir still didn't get up to leave.

"Won't you be late for your deliveries?" she said when Billee sat licking her paws after the hearty breakfast.

"I will pedal faster today." He let out a relaxed breath like he was ready to sit for a while.

The longer he waited for an answer, though, the more confused Rozeena became. She searched for a logical answer but could only come up with one, and it wasn't a very smart one.

"It's not that Faysal will grow taller if you give my milk to Billee." She swallowed and whispered at the air between them. "It's that I won't grow any taller."

"Hmm. I see. And why don't you want to grow?"

"So that Faysal won't feel . . ." But she bit her lip before completing her thought. Faysal didn't feel anything but happy right now. He wasn't even teased for his height, not yet at least.

Kabir rubbed the white bristles on his chin and turned to inspect his bicycle leaning against the house. "Look at it. It can't even stand up on its own."

She followed his gaze and nodded, grateful for the change of subject.

"And I hang my milk canisters—some heavy, some empty—on it too." He paused while Billee squeezed between the bicycle's pedal and wheel for a back scratch. "How do you think I make the bicycle work for me if it can't even stand by itself?"

Rozeena was determined to be smart this time. "Well, you make it stand. Then you ride it." But she knew he wanted more, like it was a riddle. How does it stand and move without tipping over? "You balance it!"

Kabir's walnut face broke into a wide smile. "Yes, that is right. I balance it. When I start pedaling, I have to push on one side, and then the other. I let my front wheel swing left and then right and then left again, by letting go of one side and then the other. If I push on both at the same time, or let go of both at the same time, I won't get anywhere, will I? Sometimes when I am not careful, I wobble down the street. Once I even fell and lost it all. All the deliveries for that day. But I learned my lesson. You have to have balance." He got up then, straightened his kameez over his dhoti, and pulled the handlebars off the wall before turning back to Rozeena. "It is good to care for your brother, but you have to drink your own milk to grow strong and care for yourself too."

Rozeena nodded and watched him climb onto his bicycle and ride away without a single wobble. He had years and years of practice on how to balance.

But some weeks later, the lesson hadn't worked for Rozeena. She'd let go a little, and it had ended with something she couldn't even speak of. No one could. It had ended in the worst way. She would never, ever let go again. That was the only way to be secure.

Rozeena shook her head, discarding the past. "I can't do it, Aalya. I have to make the sensible choice, the safe one."

"You don't need to tell me about making the safe choice."

Rozeena sighed. "So, you understand."

"Of course not." Aalya's tone stung. "There is nothing right, or sensible, about refusing to care for a patient."

Rozeena opened her mouth to protest, to scream that Sweetie will not tolerate another mistake, that she has the power to shut down Rozeena's clinic and dissuade all the new patients, Saima included. And if Rozeena dares to ruin Sweetie's reputation by treating another one of these hakim patients and risking another terrible outcome, Sweetie will upend their lives in Karachi in an instant. She'll send Rozeena and her mother to Lahore simply to remove any gossip, and by association, any blemish on herself or her precious son and business.

But Rozeena shared none of this.

Eventually, Aalya said, "Do what you want, Rozee," and shut the window against the night.

Exhausted, Rozeena slid down the cold concrete of the boundary wall and hugged her knees just as she did all those years ago as a child in Delhi. She was still shaken by the sudden memory that had risen in her, one she'd pushed deep down as far as possible. Now, even though her chest ached at having to turn away patients from her gate, she knew it was her only choice. She couldn't risk another incident, another mistake followed by Sweetie's consequences.

It was the only way for Rozeena to protect her home and family.

16

NOW, 2019

Rozeena presses the hot phone screen against her temple. "Is that you, Haaris?"

Another loud throat-clearing reaches her. "Yes. It's me. Can you hear me? Have you had your dinner? Were you asleep?"

He sounds nervous with his stream of questions. "I've had dinner. I was watching TV, a documentary on sea creatures." She presses the mute button on the remote, and the house goes silent. She can see the lit foyer from her sofa, but the kitchen and dining room beyond are dark. "I'll be going upstairs soon."

"I won't keep you then."

"You're not keeping me from anything, Haaris."

He takes a couple of breaths before speaking. "I heard what happened at the luncheon, how Zara left with you without telling anyone."

"Ah, yes. But all is well, thankfully."

"Yes, yes. And then Zara told me about the day she visited you when she wasn't supposed to." He pauses. "I apologize, Rozee. Your son was there, and Zara shouldn't have—"

"Mansur. His name is Mansur." Remember?

His voice dips, and Rozeena wonders if there's someone else listening on his end. "Mansur. Of course. Zara is so interested in the gardening work that she didn't think to check her WhatsApp before arriving at your gate."

Does Haaris know this is a lie? Zara was eager to leave her parents, not to garden. It has become obvious to Rozeena in just a handful of visits.

"She also said Mansur is friendly, and a doctor, like you," he continues.

Rozeena waits to see where this is headed. Now that he's mentioned Mansur, she's uneasy.

"Maybe it's time for me to meet him."

Her breath catches. "I don't think . . ." She hears a woman's voice on the other end, but the words are unclear, too far away. Rustling follows, and Haaris's voice becomes muffled, distant.

"Sorry, Rozee. I'm back now."

"Was that your wife?" The question slips out before she realizes.

"My daughter. She's visiting from New Jersey while my son is in Karachi. They both go to Karachi every year with their families. It's good to keep that connection for the grandchildren." His voice cracks, probably remembering his lost grandson.

"Yes, I've heard from Apa's friends that your children come here often. But they never mention your visits to Karachi."

There are footsteps. The woman's voice asks Haaris where he's going, and he replies, "The deck."

A couple of thuds later, there's a sigh, and Rozeena imagines him sinking into a chair outside. It's daytime in Minnesota, the time between breakfast and lunch. Rozeena turns away from the lit foyer, past the mute TV, to the large windows facing her dark garden. Vague outlines of trees are visible, as well as the smooth curve of the dense bougainvillea atop her front boundary wall. The smaller plants are completely shrouded in the night.

"There was no reason to return, Rozee. My in-laws all migrated to the US, and my family, including Apa, used to visit regularly."

"So why now? Why are you really coming back?" His mention of Mansur has made Rozeena more wary.

"Because life is short."

She laughs at this non-discovery, especially at his age. But Haaris doesn't join in. "Oh, you're serious."

"Of course I am. Look at the tragedy that's happened in my family." His volume rises, and she's not sure if it's because he's outside, away from his daughter, or if it's anger.

"Yes, a terrible, terrible tragedy," she says quietly. "What I meant was—"

"I know what you meant." He sighs. "Perhaps I've just been thinking more these days, of our mortality."

He lives in a different world from hers if he needs to be reminded of mortality at eighty-three. "So, you're coming to say goodbye?"

"In a way."

She frowns, trying to concentrate on what he's not saying. "And your wife too?"

"No, not her. She's not too well."

"Oh, I'm sorry." She doesn't ask if it's serious. Everything is serious at their age. "But how can you leave her alone then?"

He's silent for a whole minute this time. "She lives with my daughter and her family in New Jersey. Permanently."

Rozeena raises her brows. "Why?"

"It was better that way, for the two of us."

"Has it been like this for many years?"

"Since the children grew up."

That's at least twenty-five years now. There's rustling on the other end of the phone again.

"Hello? Asalaam aleikum, Rozeena Aunty?" His daughter's voice comes through loud and clear.

Rozeena tenses and pulls her back off the sofa. She hears footsteps, perhaps on stairs, as the woman continues.

"This is Farah, Haaris's daughter. I hope it's okay if I say hello?"

"Of course. Waleikum asalaam. How are you?" Rozeena offers condolences.

"Thank you. Yes. It's been difficult, to say the least." Farah sounds a little out of breath. "I just walked down from the deck to the backyard. Abba is waiting anxiously for me to return with the phone." She laughs. "I don't know what he thinks I'll tell you."

Rozeena wonders too.

She waits, staring at the muted TV and the otherworldly sea creatures that live where light hardly reaches—bulging eyes on either side of huge fangs; miniature skeletons that change colors, blue, red, green.

"I'm worried about him," Farah says. "I mean, I'm happy that he's getting in touch with old friends, so this new connection with you, Aunty, is a good thing. Thank you."

"Why are you worried then?" Rozeena's voice sounds too loud in the house. She unmutes the TV and lowers the volume to a buzz in the background. She needs the company.

"It's been a hard time for all of us since Fez, as you can imagine. But Abba was especially close to him." Her voice drifts off, as if speaking to herself. "Maybe it's a grandchild thing."

Rozeena shakes her head. She loves Mansur more than she loves his children. It's very, very close, but still. "Yes, it could be a grandchild thing," she lies.

"No, actually, maybe not. He's not the same with Zara or my children. Fez looked like Abba, you know? And they had the same interests too."

Now Zara's comment about Haaris's big green thumb makes sense. It's hard for Rozeena to imagine, though, that Haaris would be interested in such things.

"It will take time," she says gently. "Loss stays with you."

"Yes, but Abba has changed overnight in some ways. When he thinks no one is around, he gets a slight stoop, like he's tired. And sad. He snaps up straight and proper in front of us." She swallows loudly. "Sometimes he doesn't shave for weeks, until we convince him to."

"That's worrying indeed." Rozeena doesn't know anyone of his generation who doesn't shave for weeks, unless it's someone with a proper beard, and then the beard is always well-groomed. "Is he unwell, physically?" She can't stop herself from asking though it feels like prying.

"Nothing like diabetes or anything, but I did suggest therapy. He says he doesn't need anyone telling him what's wrong with him." Her voice turns small. "I see him cry sometimes."

"Oh, I'm so sorry, Farah." It's difficult to see your parents cry at any age. "Grief is—"

"I know. But now he's started talking to my mother a lot on the phone. They've been separated for years, but now they're on the phone every other day, and sometimes completely silent, just holding the phone to their ears."

Rozeena doesn't want to know all of this, at all, but she must say something. "It's good to have someone to talk to. Someone who understands and knows everything."

"Exactly!" Farah is suddenly much too excited, as if it's a revelation. "There's something that they share, and I don't know what it is. But it has to do with Karachi."

"Karachi? But what? Your parents haven't been back in decades."

"I know. And then Abba comes up with this whole idea to go back to pick up Zara. I could easily go myself. I go every year to meet my in-laws."

Haaris's gruff but distant voice comes through the phone. "Enough now . . . nighttime there . . ."

"Oh, I'm so sorry, Aunty. I've kept you up so late on the phone."

"Not at all." Rozeena's mind is working hard to comprehend what she's just heard.

"I thought you should know where he's coming from. Abba is hurting, and well, I'm happy that he'll have a friend there in Karachi."

"He's told you about me?"

"Nothing at all, actually. I only know through Zara's work. I guess he hasn't really been in touch for all these years, has he? But for some reason, he needs to be now."

When the call ends, Rozeena stares at the sea creatures and remains erect in her seat, unable to lean back. Her mind is whirling, trying to sift through the intention behind this telephone call. Farah's was clear. She's worried about her father and his changing behavior.

But Haaris is easing Rozeena into something. He's appealing to her emotions. Maybe he even suggested Farah have that talk with her. It sounds like he knows Rozeena won't like what he has to say when he arrives in Karachi.

And what if it turns into something dreadful, like the last time he returned?

17

THEN, 1964

One Day Before

Haaris raised his camera to take what felt like the hundredth photograph of Rozeena.

They were at Clifton Beach again, at Jehangir Kothari Parade, but it was early afternoon, and the beach was busier than before. In search of privacy, they'd reached the vast pavilion at the end of the pier this time. Even then, solitude lasted only a few minutes before the next group of beachgoers bounded through the building and tumbled down the stairs onto the sand.

He clicked the camera again.

Rozeena stood framed between two outer pillars of the pavilion with her back to the sky and the matching blue sea, all shimmering under the bright sun. It vanquished the chill from the air, warming and relaxing her as she smiled at the camera. She tried to forget about the cinema outing with Waleed and Saima and hoped her referrals would keep pouring in at the clinic. And after her last conversation with Haaris, Rozeena still had concerns and questions. So when he called and asked her to come with him to Clifton Beach, she was hopeful for answers.

After several clicks, she reached for the camera. "Now, let me take some of you."

Haaris shook his head. "I want you in this film, only you." He smiled slowly as she stood there, the blue flowers rippling across her white sari with the gentle breeze, wisps of hair loosening from her low bun and crisscrossing her cheeks. "So, I can have you with me, always."

His words jolted her.

"Why? Are you leaving again?"

"I just came back, and you want me to leave already?"

"No, of course not." But she couldn't let it go. "What is so terrible about working in a successful business, Haaris? Why do you keep running away?"

With a knotted brow, he began fidgeting with his camera. The longer she waited for his reply, the more she regretted asking him. But she had to know, whatever the truth might be.

When he finally looked up, he gave a fleeting smile and shrugged. "It's all so dull, Rozee. What is this import/export anyway?"

"It means buying and selling." She folded her arms. "I want the real reason, the whole reason this time. We're not children anymore."

Her heart thumped against her forearms.

"You wouldn't understand. My family is different."

She pursed her lips. Aalya had said the same, as if Rozeena's life was simple and easy and carefree. Her friends knew nothing about each other anymore.

He sighed and turned to the sea. As she moved closer, she noticed he wasn't even looking at the water. His dark, curved lashes sat so close to his cheeks he could probably see nothing at all.

"You're right." His fingers moved mindlessly over the camera in his hands. "It's not just the work. It's not the work at all, actually. It's everything else that comes with it."

"Like what?"

His chest heaved with a deep breath and subsequent release. "It's difficult to be honest."

"It's all right, Haaris. You can tell me any—"

"No. That's not what I mean." He turned to face her, his dark eyes hard, unblinking, and unwavering, even in the afternoon glare.

She made sure to keep her face expressionless, free of judgment.

"We call them favors," he said. "Or we call them 'fees for services,' or simply call it a 'partnership.' Either way, we get what we want, whether it's the right price, the right contract, or the right piece of property."

"Property? How can you import—"

"That's not the point, Rozee." He expelled a terse breath. "I'm saying it's all around me, my family, my circle."

Her eyes stung, staring at him. They had talked about the complicated connections between Haaris's friends and family the other night, but she didn't know this bled into his family's business as well, the future Haaris has been trying hard to avoid. Was his father giving and taking bribes, threatening people? Worse?

"You can be different, Haaris. You don't have to—"

"Yes, I do. It's the family business, run by the family—my father, his brothers, their children. I have no choice but to run it the way they do." He looked straight at her now. "And if I stay here, I have no choice but to be a part of it."

Her breath caught. "But . . . but you can do something else."

He gave a sad smile. "I don't think so. It's what I'm meant to do, isn't it? From the day I was born."

This, Rozeena understood. She knew all about expectations. Her life was built on them.

"You see why the only way to stay away is to physically stay away?"

A lump stuck in her throat. All she could do was nod. Even in this situation, Haaris had security like she'd never experienced. He could selfishly get up and leave, and his family's money granted him freedom and comfort on the other side of the world as well.

"But I can't leave now," he said, taking a step closer, his fingers reaching for her hand.

"You can't?"

"How can I possibly leave you?" he whispered. His hand squeezed tight around hers.

"But what will you do here, if you stay?" she breathed. She could smell his Brylcreem, see his close shave.

"I'll find a way. For now, I'm in the family business until I can see what else there is."

She nodded. She needed time as well, to find a way to keep her family together, safe, and in Karachi. He, on the other hand, was looking for a way to break away from his, but gently.

He squeezed her hand again, and his hesitant smile froze on his face as he searched hers, waiting for a response. She wanted him, whenever they were ready, their duties to their families fulfilled, or at least addressed. With a quick glance to confirm they were alone in the pavilion, she pulled the rest of him into the sliver of shadow where she stood. Out of sight from the beachgoers, she closed the distance between them.

His fingers pressed into the bare flesh at her sides.

She gasped at his touch, hot, firm fingers just below the edge of her blouse. She slid her palms up his chest and felt the heat through his thin white shirt. His heart beat hard. When she circled her arms around his neck, their chests pounded together, heaving, pressed against each other until approaching voices tossed them to separate pillars like frazzled, breathless strangers.

Rozeena gripped the stone with a hand to regain her composure as laughter filled the pavilion.

Smoothing back her hair, she readjusted the loose end of her sari tight across her front and over a shoulder. Families oohed and aahed at the water and then headed down the front steps to the sand. Rozeena kept her eyes on the sea and sky before her. The gentle winter breeze swept through the pavilion, across her face and throat and chest, jostling everything in her mind, every worry she had, to make room for her to see the truth of her feelings, and what she wanted.

She turned to Haaris, waiting at a polite distance.

Their eyes locked in silent communication as another group entered the pavilion. Children scurried in between Rozeena and Haaris as if they too were immobile stone structures, turned toward each other permanently.

Later, outside Rozeena's front gate, Haaris surprised her with a big, shiny cowrie shell. She hadn't collected a single shell since her father died, eleven years ago. But now Haaris had already given her two, reminding her of that carefree time in her life, and she loved it. She caressed the shell's smooth, speckled brown mound before turning it over to rub the flat ivory underside.

"There was a third type you liked too, right?"

She nodded, wanting the days to hurry up to the one where they'd meet at the beach again, and he would complete her collection.

Rozeena was just in time for tea with her mother and Khala. "You won't be able to take the Morris today," her mother said as Rozeena slid into her chair.

"The car can't make left turns apparently," Khala added.

The knocking must've turned into something more serious. After the idyllic afternoon with Haaris, Rozeena was hurtled back to her reality.

"I'm sure it can be fixed," she said with more confidence than she felt. "But I should hurry. I can't be late." Not today, with the prospect of new patients.

Her mother nodded as she stirred her tea. "Shareef has to go to the market, so Aalya will go with you in the rickshaw. And yes, hurry. She has to pick up her father on the way."

Of course they wouldn't want Aalya coming back alone in the rickshaw after dropping Rozeena. After a couple of burning sips of tea, Rozeena rushed out the back gate where Aalya was already waving down a rickshaw. With a tight braid down her back and her simple yellow shalwar kameez she looked like a schoolgirl today, certainly more than three years younger than Rozeena in her sari. Yet Aalya was the one giving directions.

"Where are we going?" Rozeena shouted over the sputtering vehicle while trying to keep her hair from flying free.

"Not far," Aalya yelled back with a smile. "We'll get you to MPS Chambers on time."

Rozeena smiled, grateful for the absence of tension between them after last night on the roof when she'd refused to see the sick man.

They turned a corner and before the rickshaw-walla came to a complete stop, Aalya jumped out her side. They weren't far from Prince Road, but this was a new neighborhood and not in the direction of downtown. Within seconds, Aalya stepped back out of a gate, alone. Ignoring Rozeena's questions, she told the driver to go to the next one.

"What next one, Aalya? Do you even know where Ibrahim Uncle is?"

The rickshaw turned the corner so fast, Rozeena nearly fell out the doorless side.

"This one!" Aalya shouted, pointing to another black gate.

The driver slammed the brake.

Catching her breath, Rozeena centered herself on the seat. "Well, go on then. Go and get Ibrahim Uncle."

"Come in with me?" Aalya gave Rozeena's hand a quick squeeze and jumped out to wait by the gate.

"We need to hurry, Aalya. I have to be there well in time for my first patient."

They stepped through the gate together.

It was a newer house, but the garden looked much like Rozeena's, a rectangle of grass with coconut palms on one side and some plants filling the beds along the boundary walls. The lady of the house stood in the corner a few feet from the front door and faced the plant at her feet.

"Go get him, Aalya. Hurry." There was still time, but not if she didn't move.

Aalya stood staring at the middle-aged lady in the pink sari who finally looked up and in their direction. She nodded before reaching down to brush a hand over the plant's spiky, long leaves. She said something inaudible to the maali who crouched low on the ground, his hands working in the soil.

But then he straightened his curved back and stood up in his beige shalwar kameez.

It couldn't be.

18

Aalya was already halfway to her father when Ibrahim's face broke into the smile Rozeena had known since childhood. She swallowed, unable to comprehend the scene as she approached them. Still some feet away, she heard the lady speak.

"The mint with cinnamon, Ibrahim? And what's the other dried leaf?"

He spoke too softly for Rozeena to hear.

"Yes, yes. I'm boiling it all together." The lady smiled at Aalya and then turned to squint at Rozeena, before going inside her house.

"I'll wash my hands and then we can go, Rozee," Ibrahim called with a smile.

She nodded, approaching him, trying to behave normally. "Uh, what's this one called, Ibrahim Uncle? It's so unusual."

She bent over to stroke the stiff leaves, then quickly pulled herself straight, not wanting to imitate the owner of the house, the lady who employed Ibrahim as a maali it seemed.

"Ah, yes. This one is a kangi palm," he said with pride. "A young one." The stem sat low to the ground and blossomed a rosette of leaves, dark green and spiked like long fish scales. "Its parent lives in Haaris's house. The maali there gave me some young ones to plant." He nodded toward the front door. "I brought it as a gift today, along with my fresh mint." He looked Rozeena straight in the eye. "They've been good to us, for many years."

Rozeena didn't know what to say.

"We'll get a plant for Zohair's garden too, won't we?" Aalya said to her father.

He nodded, patting Aalya's fingers wrapped around his arm. Thick lines of dirt filled his nails, and when he raised a hand to the servant who came out to say the lady wanted a word before he left, Rozeena saw trenches of dark earth in his palms. Ibrahim followed the servant to the back of the house, and she wondered if he'd wash up in the servants' quarters and enter from the kitchen.

"I used to work beside him when I was younger, before Partition, and even after," Aalya said, crouching low on the grass, exactly as her father had. Her palms pressed the earth around the new plant, and she breathed in the scent of dirt with her eyes closed.

"Yes, I remember. You loved it, but Neelum Aunty said—"

"No man wants a bride with rough, laborer hands." Aalya completed her mother's stern scolding in the exact tone it had been delivered.

Rozeena watched in silence as Aalya smoothed the soil. What child wouldn't love burying fingers in dirt, adding water, and slapping piles of mud between soft palms? But Aalya had told Rozeena she enjoyed it even as she grew older, saying she found the work soothing and so rewarding. There was no doubt Zohair's garden was by far the prettiest on the street. In fact, Haaris said that not one of his relatives in Karachi had managed to grow a garden so beautiful. Ibrahim Uncle has magic fingers, he always said.

"It's a part of us, you know?" Aalya turned her head to look up at Rozeena. "We've always been maalis." Her eyes traveled across

Rozeena's face as if expecting a reaction with each statement. "I'm the first to go to school." She bit her lip, still staring. "My parents can't read or write." She bowed her head then. "I called you a hypocrite last night, but I'm the one living a lie, Rozee, every single day."

Rozeena dropped to her knees and reached for Aalya's face, cradling her cheeks. "Why didn't you tell me before? You didn't have to pretend, and Ibrahim Uncle shouldn't have to hide his—"

"What would people say if they found out? I couldn't tell you."

"But I'm not those people. I'm not the ones you need to worry about."

"So, there are people I need to worry about?" Aalya's smile was sad and fleeting.

Rozeena stiffened.

"It's all right," Aalya said. "We know we need to worry. If the secret came out, my parents would be called liars, impostors, fraudsters. No one would believe the house could be ours. They'd take it away, and worse, send us to jail for lying and stealing. My poor parents have only been honest, but who would believe servants?" She paused. "Also, everyone knows that the daughter of an illiterate maali can only marry the son of an illiterate maali, so that would be my future. And I couldn't tell you because I had to keep you safe from it, from being a part of the lie. If people found out what your parents did for us—"

"My parents? They knew?"

"I wouldn't be here if your parents didn't know, Rozee. We'd just be another family gone missing during Partition, left homeless, or . . ." Aalya jumped up and smoothed down her kameez. "Stand up. Your sari will get all dirty, and you'll have to fix more than just your hair at the clinic." Aalya's eyes flicked toward the front door. "Let's wait in the rickshaw."

Rozeena tensed at the possibility of the lady returning to tell them to move along. A servant's family shouldn't linger.

As they made their way to the rickshaw, Aalya explained how her extended families on both sides had been servants—maids, cooks, maalis, ayahs—for generations, for as long as anyone could remember. Ibrahim's father and all his brothers and uncles had been maalis. When Partition happened, Aalya's little family accompanied one of Ibrahim's employers, an old man, across the border to Pakistan. The old man needed help with the journey and promised them passage back to their village after he'd settled in.

"It didn't take long." Aalya slid back into the rickshaw. "He had documents showing the property he owned in India. He got his claim quickly here in Karachi."

That's how refugees had been accommodated on either side of the new border. Muslim refugees who fled India arrived in Pakistan and were allotted the abandoned properties left behind by Hindus and Sikhs—they, in turn, claimed the property left behind by Muslims in India. But Rozeena remembered her father saying how, even with the requisite documents, they'd been lucky to get the house in Karachi, because there hadn't been enough property to hand out. There were many more Muslim refugees than the small port city could accommodate.

"But the old man got sick with cholera like so many others during Partition," Aalya said. "He had no family in Karachi, so my parents nursed him and cared for him, but he died anyway. He knew he was going to, because instead of giving my parents passage back to our village, he gave them the house." She blinked with a shake of her head. "He offered us a new life."

It was a chance to make their own destiny in a brand-new country, the perfect opportunity to start from scratch where no one knew where and what they came from.

"I remember the day we moved from the servants' quarters to the main house. It felt huge in there, like a palace." Aalya smiled.

"The main house," Rozeena repeated quietly. She wondered how long Aalya had considered their home the main house, and if she remembered much of living in the quarters where Gul had lived with Abdul.

"And then about a week later, you moved in next door," Aalya said.

Rozeena nodded.

Abandoned homes on Prince Road had filled quickly. She imagined no one had even questioned Aalya's family about their different ways, their way of speaking and living. Refugees had poured in from all over the subcontinent, and they'd been wary of each other, tight-lipped about what they'd suffered, and eager to only look ahead, like Rozeena's father.

He'd been so optimistic, filled with so many dreams—perhaps to override the nightmares. Mohammad Ali Jinnah, the founder of the nation, had declared Karachi the capital city, and there was much to be done. Her father quickly began working in city planning, establishing infrastructure and systems for the growing population. And for Rozeena, just nine years old then, he quoted Jinnah's words, envisioning her future and independent life.

"No nation can rise to the height of glory unless your women are side by side with you."

Aalya looked past Rozeena to the gate that Ibrahim would walk through any second now. "Your father made us believe everything was possible, that everything would be all right, and we'd be safe. He helped transfer the ownership papers into Abba's name. He signed with his thumbprint. Then Zohair and his father arrived in Karachi some months later. They bought the downstairs from us, and we had money to live on. But of course Abba has had to work too." She paused. "We felt so safe living with your family next to us, on our side. And now you're leaving. Moving to Lahore?" Aalya frowned.

"What? Oh no, it's not going to happen." Rozeena shook her head. "Not if I do what I'm supposed to." She smiled reassuringly. "But who told you?"

"Your mother, of course. When your family isn't next door anymore, who'll keep our secret and keep us safe in case . . . ? Ammi is so scared that one day everyone will know, and they'll throw us out, even with all the correct papers. That would be the least they'd do. Abba would be jailed because no one would believe his thumbprint alone gave him ownership." Aalya shook her head. "The only way to be safe, forever, is for me to marry well. Powerful families take care of their own, don't they?"

Rozeena couldn't disagree. After hearing Haaris's stories, she believed they could give and take and protect and destroy. All at will.

"It's what Ammi has always said to me," Aalya continued. "I need to make a good match. I have to make the safe choice, the sensible choice, just like you did the other night, Rozee. At Haaris's ball I can meet people, or at least get introduced to those people, that society." Aalya bowed her head to her lap, and before Rozeena could say, Are you sure and what about Zohair, she added, "Help me find a good match, Rozee. Please?"

The gate banged shut, startling them both, and Ibrahim hurried toward them.

Rozeena squeezed Aalya's hand. Although Rozeena had decided not to go, not to get mixed up with these people anymore, she had to do this for Aalya, for her best friend and sister. "Of course I'll help. Anything you want. Anything at all."

With a huge, relieved smile, Aalya shifted to the middle to make room for her father.

This time when the rickshaw-walla sped off, Rozeena welcomed the loud sputtering. She leaned back in her corner, alone with her thoughts. Something had shifted inside her, but it wasn't her respect or love for Aalya and her family. Nothing had changed there. But Rozeena felt weakened, less in control. She'd been so sure of her relationship with Aalya and her responsibilities toward her. But what Rozeena had believed all these years wasn't true.

Even Neelum's words in 1947 had meant something else, something deeper, when she'd pressed her daughter's fingers into Rozeena's palm that first day of school.

Promise me you'll make her just like you, so much like you that people will think she's your little sister.

Rozeena had always believed it had been her own decision to care for Aalya like a sibling, a second chance to protect and do the right thing. But now she knew the relationship had been orchestrated by their parents, all four of them. Rozeena had only played a designated role.

And if she didn't know this huge truth about the people closest to her, what else didn't she know? Rozeena stared at her palms, lying helpless on her lap, rising and falling with each bump of the speeding rickshaw. She held her breath, feeling so insecure that she was counting the seconds until the next lurch would toss her out and onto the road.

When Rozeena reached home from the clinic that evening, she found her mother standing by the drawing room sofa with an anxious smile. She'd draped four of her more formal saris across the sofa back.

Taking in the wardrobe display, which was clearly in preparation for Haaris's ball, Rozeena said, "It's not true, is it, that the Morris can't make left turns?"

From her armchair, Khala calmly looked from Rozeena to her mother.

"You knew too?" Rozeena said.

"I have eyes and ears, don't I?" Khala said. "Of course I knew."

Her mother nodded. "Some of Neelum's ways surprised Khala when she first came to live with us."

Khala chuckled. "Remember the two stacks of dishes she brought out when she invited us for chai? Neelum carried all the saucers in one hand, and a tower of teacups in the other. Plunked them on the dining table. Who serves chai like that?"

"What Khala means is that there were many little things that made it clear Neelum's background was different," Rozeena's mother said. "Not just her speech. She's adjusted to new ways over the years. But, Rozee, I had to tell her about our plans for Lahore. They've relied on us, on your father's help in the beginning, and the feeling of safety they've had from knowing I'm here."

"Why didn't you tell me about them before?" Rozeena said.

Her mother smiled, reaching for the navy-blue sari. "It's not my secret to tell, is it? And this story about the Morris and Aalya getting a rickshaw, well, that was all her idea." She handed Rozeena the sari and matching blouse and petticoat. "Aalya said she wanted to see your face, your reaction. If she'd simply told you a story about their past, you'd come to the truth slowly."

Aalya wanted to see if Rozeena would be shocked, repelled.

"That's a good color for you," her mother said, nodding at the sari. "It's an important occasion, Rozee." She sat down in the space vacated by the fabric. "I need to make sure you know how important this is to me."

Rozeena shoved away the other saris and reached for her mother's hands, balled into tight fists. "I understand. It's Aalya's future."

"No, it's more than that." She paused. "I feel like Aalya was given to me, to help care for, after Faysal."

Rozeena's fingers went cold and stiff around her mother's hands.

She wanted to pull away but was afraid to even move. Faysal was never mentioned, and Rozeena preferred it that way.

"It would finally relieve me of my last responsibility here in Karachi," her mother continued, "if I could see her settled, Aalya and her parents safe."

Rozeena nodded. She would do anything to make that happen.

19

NOW, 2019

Your parents know about our little outing," Rozeena says, picking up her purse from the veranda chair. "I made sure to tell them, so they don't worry."

Zara doesn't look at all concerned though.

She settles into the back seat of Rozeena's car and is probably willing to go anywhere but home since gardening won't be possible today. The organic fertilizer has finally arrived, days late, and the men are busy spreading foul-smelling lumps all over Rozeena's grass and flower beds.

Within ten minutes, Rozeena's driver turns off the wide, four-lane boulevard running along the never-ending shoreline of Sea View. He parks, and the glorious Arabian Sea lies before them, a gray-blue expanse, lined with cresting, frothy waves crashing onto the soft sand.

The crowds have gathered already. It's Saturday evening, and tomorrow is a holiday for all. Families from the other side of the city spill out of public buses and vans. Children break loose and climb down to the sand before their mothers can chase after them, clutching onto their dopattas in the swirling sea breeze. In the parking area, there's blaring music competing with shouts from vendors selling cold drinks and roasted corn from carts and ice cream from coolers strapped onto bicycles.

Rozeena settles down on the two-foot-high wall between the parking area and the stairs going down to the beach. Zara joins her, pulling out a sketchbook from her satchel and squinting at the vista. Within seconds, she erupts into uncontrollable giggling. The powerful gusts have sent her silky scrunchie skidding between the parked cars behind. When she reaches up to keep her hair from cycloning vertically, the sketchbook pages ruffle until they fly right off her lap. She pounces on the sheets, trying to keep her hair off her face at the same time. Rozeena joins in the laughter watching Zara tuck the paper under an arm and grab her scrunchie before it's lost between the cars. She has no hands left to tame the whirlwind of hair twisting and dancing above her head.

"Let it go, Zara," Rozeena says, pointing at her own head. Loosened locks of gray are flung about by the ferocious summer wind.

Smiling, Zara slips the sketchbook back into the satchel and rejoins Rozeena, who now ponders, looking out to the sea. The water blends into the sky, but she stares through it all, as if there's something beyond. Her eyes begin to sting. She blinks and speaks over the rush of wind.

"You know, when I sit here with my back to the world, I can always see clearly, even if I don't want to."

"How long have you been coming here?"

"Since Partition, after my family came to Karachi. But we lived closer to the center of the city then, the north end actually, and none of this area was even developed. It was just an empty desert next to the sea, no houses or roads or anything. The closest place we could get to the water was Clifton Beach, where the Jehangir Kothari Parade is. Do you know it?"

"That huge park?"

Rozeena nods. It's all reclaimed land now, turned into a giant, manicured park as far as you can see. The water isn't even visible from the promenade anymore but the structure itself, the buildings of the Parade, have remained.

Zara stares ahead. "So what do you see today?"

Rozeena speaks slowly. "I see that I will miss you when your internship ends."

"Well, I'm not going anywhere soon." Zara screws up her face. "You're kinda stuck with me for now."

"That sounds lovely." Rozeena truly hasn't felt this useful in years. "And what about you?"

"Oh, I'll miss you too, of course."

Rozeena laughs. "Thank you, but I meant, what do you see? Maybe something about why you're here, doing this internship?"

Low, but audible, Zara speaks to the sea. "I have to do it. I owe it to him, to them."

Rozeena nods. "And what do you owe yourself?"

Zara pulls her knees up to her chin and curls into a tight ball. They sit in silence for a while. "I like taking pics and writing the blog. I like that. So that's for me, right?"

"Yes, good. And there's your drawing."

"Yeah, well, that's going slowly. I do it late at night, so I can be with my parents and do stuff with them during the day." She shrugs. "I want them to think everything is okay. That I'm okay."

Rozeena looks at Zara, so sweet and caring but also scared.

Bringing her hand to her heart, Rozeena says, "I've felt it here. What you're feeling right now, I've felt it here, for my brother. But, Zara, you were nowhere near Fez's accident. And this is not your burden to bear."

Her mouth falls open, but she doesn't turn to meet Rozeena's gaze. "You know?"

"No. I don't know much at all." She only knows Zara wasn't in that car. According to Haaris, no one even knew Fez had left the house in the middle of the night. "But I know that sometimes we believe things that aren't true. Sometimes we misunderstand events, thinking we had some control over them. We don't realize that many, many times we're powerless." She reaches over to rub Zara's back, still curved into a ball as she hugs her knees tighter. "You don't want to hold on to those beliefs and make choices that can hurt people, your parents and yourself too."

Zara swipes her fingers across glistening cheeks, damp with mist or tears or both. "Tell me more about your brother. How did he . . ." Her face crumples, and Rozeena looks away.

"Partition."

"Oh, I didn't know." Zara sounds surprised. "I mean I know about Partition from my parents and a little from school, about the British being colonizers and all. The abuse and—"

"Yes, all that is true. But even as they were leaving, when they were supposed to be ending their reign . . ." Rozeena exhales forcefully. It's difficult to speak of the violence even now.

Zara's voice is gentle. "I'm sorry. It's okay if you don't want to talk about it."

Rozeena holds her hands tightly on her lap and takes a deep breath, taking in all the salty, dewy mist of her country. If she can't talk about it after all these years, how can she expect Zara to talk about her loss, so recent and devastating?

"It was the worst night of my life, the night we fled." Rozeena's voice cracks, but she clears her throat and continues. "It wasn't only my family who suffered. So many people were massacred during Partition, because of fear, because no one knew where they belonged. The Radcliffe Line was announced with no preparation for the fallout." Rozeena remembers it all so vividly, the chaos on the streets, the homes set ablaze by shouting crowds in the night, Faysal shaking

151

her by the shoulders and telling her to run toward the safe house. "I was so young, I didn't understand what was happening, and then suddenly when I turned around, Faysal was gone. I remember thinking, 'Aren't we going to wait for him? How can we just leave?'"

Rozeena has never said this out loud to anyone, not even herself. Raising her dopatta to her eyes, damp like Zara's cheeks had been earlier, Rozeena wipes away the humidity or tears or both.

Zara scoots closer and rests her head on Rozeena's shoulder. The weight and warmth slowly soothe Rozeena.

"I'm so sorry that happened," Zara says after a while. "I didn't mean to upset you by asking."

Rozeena smooths Zara's hair off her forehead and smiles. "You know, I see so much of myself in you."

"Really?" Zara straightens with a grin. "I'm like you?"

Rozeena laughs. "Well, not in every way, but perhaps in the important ways." She doesn't want to frighten Zara into silence but has to say it. "Like how we handle heartbreak."

Zara bites her lip, and Rozeena continues.

"After Faysal died, our family was left with a big, gaping hole. No one ever spoke about his death, not one word, but somehow I believed it was my duty to fill the hole. It was a mistake." She swallows deeply, shaking her head at the guilt she's felt over her brother's death.

Zara is silent, facing the crashing waves, and Rozeena wonders if the girl has heard the confession. Surprisingly, Rozeena feels lighter after saying the words, though it's too late to fix any of her mistakes. But it's not too late for Zara.

After a few more moments of silence, Zara pulls out a wallet from her satchel.

"I know what we need, you and I both, since we're so alike." She points to the stall near the line of cars behind them. "I won't be far."

Rozeena makes sure to keep an eye on Zara until she returns with two cans of chilled Pakola, straws bobbing up from the neon-green fizzy drink.

"I love Pakola. I have as much as I can when I'm here," Zara says and sits back down.

The ice cream soda flavor is intense. Rozeena rarely has soft drinks anymore, but the sugar level certainly jolts her out of the past.

"Exactly what we need. Thank you, Zara."

Sweetness fills Rozeena's mouth, and she lets her whole body absorb it, numbing the effects of the words she's rarely spoken in her rather long life. Rozeena's family, like many other refugees, never spoke of Partition and its horrors. That's how the trauma had been dealt with. They looked ahead instead, focused on the future, and tried to forget.

But now Rozeena knows. Like the powerful waves that must reach the shore and crash onto the beach, the past too must bubble up from within us, up and out through our lips. We must speak of it instead of allowing the pressure to build inside. Rozeena knows the damage it can cause.

"Maybe tomorrow you can tell me your story," she says.

Zara keeps the straw in her mouth, taking big gulps of Pakola. She doesn't say no, so Rozeena is hopeful.

But the next day, Zara goes missing.

20

THEN, 1964

The Welcome Home Ball

S oon after Rozeena returned from the clinic, Aalya arrived at Rozeena's house to get ready for Haaris's Welcome Home Ball with her. They only had an hour before the invitation time, and a buzz of nervous excitement filled Rozeena's bedroom.

After quickly tying her own navy-blue sari, Rozeena made room for Aalya in front of the mirror. It covered the entire length of the wardrobe's single door, so they had full view of the sari to check if the pleats fell correctly. Rozeena had chosen her mother's shocking-pink one for Aalya, thinking it would enhance her natural complexion. As Rozeena concentrated on making perfect folds, ensuring the fabric draped seamlessly from Aalya's waist to the floor, Aalya bit her lip and fidgeted.

"Don't worry," Rozeena said with a reassuring smile. "I do this every day for the clinic. I know how to tie saris."

"Oh, it's not that, Rozee." She twisted her mouth. "But what if tonight isn't enough? What if—"

"Sshhh. Don't say that." She raised a finger to Aalya's pouty lips.

After carefully hanging the loose end of the sari over Aalya's shoulder, Rozeena took her hand.

"Tonight is just the beginning. There'll be many more nights and parties where you'll meet people." Rozeena grinned. "Think of tonight like your first day of school. Do you remember?"

Aalya's face relaxed into a smile, and she pressed both their hands together, melding them into one like her mother had done that day.

"Of course I remember," she said. "I stepped onto the school bus feeling safe and strong because we were joined like this, like sisters."

Rozeena nodded, and in that moment their recent silences and arguments flitted away like weak clouds. The sky was clear once again. Their bond was secure. She stepped back and nodded approvingly at Aalya, shimmering in her simplicity, in her natural beauty. But Rozeena had a finishing touch.

"Ammi's lipstick," Rozeena said, holding it up. Neither one of them wore makeup, and wouldn't until marriage, as was done in families like theirs. But Aalya's mother had given permission for tonight.

Rozeena dabbed the bright pink onto Aalya's lips, and the shade matched her sari perfectly. As Aalya giggled at the mirror, making faces and smacking her unfamiliar lips, Rozeena spotted her nails, coated with fresh pink Cutex, and wondered if it was another gift from Zohair. But Rozeena wouldn't comment on it. It was too important a night.

"Neelum Aunty is waiting to see you all dressed up," she said with a wide smile.

Aalya nodded and headed to the door. "And then let's meet on my roof before we walk over to Haaris's?"

Rozeena immediately agreed. They'd never missed spying on a rooftop party at the Shahs' before, and they wouldn't start today. They'd spent too many childhood nights gazing down at the dancing, the revelry, the glimpses of lifestyles they'd only heard about. It felt like a necessary ritual tonight. But this time they'd go straight from Aalya's rooftop to Haaris's. It would be a true transition for Aalya, one that would secure her future.

And what about Rozeena's?

Before going next door, she telephoned Haaris to tell him she'd be at his party tonight.

"You're coming? Why?" His surprise was obvious. "I mean, that's wonderful, Rozee. But why did you change your mind? Did something happen?"

She couldn't tell him the true reason, the secret that was only Aalya's to tell.

Forcing laughter, she said, "Are you saying you don't want me there?"

She could hear people milling about him. Was he in his drawing room like she was in hers? Servants' voices and a woman's too floated through the receiver, perhaps his mother giving last-minute instructions. The party preparations would be lush and perfect, like the Shahs themselves.

"No, no. Of course not." He lowered his voice. "I want you here, Rozee."

Her heart raced, flooding her with warmth. These were the words she'd wished for, the ones that gave her hope for their future together.

"I want to be there to celebrate your return, Haaris, like your other friends." Although she knew this wasn't the whole truth, it was close enough to what she could give him right now. And she hadn't overcome her annoyance with Saima's manipulation but had to be there for Aalya.

"My other friends? You're nothing like them."

She flushed hot, grateful her mother and Khala weren't in the room.

"And with you at the party, Rozee, we'll be celebrating much more than my return."

She tingled with anticipation now. Yesterday at Clifton Beach, they'd made a commitment to each other, unspoken but definitive. Would he say the words out loud tonight and tell her he loved her? Would she?

Minutes later, Rozeena climbed Aalya's concrete stairs past her landing and all the way to the roof.

"Shouldn't you be in the front, spying on the party?" Rozeena said, seeing Aalya leaning against the back boundary wall, staring out behind their homes.

Aalya pointed at the market. "When did God Bless become so big?"

Rozeena noticed too. The market was dotted with many more lights, its main street looking longer than ever.

As children, the four of them had lovingly translated Khuda Rakh Colony to God Bless Colony, and the five-minute walk to its main street, where the little general store always had toffees, had been the ultimate treat for them. But as they grew older their shopping shifted to other places, because only servants went to God Bless regularly, for fresh vegetables and other simple household necessities.

Aalya turned to her, eyes round. "I don't even remember when we went last, all together."

"It's all right," Rozeena said softly, guiding Aalya across the roof to the front. "It's normal to grow out of those childish things. Hasn't Haaris finally come back from Liverpool? And Zohair has his new work at the railway station, and his other big plans too."

She glanced at Aalya's face for a hint of sorrow, or regret, at the mention of Zohair, but just then, below them on Prince Road, several cars stopped in front of Haaris's gate. Women stepped out wearing sleeveless blouses over matching jewel-toned hipster saris—sapphire, emerald, and ruby. How did the saris sit so low without slipping off? Rozeena and Aalya burst into laughter tugging at their own saris already tied high on their waists. How different they looked with no more than an inch of flesh showing below their blouses. Music started up on Haaris's well-furnished and brightly lit rooftop. Elvis blared loud and clear, and the silky saris warmed up to the beat, swinging and twisting to Elvis's deep, deep voice.

Rozeena searched for Haaris but couldn't spot him in the huddles of suited men. Aalya stared intently at the crowd as well, and Rozeena wondered if she was looking for Zohair, or if Aalya's future husband was somewhere in the crowd of people.

"Are you ready?" Rozeena turned to Aalya, grabbing her hand and squeezing it.

Aalya pulled her gaze away from the party, and for a moment Rozeena sensed a hesitation. But it was quickly replaced by a smile and nod.

"Definitely. Yes."

Across the street, they followed Haaris's guard to the back of the house, passing by two giant tamarind trees, their canopies perfectly trimmed, before reaching the stairs. The music bounced against their heads as they stepped onto the roof. The buffet was being set up on one side, and on the other, the chatter of guests competed with the music. A cloud of perfume, unrecognizable other than it was something flowery and strong, engulfed Rozeena. A uniformed waiter passed in front with a tray of golden-brown drinks she didn't recognize. Perhaps it was the Johnnie Walker she'd seen in a newspaper ad recently. Aalya squeezed her hand, and Rozeena gave her a reassuring nod, searching for someone familiar in the clusters of guests, laughing, dancing, drinking.

Zohair caught her eye from across the dance floor and bounded over, curls flopping on his forehead, eyes fixed on Aalya. She let go of Rozeena's hand and took a step forward to meet him. Rozeena pretended to fidget with her bun, jabbing it with her index finger here and there, not wanting to leave Aalya's side.

Where were the eligible bachelors?

Saima headed toward them, with a train of three dark suits behind.

She drew everyone's eyes to her with the rippling, burgundy chiffon sari and heavy ruby necklace draped over her collar bones. The center pendant reached low into her neckline. As Saima weaved around bodies twisting and thumping to the beat, Rozeena recognized Haaris and Waleed as two of the men following her. Waleed didn't cast a single glance toward Rozeena as he neared, not even to acknowledge their outing to the cinema.

His focus was entirely on Aalya.

Haaris was dragged away by one of his guests before he could reach Rozeena.

Embracing Rozeena, Saima cooed, "There's someone I want you to meet." She pulled back and gestured to the third gentleman who'd followed her across the roof. "Javaid is a veterinarian, a bit of a black sheep in his family, but we still like him." She laughed openly at her teasing. "Anyway, I thought you two might have something in common."

She fluttered a hand between them, the similarity of their professions not needing further explanation, and then slid away, linking arms with Aalya and Waleed.

Rozeena watched them walk away.

Waleed seemed enthralled. His head tilted low in Aalya's direction. Saima had easily shifted her matchmaking efforts. A couple of men grabbed Waleed for a photograph. He posed, while Aalya stood by with Saima. When the camera flashed, his head was turned toward Aalya, a smile flickering on his lips. Rozeena now wished she'd spoken to Waleed the other day, at least to know what sort of person he was. But it was only a first step, and in the next few weeks Aalya would get to know him and others, attend more events too, and hopefully find someone suitable.

Feeling a little relaxed, Rozeena gave the veterinarian an easy smile. "I assume Saima calls you the black sheep because you're not a real doctor."

Javaid laughed, a good sport and quite used to the mockery apparently. He had a kind face and knew about medicine, so they chatted while Rozeena kept an eye on the time and on Aalya from afar. Her mother had insisted they return no later than ten p.m. It wouldn't be respectable otherwise.

Haaris caught Rozeena's eye every five minutes from within various huddles of friends. After the first couple of times, Rozeena shifted her position to make sure she'd remain in his line of sight. It was nothing more than a check-in, a slight lift of the corners of his mouth, an infinitesimal nod. She returned it each time. If Javaid noticed, he was polite enough not to mention it.

As soon as a group of men whisked Javaid away, Zohair landed by Rozeena's side.

"Why aren't you with Aalya?" He kept turning his head to follow her movement across the roof. She was still linked to Saima but now in a group of only women.

"She's meeting people, making friends." Rozeena shrugged. "Aren't you doing the same?"

"I'm meeting people for my business ideas, not for . . ." He pursed his lips and stared at Rozeena, waiting.

She swallowed and kept herself from divulging even a hint of the true reason behind Aalya's urgency. Rozeena was certain Zohair adored Aalya. He'd care for her and support her in every way. And he was good, so very good. A lump lodged in Rozeena's throat. She desperately wanted to tell him all of this, but how could she? After what she'd learned, Zohair wasn't good enough. Marrying him wouldn't keep Aalya's family safe enough.

Sighing, he blew air from his mouth, the soft curls on his forehead lifting like they did when he was a child. He headed back toward Aalya and latched on to the group of men closest to her.

At nine forty-five p.m., Aalya pulled Rozeena away from the buffet.

"Waleed wants to walk me home. What should I say?" She bit her lip.

Rozeena set her plate down on the nearest table and swallowed her last bite. "Let's go."

"He says he also wants a view from my roof," Aalya continued. "I was pointing out the house and how we used to spy on these parties as children, and he said he'd like to see the view from up top and do a little spying himself. He has this new camera." She raised her eyebrows.

"Do you want to show him the roof?" It was Aalya's choice, her decision.

"I think so. We could go as a group."

"Yes, definitely as a group. You can go ahead, and I'll follow a minute behind, all right?" This way they'd have a little privacy but not remain unchaperoned. "And he is Haaris's friend." Rozeena furrowed her brow, intent on giving the best advice. "He's divorced but was perfectly decent that day at the cinema. I know his sister Saima. Her son is my patient."

Aalya nodded, equally serious. "I'll say yes."

Rozeena watched Aalya head to the staircase. Waleed followed right behind, but then two couples intercepted him, and he stepped aside to meet them. This time when Haaris caught Rozeena's eye from across the roof, she waved and pointed to the staircase just as Waleed started down after Aalya.

Haaris hurried over to accompany Rozeena down the stairs.

The music and laughter receded as they reached the ground, their steps falling in unison and stopping altogether near the tamarind trees.

Rozeena smiled. "It was actually nice, your party."

He laughed. "You seem surprised."

"I didn't know what to expect, that's all." She looked up at the canopies overhead. "We're so different."

"Not that different, Rozee." He moved a step closer. "I think we're a perfect match, don't you?"

She reached for his arm, ensconced in his dark suit jacket. "It always feels right with you." But everything around him was so perfect, so rich, so easy.

He reached for her other arm, keeping his eyes on her. Her lips quivered as his warmth ran up her bare arm, fingers wrapping around her cool skin, caressing her all the way up and then back down. Her breath, trapped inside, burned hot.

She stepped closer. "I need some time, that's all."

His chest smelled of other people's cigarettes. He rubbed his face against the top of her head, and she got a whiff of his fresh Brylcreem, clean and sweet. She reached around his waist inside the coat, and his arms wrapped around her back. Her eyes closed.

"Time for what, Rozee? We can do it together, whatever it is." His heart beat fast in her ear.

Her voice was sleepy, like she didn't want to move even a bit. "I need to take care of Ammi and the house. Let me get it settled. Let me be ready. Then—"

"I hope she approves of me."

Her eyes flew open. Slowly, she pulled away. Haaris was smiling, like it was a joke to wonder about her mother's approval.

"What about your family?" She glanced up, all the way to the roof, to the people whose lives were like brightly lit dreams in the sky. "I'm not like your other friends."

"Exactly. You're not." His hands cupped her face. "I'll tell my parents tonight, after the party. They'll be happy for us. I know they will." His fingers brushed her cheek, then her throat. "I love you, Rozee."

She stilled his hand and raised it to her lips. "I love you too, Haaris." His palm was hot and smooth and hard against her kiss. She heard his soft groan like it came from within herself. As she wrapped her arms around his neck, he brought his lips down to hers. He tasted sweet, and salty too. They melted into each other, and when his mouth moved to her cheeks, she was left panting. He kissed her eyes, neck, throat until it was unbearable. She pulled him back to her lips, and they crashed into each other again. From mouth to chest to thighs, every part of them touched.

"Rozee?" a voice called from behind the house.

They tore apart from each other just as Zohair turned the corner, running toward them.

"Rozee! Where's Aalya? I can't find her upstairs."

She gasped. "She's on her rooftop, with Waleed."

"What? How could you let her go alone with him?" Zohair hurried ahead of Rozeena as they crossed the street.

She didn't explain that Aalya had wanted to go, that she didn't mind Waleed's company.

Rozeena had to run to keep up with Zohair as they crossed his garden and went straight to the stairs at the back. When they reached the rooftop, they saw clearly under the light of the near-full moon.

Two tangled bodies pressed against each other at the far end of the expanse. Rozeena stood confused for a second, and then saw Aalya twist away from Waleed and fall to the ground. Instantly her legs began kicking wildly at him. Her screams reached Rozeena, even over the music from across the street.

Zohair set off like a locomotive, shooting across the roof, gaining speed and momentum. Rozeena ran behind him, yelling for Waleed to stop, but he reached down for Aalya's shoulders, for the front of her blouse, snatching, grabbing. Zohair charged at him with the force of his entire being. He slammed against Waleed, lifting him off the ground so high that Waleed bent backward over the front boundary wall.

There was no way to stop then, or even slow down.

Smashed against each other, both men disappeared over the wall.

Across the street, the music stopped, and screams rose into the night.

21

NOW, 2019

Rozeena waited for Zara on the veranda, as usual—the Country Time lemonade chilling in the fridge, and Pervez stationed outside the gate, expecting Zara's car any minute. But she never arrived.

Rozeena made the first phone call at exactly five thirty p.m., thirty minutes after Zara should've arrived for her gardening internship. Zara's mother started screaming instantly, crying for her husband and Zara and the driver and anyone else who would listen. Their driver was missing too.

Seconds after her next call to Mansur, Rozeena's phone rang. It was Haaris.

"Did you say anything to Zara?"

"What do you mean, Haaris? Are you asking me if I told her to run away?" Standing in the center of her veranda, Rozeena slammed her hand on the chair back.

"No, no. Of course not," he said quickly. "Just trying to see if any conversation of yours could give us an idea of where, or why—"

"I'm assuming your son tried calling the driver's mobile number?"

"Yes, of course he did. It's turned off. And Zara doesn't have a local mobile number. They're trying to call her through WhatsApp but it's not working. Has she been late before?"

"No. Never." That's why Rozeena sounded the alarm.

"Maybe she stopped at the market for something," Haaris said to himself, before ending the conversation.

Mansur paces the veranda tiles now, while Rozeena takes a step forward, then back. She holds her head in disbelief, then sits down, gets back up and collects her purse from the table.

"Where are you going?"

"To drive around the neighborhood, Mansur. We must do something."

On the way to the car, Rozeena wonders if there's something to Haaris's accusation. Could this be her fault?

"You're right," Mansur says. "We might as well search the streets, the neighborhood. We'll go in my car, and your driver can take yours in the other direction. Pervez recognizes Zara, doesn't he?"

"Of course, and the driver and car as well."

Mansur suggests they go to Zara's parents first and offer to help. Perhaps they know more by now or have a plan. But the more Rozeena considers Haaris's words, the more she believes they could be true.

"No, her parents must be out driving around themselves. We have to go straight to Sea View." She gives Mansur a firm nod.

"Why Sea View?" But he complies immediately, taking a sharp left.

"Because Zara likes faces better than plants."

Her son knows better than to ask for an explanation. She'll only offer one when she decides it's time. For now, she directs him to roughly the same spot she brought Zara to, where Rozeena prodded her for answers, pushed her to see what she really wants, why she's really doing a gardening internship and for whom. Perhaps Rozeena pushed too far.

As they park, Rozeena's phone blasts its ringtone and vibrates in the purse on her lap. The screen flashes Haaris's name again.

"Have they found her?" she says without preamble.

"No, not yet. I was going to ask if you thought of any place she might be."

Mansur has stepped out already, his door ajar, so laughter and shrieks from the evening crowd at the beach waft into the car. He ducks his head back in and mouths, *Are you coming?*

"Maybe. I have to go, Haaris. I'm out looking for Zara, but I'll call you with any news."

Her son's eyes widen, and his arm shoots toward her, fingers rigid, reaching for the phone. She admonishes herself for saying Haaris's name out loud and doesn't want to hand Mansur the phone. But his lips pull down at the corners. His hurt pains her, shames her into giving it up.

Mansur says salaam and introduces himself and then quickly gets back inside, slamming his door shut against the commotion outside. His hair is disheveled from the sea gusts, worse than what he used to wake up with as a child. But Rozeena clasps her hands together on her lap. She cannot fix her son's hair any more than she can keep him from speaking with Haaris.

"Yes, my mother has an idea of where she can be, I think." He turns to her with a questioning nod, and she smiles back in response. "Of course. As soon as we know anything. And please, let us know if her parents . . . Yes, thank you."

He ends the call, and Rozeena speaks quickly because she's kept a secret from her precious son, a valuable secret.

"Haaris calls once in a while," she confesses, tucking her phone back into her purse. "But since he's coming to Karachi himself soon,

I thought you could just meet him and ask your questions in person. He might be more inclined to talk then."

Her excuse is feeble. From the tone of this telephone conversation, Rozeena has obviously been chatting on the phone with Haaris regularly since Zara has been here, at least.

"Did he say that? That he'll talk in person?"

"I think he will." She lies too easily, but only for Mansur's good.

Her son sits back in the driver's seat with a deep sigh, staring out at the gray-blue expanse before him. The white foam rises high along the beach as each wave pounds the sand. The summer sea is too rough for swimming, so bodies crowd the beach, filling it with their colorful flapping clothes, swirling hair, and faces turned upward. Gray clouds have blocked out the sun. It might even drizzle, the beginning of the monsoons.

"You don't think she'd wade into the sea, do you?" Rozeena squints to see for bobbing dark heads.

Everyone knows it's the wrong season for swimming. But Zara has probably not seen the warning signs or read the *Dawn* articles recording daily drownings.

Rozeena refuses to wait in the car, so Mansur has to slow down to match her pace on the sand. His socks and shoes are in one hand because he forgot to leave them in the car. He has Rozeena's elbow in the other. She keeps her sandals on, afraid of sharp objects jabbing her. They enter the crowd to search for Zara. The closer they get to the water the saltier the air gets. It's louder here too, with the roar of the sea, but it also becomes easier to walk. Instead of sinking into dry sand, their feet are supported by the taut, wet surface.

Crowds thin as Rozeena and Mansur exit through the mass of bodies. There are only a few brave souls moving ahead of them, near the water's edge. Some sit, waiting for the sea to rush up their legs after the waves crash and lose momentum. Others run toward the growing wave, taunting it, and then turn back to outrun it as it chases them.

She feels cool drops on her face and shivers staring up at the gray clouds that have turned the sea the same color. When she lowers her eyes, she spots three heads in the water. Mansur drops his shoes and runs toward them.

He's only knee-deep in the rough sea, when three young men rise up to stand. Rozeena looks left and right, but there's no one else in the water as far as she can see.

"What if she went in to get her feet wet, and . . ." She swallows, looking up at Mansur, back at her side. "The sea is so rough."

He stares ahead. "We can't stay here thinking these things. There's no point."

She nods, grateful that he's making these decisions. It's getting harder for her not to despair. She turns away abruptly from the sea, refusing to look at it and consider what might be. When they reach the car, she spots the stall.

"Where are you going?" Mansur calls after her as he puts on his shoes, but she doesn't stop to answer.

Rozeena reaches the young man selling Pakola and catches her breath after the long, fast walk. "Have you been here all afternoon?"

He nods.

"An American girl, in jeans and a T-shirt, did you see her today?" Rozeena assumes Zara is dressed as usual, and although she speaks Urdu and looks Pakistani, there's no doubt she's from somewhere else.

Mansur is by her side now and waits for an answer too while the stall owner serves Coke to a group of seven.

"She had a bag, a big brown one perhaps," Rozeena says when he's free. "And she likes Pakola."

"Yes, yes. She was here." He nods. "I remember because she wanted a rickshaw." He shrugs. "I told her, just wait around for one."

"And did she?" Mansur says quickly.

"I think so. Many people are coming and going all the time. There are always rickshaws and buses, and cars too. Good for business." He grins.

Rozeena turns to the vehicles, searching for a rickshaw, any rickshaw, while Mansur shoots off more questions.

When was she here?

Do you know where she was going?

Was she with anyone?

Are you sure it was her? How tall . . .

The stall owner is certain it's been less than an hour since he sold her the drink but doesn't know where she was going, or if she found a rickshaw.

Rozeena returns to the car while Mansur runs around questioning people in the parking area, speaking to other vendors and checking with rickshaw-wallas. She leans back in the passenger seat, exhausted, both mentally and physically, and wonders where Zara could have gone.

It'll be dark soon.

What will they do then?

22

THEN, 1964

The Welcome Home Ball

Rozeena pressed her palm against Aalya's mouth and pushed
her down to keep her hidden from sight.

People across the street had seen the men fall. Within seconds, shouting had replaced the screams, and with no music blaring
now, voices traveled far and clear. Guests yelled down from Haaris's
roof to their drivers on the road.

"Hurry! Bang on the gate."

"No, not that gate! The house over there, where the people fell."

Aalya tried to reach up for the boundary wall.

"No." Rozeena held her tight. "They mustn't see you. Not here.
Not like this."

Aalya's blouse was torn open, a sleeve ripped and hanging off her
left shoulder. Three deep scratches dug across the top of her right
breast. Blood inched down.

Banging started at the gate, and more shouting from Haaris's
roof. Guests were headed down to investigate the incident.

Did they know who'd fallen yet?

Rozeena gathered the loose end of Aalya's unraveled sari and threw it over and around her shoulders, binding her bare arm as well. Aalya turned rigid in the cocoon for a second. Then the shuddering began.

"My fault . . . I . . . he . . . he said photographs and I . . . I said . . ."

Rozeena pulled her into her arms, trying to hold her together. "No, no, no. Nothing is your fault, Aalya." It was only Waleed's fault.

But Zohair.

Rozeena resisted the urge to look over the wall herself.

"We have to go," she said with a twist in her gut. "Downstairs to the garden."

Aalya continued to vibrate in Rozeena's arms. It was too much of a risk to take her to the front like this. Aalya's eyes weren't even focusing, irises hopping from one spot to the other. She couldn't be trusted to follow instructions, play a charade.

"Listen to me." Rozeena's tone was stern now. She had no choice. "We have to get downstairs before someone notices we're missing from the party." She squeezed Aalya's shoulders until at least her eyes stilled.

Then, holding hands, crouching low, and hugging the boundary wall to remain in the shadows, they ran back to the stairs. But just as they started down, the door to Aalya's house flew open below them. Her parents, of course. They must've heard the commotion, maybe even stepped out on the corner balcony to see what had happened. They must've checked Aalya's bedroom too. She should've been back home by now. Rozeena waited until the tops of the parents' heads reached the ground and turned the corner.

The front gate banged open.

Voices grew louder, closer.

As Rozeena and Aalya emerged from the side of the house, a crowd of mumbling men and women blocked their view and their passage ahead. From somewhere in Zohair's garden, a man barked instructions.

"Move back. Stay back."

There was shuffling in response. Suddenly, a woman's wailing pierced the night, loud and sharp, until it died down to an exhausted whine. The ensuing silence quickened Rozeena's heart as she wondered why no one was doing anything.

She could only see the backs of unmoving guests. There was no discussion about what to do next, about making room so Zohair and Waleed could get up and move along. Threading her fingers into Aalya's, Rozeena shouldered her way through the spectators. A flash blinded her. She blinked rapidly and searched for the source. Who was taking photographs? Before she could spot the camera, her eyes landed on the tiled veranda by the front door.

Waleed lay flat on his back, his limbs spread out like spokes of a wheel. Zohair was splayed too but facedown across Waleed's chest. That's how Rozeena had seen them last on the roof, Zohair barreling toward Waleed, chests smacking, and both flying over the wall glued to each other. Their bodies formed a giant X to mark the spot now. From beneath Waleed's head, a pool of dark red ballooned onto the black-and-white tiles like a collapsed parachute.

His eyes were closed.

She couldn't see Zohair's eyes because he faced the tiles.

His father knelt beside him. Rauf's hand hovered above Zohair's head, and then he bent over and kissed his son's curls. The man barking instructions ignored Rauf, perhaps knowing he was the father.

"They mustn't be moved! Don't touch them," he yelled at everyone else approaching the veranda. "Their heads and necks and spines, extremely delicate."

A quick glance up at the roof told Rozeena how impossible it would be to survive such a fall, especially if you went down headfirst, which both men did. Rozeena spotted Haaris pushing through the crowd, and then he froze—mouth open, empty hands reaching forward before he ran to Rauf and dropped to his knees next to him.

Undulating wails rose again. Rozeena took two more steps ahead and spotted the source. Saima knelt on the tiles on the far end of the blood pooling from Waleed's head. Rocking back and forth, she flung her arms up in the air, shaking with tension, like she was keeping herself from crawling over the blood toward her brother's head.

"Do something! Why don't you do something?" she cried at no one in particular.

Haaris answered softly, "I called the ambulance, Saima." He kept his eyes lowered like he was speaking to the men on the ground, telling them to hold on, wait, breathe. "It's coming. It's coming."

Saima ignored his words and continued to ask why no one was doing anything. She swung her head left and right and nearly swept right past Rozeena but stopped and came back to her. Saima frowned as if trying to remember something important. Then, noticing Aalya, her eyes grew round. Was it recognition, or was it anger? Saima rose from the ground, yanking her sari from under her heels and ignoring the loud rip of chiffon. She took two steps toward Aalya, but before she could reach her, Aalya's parents pounced upon their daughter. People turned their heads at Neelum's soft cries of relief, as mother and father quickly dragged Aalya away, back through the throng and to their staircase behind the house.

Rozeena breathed relief that at least Aalya was safe, for now. People had seen her here, like all the other party guests who'd run across the street after it happened. It looked like Saima had lost her train of thought. She dropped back onto her knees by Waleed's blood.

The ambulance arrived.

All heads turned to the gate. Haaris shot up to his feet. The gate was pulled open all the way to allow for the ambulance to drive up to the edge of the grass. As the crowd parted for the stretchers, Rozeena got pushed to the side. One by one, they carried Waleed and Zohair into the vehicle, carefully lifting and maneuvering them to support their necks, their backs and heads. When the St. John ambulance sped away toward National Hospital, Haaris's guests began milling about. Some filtered out of the garden. Those remaining were louder now, not bound by the etiquette of tragedy, freely expressing their shock and predictions of the victims' states.

"No one can survive that fall."

"That other fellow," a voice said from the group. "Who is he? Do you know him?"

"Never met him before. Is this his house?"

"But why was Waleed here?"

In unison, heads turned to the roofline. "Why was he up there?"

Rozeena pushed her back into the wall of Zohair's house, feeling the intrusion of these strangers who photographed the devastation, trampling like beasts in the garden.

Standing at a distance, suddenly separate from the mass, she shivered in the night, but her armpits were damp, and her forehead and nape slick with sweat. She swiped at her face and wiped her hands on her sari. When she took a deep breath to calm herself, the scent of Ibrahim's jasmine entered her, but it was sickly sweet, nauseating.

Ibrahim appeared from the side of the house and nodded at Rozeena. The guests quickly hushed each other, pointing at him and then at Rauf who'd emerged from inside.

"Haaris has gone to get his car." Rauf's voice was barely audible. The two fathers were going to the hospital together.

The last of the crowd trickled out, leaving the gate wide open behind them. Rozeena rushed to shut it. As she did, she saw couples heading toward their cars, practically bouncing with elation at the surprise events of the night. Saima wasn't among them. She'd left right away, following the ambulance.

"You can't do anything now, Rozee." Haaris left the engine running on the street and hurried toward her. "Go home, and don't say . . . Don't talk to anyone about—"

"Rozeena?" Her mother and Khala stepped out of their own gate down from Zohair's.

"I'm coming." She nodded vigorously. "Please. Go back inside." They listened.

Rozeena and Haaris turned around to face an empty garden now, and the pool of blood on the veranda. Ibrahim and Rauf walked toward them.

"I want to come with you, Haaris," Rozeena said. Her eyes flicked up to Aalya's corner balcony. She pulled them back down.

"There's nothing you can do," he repeated. "Just remember—"

"I know. Of course I won't say anything, to anyone. But you too, Haaris." She swallowed, wondering what he knew and what he assumed had happened.

He mustn't say anything about how Zohair came looking for Aalya, and how they'd run after her and Waleed. It was just minutes later that both men fell to the ground.

"I don't know anything," Haaris said with a blank stare.

Her mother reached for Rozeena's face, cradling it as soon as she entered the gate. "You're all right. You're safe." Her voice was hoarse but relieved.

After telling her mother and Khala whatever she could, Rozeena telephoned next door.

Neelum answered, sounding incredulous, in shock. "How did this happen, Rozee? How could it happen?"

"I don't know." She shook her head into the receiver. "I just don't know. Can I speak to Aalya?"

"She's still in the bathroom, taking a bath. At this time of the night." A pause and muffled voices. "Here she is now. Talk to her."

Aalya took the phone.

"Should I come there? I can sleep there tonight," Rozeena said.

But Aalya insisted she didn't need it and then fell silent.

"It wasn't your—"

"Maybe they're . . . Maybe he's going to be all right?" Aalya whispered.

There was no denying the gravity of Waleed's head injury and the loss of blood. If the music hadn't been so loud, they would surely have heard the crack of his skull against the tiles. Rozeena squeezed her eyes shut and shook her head to remove the sound from her mind, and the image.

But Zohair had a softer landing.

"Yes, maybe."

"I should go. What if they're trying to call from the hospital?" A tinge of hope had risen in Aalya's voice, and Rozeena admonished herself for having encouraged it.

"All right, but, Aalya, don't say anything to your mother, or anyone else. Talk to me. Only me."

23

NOW, 2019

Zara was here at Sea View not long ago. Rozeena must hold on to that hope, a sign that if she thinks hard, she can guess where the girl might have gone next.

Her phone pings, then pings several times again before Rozeena can retrieve it from her purse. She's lost track of time, sitting in the car while Mansur runs around trying to find anyone who might've seen Zara.

Rozeena's phone shows Mansur has made a message group with Zara's mother and another number, probably her father. The parents are on their way to Sea View right now. Their driver has finally arrived back at the house after dropping Zara at Sea View and stopping at the market. Apparently, she borrowed his phone and turned it off before returning it to him. By doing so, she gave herself some extra time.

As Rozeena reads these messages, Zara's photograph pops onto the screen.

Show it to the drinks man. Did he see her for sure? We're 2 minutes away.

Rozeena's index finger lands on Zara's face, on her cheek, across her smile.

Tell me you're safe.

Ya Allah. Make her be safe. Please.

Rozeena swallows a huge lump in her throat, unsuccessfully, and squeezes her eyes, refusing to see or think of what might be. No, Zara is not lost, not hurt, not being hurt by anyone. Mansur makes the next several decisions, and Rozeena lets him because she doesn't know what more she can do. Her head pounds with worry like it will explode.

She returns to her house while Mansur and Zara's parents and all their other friends and relatives search places Zara frequents— restaurants, art galleries, movie theaters, shopping malls—all while Rozeena sits on her veranda watching the sky change color. In thirty minutes, the sun will set, and the long, dark night will start. Rozeena doesn't look at her phone anymore. There's a new, larger message group, and the pings have been repeating the same message over and over again.

Not here.

Not here.

Not here either.

Pervez hovers by the gate, one foot out and one foot in. Mansur insisted he stay with Rozeena, in case. He didn't have to expand on his reasons—in case she needs to be rushed to the hospital. It's never once happened yet, but she is eighty-one, Mansur reminded her.

When Pervez arrived at Sea View to pick up Rozeena and bring her home, he first interrogated Zara's driver who'd arrived minutes earlier with her parents.

"He's an ignorant man," Pervez said later of Zara's driver, shaking his head with a deep frown. "How could he drop Zara Bibi and leave? Who can do that? Even if she told him to leave, he should have stayed. And he should have checked his phone. What is it for if it's off?"

Rozeena doesn't blame the poor man though. Who knows how often, and in what way, he's been admonished for not following instructions.

Pervez is itching to join the search party, but like Rozeena he's been told to do nothing.

She drops her head back on the chair and tilts her face to the sky, like Zara does. The land disappears from sight, even the tops of the coconut palms are mostly gone. Taking deep breaths, Rozeena waits for the magic to begin. Maybe she can be brilliant and make discoveries while doing nothing, like Isaac Newton.

The sky above feels heavy on Rozeena's head, pressing. Her eyes close and she goes within, odd bits flashing in her mind.

Zara's eyes, so much like Haaris's.

Mansur's sweet worry wrinkle above his nose.

The crunch of hot potato samosas.

Zara lounging and eating, more than gardening.

Rozeena bolts up straight, and the sudden movement makes her dizzy. She squeezes her eyes shut and calls for Pervez.

"The nursery. Atif's Nursery," she says to him. She has no time for extra words.

Pervez runs back to throw open the gate.

Atif's Nursery is definitely not on the search party list. As Pervez reverses out the gate, Rozeena calls Mansur from the back seat. It's not more than a ten-minute drive from her house, she tells him. He hangs up quickly to inform everyone else. But within two minutes, Pervez is stuck in traffic. Frustrated, he swings the steering wheel this way and that to somehow squeeze through. But it's the worst time to be on the roads, evening rush hour.

Message after message with ETAs to Atif Nursery ping on her phone, questions about its location and fastest routes and information about traffic jams.

Traffic has completely stalled on Gizri.

If we had motorcycles we'd get there faster.

Rozeena shakes her head at the futility of that last comment. These types of people have SUVs and other fancy cars. Never once would they envy the poor commuters weaving through dusty traffic under the hot sun with a family of four balanced on the slim seat of a motorbike.

She puts the phone away and turns her focus to the outside, checking faces on the street, in the cars, and buses and rickshaws too, until she's seen them all.

Zara is not here.

The traffic is at a complete stop.

And the sky has turned dark.

"I'm going to walk the rest of the way." She grabs her purse and unlocks her door.

Pervez spins around. "No, no, no. You can't. It's dark and where will you walk? On the road?"

"Yes, why not? Nothing is moving. I can't get run over."

Apparently, an oil tanker has slid across the three-lane boulevard. At least that's what pedestrians coming from ahead are announcing to everyone. All traffic will be stopped for who knows how long. Now, even the continuous honking has died down around them in acceptance.

"I am coming with you," Pervez calls from behind.

She waits for him, noticing that drivers of other cars, buses, and transport trailers have left their vehicles too. They've gone ahead to investigate.

Pervez's hand hovers by her elbow, the one free of her purse, as they begin weaving through the traffic. Most cars and rickshaws have cut their engines to save petrol, though exhaust fumes still blow toward her with the strong breeze. Luckily, the tall, arching streetlights are bright and plenty. As they walk, Pervez calls Mansur to give him an update, and instantly Rozeena feels the ping vibrations go off in her purse pressed between her arm and chest.

"Mansur Sahib says they are all behind us, stopped in the same traffic," Pervez says.

Rozeena quickens her pace despite the thick humidity pushing against her. She's panting by the time they reach the tanker. A crowd has formed around it, no white uniforms of the traffic police in sight. Men yell instructions to the tanker driver. Some climb up the side. As Rozeena and Pervez navigate around it, she sees men peering underneath the giant cylinder. At least they're trying.

Only motorcycles and a few people, like Rozeena and Pervez, are trickling through to the other side. It becomes quiet as they move past the tanker. Atif's Nursery is on the corner, but the main entrance is closed, so they go around toward the side entrance, the one Rozeena usually uses.

The small residential street is dark, but Rozeena hears laughter.

There are bodies circling, dancing in the middle of the street.

The gates of all the homes are shut, families and cars safe within their boundary walls, except two cars, parked on the street near the laughter, engines running.

"No! Just leave me alone!"

Zara.

Pervez breaks into a run.

The laughter is louder now, the voices of men.

What's happening up ahead?

What's happened already?

Rozeena has to keep an eye on the road too, as she fast-walks toward them. She's suffocating in the humidity, fire building inside her, running down her temples in lines of sweat.

She stops, wanting to fall to the ground. There's nothing left in her to go on. Men run out of Atif's darkened nursery now. Under a dim bulb, she sees sticks waving high above their heads. She starts moving again, as fast as she can, but it's as if her legs are sinking in quicksand.

Pervez has reached the crowd, and Rozeena can only add her strong voice from a distance. "Zara!"

Some heads turn toward her. She raises an arm, makes a fist, wanting a stick instead.

"Aunty? Aunty!" Zara screams back.

Seven or eight bodies disperse like scurrying ants, running in the direction of the two waiting cars. She hears men, boys, yelling.

"Let's go! Move!"

The cars screech as they pull off the curb. Red lights disappear down the road.

Zara is crying loudly now. She's fallen onto her knees in the middle of the street. Pervez stands before her, arms outstretched, making himself as big as possible, a wall around her. As Rozeena nears, she recognizes the other three men. They're from Atif's Nursery. Their sticks hang beside them. Mouths hang open. They nod at Rozeena.

"Come inside," one says.

"No car?" The other searches behind Rozeena, confused she's on foot.

"Zara." Rozeena pants, reaching for the girl's head.

She jumps and lunges for Rozeena's neck pushing her back, nearly off her feet. Pervez instantly moves behind her, supporting Rozeena's back with a palm until she's stable again. Zara's words are unintelligible. She blubbers, sobs, cries for her mother, says sorry over and over again. Rozeena hears Pervez on the phone with Mansur.

We've found Zara Bibi. We've found her, Alhamdulillah.

"Let's go inside the nursery, all right?" Rozeena strokes Zara's head, which has slipped down to Rozeena's chest.

The girl is hunching lower and lower, trying to fit herself inside Rozeena. If only she could hold Zara inside and protect her from the world.

24

THEN, 1964

One Day After

When he returned from the hospital the next morning, Rauf's cheeks had sunken even further, but his eyes shone. Zohair had survived the fall. His injuries were severe, but he was alive.

Rozeena and Aalya stood stunned by what could only be a miracle. Everyone around them thanked Allah. They'd gathered in Zohair's garden, forming a tight circle in the area between the gate and fountain. Rozeena's mother and Khala were there too, as were Aalya's parents, and Haaris as well.

When the chatter quieted to a hum, Haaris somberly announced that Waleed's funeral was today at noon, directly after Zuhr prayers.

"Since it's Sunday, everyone will be there," he added.

The party in the garden nodded, knowing they too would have to attend the funeral even though they hadn't known Waleed or his family or any of his relatives, close or distant. But Waleed had died in this house, right there on the other side of the fountain, the spot everyone avoided even glancing at by staying close to the gate.

"There'll be a police inquiry too," Haaris continued, with his head bowed. Apa's husband was in the police, so Haaris had gotten the news directly from him even though the incident didn't fall in his district. "It's routine, of course, but also because Waleed's family is demanding to know what happened. They're not satisfied by calling it an accident. So, it's best that we just leave everything like it was last night."

His eyes made their way through the rippling fountain and straight to the black-and-white veranda tiles. Dried blood marked the spot below the roofline. He looked up, like Rozeena had done when she'd entered the gate. But even in the daytime, there was no evidence of a weak wall, no crumbling wedge or chunk broken off. There was no easy way to explain away the tragedy.

She wanted to rip the roof apart with her hands and fling it to the ground.

"The police were at the hospital," Rauf offered quietly. Aalya sucked in a breath, and Rozeena flashed her a look, pursing her own lips. "The doctors told them to come back later, when Zohair is stronger. But I don't think they'll wait too long."

No one asked the important question. Had Zohair told Rauf what happened on the roof last night? Even Khala remained silent, grateful for Zohair's life and seemingly comfortable with these incomplete bits of information. But each gulp of winter-dry morning air scraped down Rozeena's throat, jagged and sharp with the fear of what was to come for Zohair, and for Aalya.

Finally, they dispersed, agreeing to meet in a few hours to leave for Waleed's funeral together, except for Rauf who would head back to the hospital. Rozeena accompanied Aalya to the side of the house, the alleyway to the back. They stopped at the mouth, waiting for her parents to reach the other end, out of earshot.

"Zohair is alive." Aalya gave a tremulous smile.

"He's alive, yes." But nothing will be all right, Rozeena thought. "Are you—"

"Don't worry about me." Aalya blinked away tears.

Rozeena wrapped her arms around her friend, her sister, and gently rocked with her, making sure to avoid the deep scratches on her chest, probably still burning and raw.

When Aalya wriggled free to follow her parents home, Rozeena turned around and found Haaris alone in the garden sitting on the fountain's ledge. She joined him, facing the front boundary wall. Neither one wanted to face the veranda.

"What's that smell?" Haaris wrinkled his nose.

She inhaled, and the rot rushed into her as well. She saw it then.

"They did this." Her lips quivered. "Your friends."

The line of jasmine bushes along the left boundary wall lay crushed. Haaris's guests had packed into the garden, stomping on the plants, craning their necks and climbing over everything to get a glimpse of the gruesome sight on the veranda. Now, deep, empty wedges accentuated the once-round bushes. Broken twigs and torn, yellowing buds littered the soil below. The petals rotted under the rising sun, their perfume turning sharp and foul.

"My friends," Haaris said quietly, staring at the mess. "What happened up there, Rozee?"

She spoke to tight fists on her lap.

"Waleed wanted to see the view of the party from the roof, so Aalya took him up."

He frowned. "She was on the roof? But I saw you and Aalya here in the garden when—"

"Just listen." Her eyes stung, and she croaked the next words out. "When Zohair and I got to the roof, Waleed had his hands on Aalya."

Haaris snapped straight. "He had his hands on—"

"So Zohair ran. He ran across the roof and slammed into Waleed. Zohair saved her." She turned to Haaris. "He did. Aalya was hurt, but less than she would've been if . . . But when Zohair pushed Waleed, they were so close to the wall, and Zohair was so strong and so fast and so angry . . ."

Haaris raised his hands between them. They trembled, begging her to stop. When he dropped them to his knees, his eyes were lowered, his lashes thicker than usual, perhaps because they were wet.

After a while he cleared his throat, retrieved his voice. "But you were down here in the garden, both of you. I saw you. Everyone did."

"I thought it was best to say we were never there. I hardly had time to think. I just wanted Aalya to be safe, untouched by it all. But now Zohair is . . . and Waleed . . ." She squeezed her eyes shut and shook her head. "I should've been there, with them up on the roof. I wasn't supposed to let Aalya and Waleed out of my sight." Her face crumpled. She wrapped her arms around herself, rocking back and forth. "But I stopped under the trees."

"With me." His voice was gruff, pained.

She opened her eyes to his hands gripping his knees, knuckles sharp under the skin.

"We have to fix this, Haaris."

"Waleed is dead. How do we fix that?"

He was right.

"And his family will insist someone is punished, severely."

"But Zohair was only trying to stop him." She shook her head. "It was an accident. Only an accident."

Haaris pushed himself off the ledge and started pacing before her, talking it through. "All right. It was an accident."

Nodding, she loosened her fists and sat up straight. "That's right. Zohair didn't plan it. No one would purposefully fall, would they?"

He stopped. "Waleed's family can still blame him. We'd all want to blame someone if this happened to us."

"But it was self-defense or defending someone else. Anyone who was up there would see that clearly." A sudden breeze sprayed fountain water onto her back making her shiver from scalp to toes. Aalya had been up there. Aalya had seen everything. It had happened to her.

No. Rozeena rubbed her arms through her kameez. Aalya had to be kept safe from now on. "Has Zohair said anything to Rauf Uncle? Has he said who else was on the roof?"

Haaris shook his head. "I don't know. I'm going to the hospital right after the funeral."

"What will you say to him?"

With hands on his hips, Haaris frowned at the grass. "I don't know. But we have connections, my family."

"Doesn't Waleed's family have connections too?"

He looked up. "Yes. And they'll use them."

"But only we know what really happened, and depending on what Zohair says . . ."

She wanted to ask who would win, which family could bribe and lie and cheat justice better? But it was all so vile, so criminal, and it was exactly what Haaris hated about his life here. It was the level of power and control Rozeena had never experienced, but now she wanted it all.

That afternoon, their cars joined the long line crawling toward Waleed's family home. Haaris's parents were in front, followed by Haaris in his car with Aalya's family, and then the old Morris, still making the odd knocking sound but turning left without difficulty.

The houses in Amil Colony weren't new, but they were massive, set on plots large enough for four average-sized homes. The gate to Waleed's home stood open, and a steady stream of mourners were being dropped off in front. After draping her white dopatta over her head, Rozeena held Aalya's hand and followed the crowd.

Inside, incense tinged the air in every room. When they approached the drawing room where close family sat, the scent became sickeningly saccharine. Wisps of smoke rose from sticks burning in every corner.

All the heavy, carved furniture in the two adjoining drawing rooms had been pushed back against the walls. Crisp white sheets covered what felt like thick carpets underneath. The front room, the one with Waleed's immediate family, was packed more tightly. Women dressed in white sat shoulder to shoulder on the floor, legs folded to their sides or underneath, heads covered casually but necks bent intently over the Quran or tasbeeh, fingers clicking the colorful prayer beads. There was a buzzing murmur in the room, which was hushed every few minutes by a cry or a moan. Pitying faces stopped their prayers and shook their heads in commiseration with Waleed's mother and sisters who occupied the main sofa. The remaining sofa seats were taken by the elderly. Men prayed in rooms across the hall.

Rozeena's and Aalya's families attached themselves to the single-file line moving slowly toward the main sofa to offer condolences. Waleed's mother wouldn't recognize them but would assume they were friends of some relative, or perhaps in-laws of a distant cousin. Funerals were never by invitation, though attendance was required by all.

Nothing could be done to stop her mother from meeting Waleed's family, but Rozeena grabbed Aalya's hand and pulled her out of the line before Saima could spot them. Something had flashed across Saima's face the night before—surprise, recognition, accusation?—when she'd caught sight of Aalya standing in the crowd near Waleed's body. Whatever Saima thought she knew, this wasn't the place to witness that discovery or try to deny it.

With Aalya in tow, Rozeena ducked into the adjoining room.

They squeezed into a space by the entrance of the more sparsely populated drawing room. Sitting on the white sheets, they pressed themselves against the wall by the edge of an empty sofa. Rozeena kept an eye out for her mother who'd come searching for them soon. They weren't planning on staying long. Closer friends and family would stay until the men returned from the graveyard and a late lunch was served.

A young woman and perhaps her mother entered the room and paused.

Hush fell over the mumbling prayers. People stared without reservation, some frowned, others pursed their lips. Rozeena was grateful she and Aalya hadn't received such attention. But then the newcomers' eyes landed on them, and the women headed to the empty sofa. They settled in as if they were not only welcome but deserving of the premium seating.

The murmured prayers started up again, heads bowed, though eyes still darted toward the newcomers off and on. When the older woman rose to retrieve a tasbeeh or a chapter of the Quran from the central coffee table, a hoarse whisper came from the sofa above.

"Who are you?"

Rozeena blinked up at the woman. Apart from the hint of dark circles under her eyes, she was younger than her voice sounded, and attractive, even wiped clean of makeup for the funeral prayers.

"A family friend," Rozeena whispered, looking around, wondering if the woman knew everyone else in this room. Haaris's circle was not only powerful but tight-knit too, and blunt.

"Whose friend?"

Rozeena scrambled for the most innocuous and honest answer. "I'm actually a pediatrician. I see Saima's son."

The explanation silenced the woman for some time until she said, "So you see the family's children?"

Rozeena nodded, keeping her eyes averted.

"And is that your sister?"

Aalya lifted her head to meet the woman's gaze.

"Yes," Rozeena said, and quickly returned her focus to the tasbeeh between her fingers, clicking the green beads mindlessly so the woman would hesitate to interrupt again.

Aalya too held a tasbeeh, but the woman had nothing, no tasbeeh in her hand, no chapter of the Quran on her lap. The older woman still hovered by the coffee table listening to the ladies explain which pile was read and which was to-be-read.

The woman bent over her armrest, low and close to Rozeena's ear.

"Do you really believe all these prayers will convince Allah to let Waleed into heaven? Do you think the prayers of his family, friends, and random strangers"—gesturing toward Rozeena and Aalya—"can erase his sins?"

Rozeena held her breath, hoping it was a rhetorical question. But the woman tapped pink manicured nails on the wooden armrest and raised her eyebrows expectantly.

"Well, they say—"

"They say?" The woman's lips curled as if she'd tasted something vile. "I say Waleed got what he deserved."

Aalya's arm tensed against Rozeena's. Neither one asked for elaboration.

The older woman returned with both a chapter of the Quran and a bright red tasbeeh, and the young one sat back on the sofa, silent and calm, as if nothing had been said. Rozeena nudged Aalya. It was time to leave. This room wasn't any safer than the first.

Before they were out of earshot, Rozeena heard the older woman speak. "Here, take a tasbeeh at least, Kulsoom, and enough chitchatting. *Log kya kahenge?*"

Kulsoom stared blankly across the room. Her lips quivering with what could be either sorrow or rage. Her thumb began clicking the beads. But Rozeena doubted Kulsoom recited any prayers for Waleed or his soul. Rozeena and Aalya left the house to wait in the car until the rest of the family completed their duty inside. Finally, the men started to leave for the graveyard, and Rozeena spotted Haaris exiting the gate.

"Stay here," she said to Aalya, and hopped out of the car to catch him before he left.

"I met someone in there." She was panting after her fast walk back to the gate. "Kulsoom."

His eyebrows rose. "What did she say?"

"Why? Who is she?"

"Waleed's ex-wife."

Rozeena frowned, considering the information. She recounted the conversation, pausing if someone was close enough to hear.

Several heads turned their way.

Haaris nodded and raised a hand to indicate he was coming. "Did she know you were at the party last night?"

"I didn't tell her, so probably no."

"She didn't ask about the party and Waleed?"

Rozeena shook her head. "Does everyone already know the . . . the accident happened at your party?"

"Kulsoom obviously knows because she knows everyone who was there. She was invited too, but her mother called to say she'd developed food poisoning or something. Understandably so. The divorce is still so recent."

"I see." She had to ask, especially after what Kulsoom had said. "Why did they get divorced?"

He chewed on his lips, then shook his head with a shrug, as if the rumors he'd spoken of were useless allegations against one another.

"And why was she invited to your party?"

This question rankled him. "Why wouldn't she be, Rozee? I've known her family for as long as I've known Waleed's." Sighing, he added, "Everyone knows everyone. There's no way out."

Rozeena returned to the car with no real information other than Haaris's displeasure at knowing all the influential families of the city. It was a tight group, and as she got back into the Morris, Rozeena understood why Saima had been introducing her brother to women outside that crowd. Waleed would've found it difficult to convince a young woman from his own circle, however wide he drew it, to agree

193

to marriage. Theirs had been a divorce of relative equals. Kulsoom's family seemed to have substantial power and influence too. Neither side had come out the clear winner. Neither side was safe from accusations, spoken or insinuated.

But Waleed had done something that made Kulsoom condemn him to hell in front of a stranger.

Rozeena's eyes flew to Aalya, who stared blankly out the window. Her dopatta had slid off her head, but she held the two ends together at her chest. She'd done this the whole afternoon, even though her kameez already covered the deep scratches.

Sliding over to Aalya's side, Rozeena pushed an arm behind her and wrapped the other around her waist to hold her tight.

"I shouldn't have let you out of my sight." Rozeena closed her eyes and bowed her head to Aalya's shoulder. "All of this . . . it's my fault. I should've kept up with you, run ahead. I should've . . ."

Aalya's shoulders shuddered as she began to whimper. She let go of her dopatta and covered her face with her hands. Her cries grew louder, groans turning into panicked hiccups. She'd held it in, kept it inside, the fear, the attack. Everything. Now it exploded from her insides. The drivers waiting by cars outside all stepped away, probably thinking Aalya was overcome by grief for the deceased. Rozeena sobbed with her, squeezing Aalya tighter, imagining her fear when she was up on her roof, alone with Waleed touching her, clawing at her.

"I'm here," Rozeena cried, tears streaming down her face, into her mouth, over her chin. "I'm here now." She gasped for air. "I'm here for you. I promise."

But she hadn't been before.

25

THEN, 1964

Two Days After

The next morning, Rozeena rubbed at the chill on her arms as she read the *Dawn* news item for the fifth time.

WALEED KHAN DIES AFTER FALLING FROM ROOFTOP, POLICE SAY

Waleed Khan, son of industrialist Wazir Khan, died on Saturday after reportedly falling from the roof of a double-story house on Prince Road, Shikarpur Colony, in the jurisdiction of Jamshed Quarters police station. According to initial information, Waleed Khan and another individual, Zohair Ahmed, both fell from the roof of a house near Imtiaz Shah's residence, where both men had been attending a party. Waleed Khan died at the scene of the fall. Zohair Ahmed was taken to National Hospital for his injuries.

Guests of Imtiaz Shah who witnessed the fall are being questioned, as are the residents of the house where the fall happened. Police plan to also question Zohair Ahmed to determine the events leading up to the fall and identify any other individuals on the roof at that time.

Police are investigating this case from three angles: accident, foul play, and suicide.

Suicide?

Rozeena wondered where that possibility could've come from, and if the police thought it was a double suicide, or that Zohair fell trying to save Waleed. She didn't dare discuss it with her mother or Khala. The less she spoke of that night, the less chance of getting questioned about her own whereabouts at the time.

Her mother and Khala continued to stare at the same news item in the Urdu language *Jang*, placed between them on the dining table. The first time they both looked up was when Shareef entered with a telegram.

Arriving 2 Dec STOP

"Is that all? No explanation?" Rozeena took the slip of paper from her mother. Shehzad would be here in less than a week now, instead of two.

Khala scoffed. "It's short because Shehzad can't spend extra rupees on explanations. What will Sweetie say if he wastes money on us?"

Her mother sighed. "There's no need for an explanation. He must've seen the newspaper this morning." Her eyes returned to the article.

The address of Aalya's house wasn't given, nor was Rozeena mentioned by name. But there was no mistaking her own face, eyes wide and staring down at the dead body. Rozeena remembered the blinding flashes. So many of Haaris's friends had the same Instamatic camera with the pop-up flash. *Dawn* and *Jang* had both managed to get surprisingly clear photographs of the two bodies and three women, albeit from a distance. Aalya's profile was partially hidden behind Rozeena's, and Saima's was bent low over her knees as she crouched by the edge of Waleed's blood.

At least the crime had been photographed in black and white.

Accident. It was an accident.

The crime had been committed by Waleed, against Aalya.

There was sudden banging at the gate, and Rozeena braced herself for the police.

She'd met with Haaris and Aalya in Zohair's garden the night before and discussed what they'd say. Both Haaris and Aalya thought a self-defense case would make the most sense. Aalya would have to be placed on the roof, as the one needing defending. But Rozeena believed nothing good would come of telling the truth, and Zohair had made the same decision. Earlier that day, Haaris had spoken briefly with Zohair at the hospital, and even in his weakened state he'd insisted Aalya not be involved in the story of what happened. When Haaris asked Zohair how he'd explain the fall to the police, Zohair had gone silent before saying he'd handle it without implicating Aalya.

Although Aalya had been reluctant at first, she'd been convinced it was for the best, especially after hearing Zohair wanted it too. And Aalya knew that even a little digging into her background could unearth her family's secret, and fraudsters and liars could be labeled murderers in no time.

So, it was decided they'd say Aalya was with Rozeena at the party when they heard the screams and rushed over to see what had happened along with everyone else. Relief had swept over Rozeena. For now, all four of them had the same story for the police interviews that were surely coming for everyone who'd attended the ball.

But after a few minutes, Sweetie and not the police walked through the double doors of the drawing room. She tossed her white shawl on the sofa and proceeded to the dining table.

"I'm on my way to Waleed Khan's family home," she said, nodding at them all before sitting down next to Khala. She waved at Shareef to bring her tea. Rozeena felt a rush of cold from the brisk, harsh swish of Sweetie's arm, even from across the table. "Tragedy doesn't end with the burial. Our families have known each other for decades." Sweetie sighed heavily.

"I'm sorry. It's so very, very sad," Rozeena's mother said. "And yes, I saw you yesterday sitting with the family."

Rozeena had obviously missed Sweetie near the family sofa at the funeral prayers since she'd ducked into the other room with Aalya.

"I see you received Shehzad's telegram." Sweetie raised an eyebrow at the scrap of paper lying in the center of the table. She'd probably told him to move up his arrival date. "I'm most concerned about you, Rozee."

"Me? Why? I'm—"

"A silly, silly girl, that's what you are." Sweetie shook her head. "You think you weren't seen yesterday talking to Kulsoom?"

"What? What were you saying to her, Rozee?" Her mother's brow furrowed.

Khala's mouth parted, eyes darting from face to face.

"Does everyone know who this Kulsoom is?" Rozeena asked. "I didn't know until Haaris told me later."

Sweetie waved away Rozeena's question. "Tell me what Kulsoom said to you."

"Nothing," she said, and then remembering they'd been seen, quickly added, "I mean, she asked how I knew the family. She didn't know who I was, just like I didn't know who she was. I told her I was Saima's pediatrician."

"You understand that Kulsoom is someone with obvious hatred for Waleed and his entire family, don't you?" Sweetie said. "She could do anything."

"But she wasn't even at the ball," Rozeena said.

Sweetie's eyebrows rose higher and higher on her head. "You presume to know so much, like you're one of . . ."

Us? thought Rozeena.

Interlacing her fingers on the table, Sweetie emphasized her words with a periodic thump of her large double fist. "Kulsoom's brother and cousins"—thump—"were at the party. They're being questioned by the police. Do you understand what that means? They're being questioned first and foremost. And you and Kulsoom"—thump—"were seen chatting at Waleed's funeral. In fact"—thump thump—"you're the only person she spoke to in that entire house, other than her own mother." Thump.

Rozeena shifted in her chair, squirming under three pairs of eyes. No wonder Kulsoom and her mother had chosen to sit next to them, the strangers who hadn't already judged them.

Shareef entered with the teapot, and its snaking steam added to the rising heat inside Rozeena. "I didn't know. I'm sorry. But why was she at the funeral if there's so much hatred?"

Sweetie's shoulders relaxed slightly as Khala's thick arms moved surprisingly fast to pass milk and sugar to her.

"Because they belong to the same people, the same circle, and have to keep up appearances, don't they?" Sweetie said. "We all do. And you, Rozee, have somehow become part of it now." She stirred her tea with purpose. "But you need guidance, and that's why I'm here."

Sweetie took several slurpy sips, too impatient to wait for it to cool.

"I'll be back to stay tomorrow," she said. "But the driver will bring my suitcase this evening." Rozeena and her mother exchanged glances. Sweetie only stayed with them when Shehzad visited. "I want to make sure there are no missteps, no misunderstandings from now on. Best to keep a close eye on things." Her gaze wandered in the direction of Aalya's house.

"Of course," Rozeena's mother said quickly. "You're welcome anytime."

With a nod, Sweetie took a few final sips and pushed away the still-steaming cup. "Go and get ready now, Rozee. You're coming with me. I'm taking food for the Khans. I stopped here to pick you up so you can see your friend Saima and offer her some support." She gave a firm nod. "Grieve appropriately."

Rozeena's mind leapt from excuse to excuse, but there was no way out of Sweetie's plan. She was determined to distance herself and Rozeena from the house next door and everything that occurred there.

After quickly changing into a white shalwar kameez, Rozeena followed Sweetie out the gate.

"Didn't I warn you about these neighbors, Rozee? Just look at what happened there."

"But they don't even know Waleed, and you said yourself it was Kulsoom's family that . . . I mean . . . you said hatred . . ." Rozeena needed to dissuade Sweetie from digging around Aalya and Zohair.

Blankness spread over Sweetie's face, as if she was seeing inward rather than the car in front of her. "Yes, I did say that. But people are saying all sorts of things. We have to make sure they say the right things, the best things. For us."

When they arrived at Waleed's family home, all Rozeena could focus on was the inspector—his khaki trousers and charcoal shirt with bars and badges on lapels and shoulders. He sat at the edge of a heavily carved armchair with rich burgundy upholstery at the far end of the drawing room. Saima sat on the matching long sofa next to him.

Sweetie's food dishes had been whisked away from the foyer straight to the kitchen.

"Won't you join us?" Saima said from her seat. Her eyes landed on Rozeena.

"Oh, we don't want to interrupt." Sweetie nodded at the inspector and took a step back. "If your mother is resting, I'll come back another time."

"Don't mind Inspector Mirza." Saima waved a hand his way. "He's here to keep us informed. His assistant sub-inspector is out gathering information, interviewing people and such, carrying out the investigation. Isn't that right, Inspector Sahib?"

Inspector Mirza straightened his back further and nodded, while Saima let out a sigh and sank further into the sofa.

"My father-in-law knows the inspector general of police so he was here last night too, telling us that everything that can be done, is being done." Saima inhaled and released a long breath. "As if that will bring Waleed back." She squinted at Rozeena and Sweetie, or perhaps at the daylight streaming in the large windows overlooking the garden.

They crossed the room, settled on the sofa across from Saima, and waited while she stared over their heads. Rozeena remembered being similarly and suddenly absent when her father died. She'd startle into the present, unaware of the passage of time, a minute or an hour. Next to her, Sweetie adjusted the white shawl over her shoulders while her eyes darted from the inspector to Saima and back.

"Rozeena, you were at the ball that night too." Saima pulled herself straight with the realization. "Weren't you?"

"Yes. I was." She spoke without hesitation, easy when it was the truth.

"Did you know this, Inspector Mirza?" Saima raised her brows.

His dark, full mustache hid any inflection of his lips, but he reached for the papers next to his tea on the table before him.

He nodded. "We have a list of all the guests. Your name?"

"Rozeena is my niece." Sweetie spoke fast, addressing Saima. "And family friends with the Shahs."

Saima frowned. "Yes, of course, Sweetie Aunty. I think I did know that, but I . . ." She gave a little shake of her head. Rozeena knew the jumbled thoughts, the fog and lack of coherence.

"Rozeena Masood, from Prince Road?" Inspector Mirza said.

"Dr. Rozeena Masood." She lifted her chin and pushed back her shoulders to compensate for her simple shalwar kameez and youth. "Pediatrician. My clinic is in MPS Chambers."

At this the inspector raised his brows.

"That's right. MPS Chambers." Saima nodded with clarity now. "We own MPS Chambers. One of Waleed's earliest projects." She blinked at Sweetie.

"Yes, I remember, Saima. Our families worked together on that one."

Saima frowned at Rozeena. "You're lucky to have found a clinic there. We're always getting requests from young doctors for a chance to set up at MPS Chambers."

If Rozeena groveled with gratitude it would be too much, too suspicious. But now she worried for the clinic itself. Saima could not only stop the referrals, she could take away the clinic on a whim.

"ASI Iqbal is at Prince Road right now, interviewing all the residents," Inspector Mirza said.

"Right now?" Rozeena shifted forward in her seat. "Maybe we should go back and—"

"Tell me, Dr. Rozeena, did you know Waleed Khan and Zohair Ahmed?"

It sounded like a casual question, but when Rozeena glanced at Sweetie, her eyes pulsed a warning. This was an interview, an interview with the police, the one ASI Iqbal would've conducted at Rozeena's home if she'd been there right now.

"I met Waleed once before, with Saima."

"Yes, but you came to the party with Aalya, didn't you?" Saima had already gathered some information. "She lives in the same house as Zohair Ahmed."

"Zohair lives in the downstairs portion, and Aalya up . . ." Rozeena pictured the stairs, the roof.

Shutting her eyes, she took several deep breaths, hands holding each other on her lap. Her fingers were cold even though the sun was higher in the sky now, warming up the room through the wall of windows.

Sweetie filled the silence quickly. "Such a terrible, terrible tragedy." Rozeena opened her eyes to see Sweetie shaking her head.

Inspector Mirza continued with no sign of emotion. "Did you see or speak with Zohair Ahmed at the ball?"

Rozeena nodded. "We met when I entered with Aalya, but then he mostly mingled with the other guests."

"And what did you see happening across the street?"

Saima leaned forward, waiting.

"Nothing. Nothing at all. Everyone started shouting that something had happened, and that we should go downstairs. I didn't know where or what had happened." The lie fell from her lips.

"Did you see Waleed Khan and Zohair Ahmed leaving the party?"

"No. I didn't."

"Did you know they went across the road?"

"No. I didn't."

He checked his notes. "And what did you do when everyone started shouting that something had happened?"

"We followed the rest of the crowd across the road."

"We?"

Rozeena blinked. "Aalya and I."

Sweetie cleared her throat, and it turned into several loud coughs, reminding Rozeena that she was supposed to be distancing herself from Aalya.

"Only because her mother asked that I accompany her," Rozeena explained to both the inspector and Saima. "Aalya is—"

"So young, unmarried, and not a doctor like our Rozee," Sweetie interjected. "So obviously her family didn't want her going alone."

Rozeena nodded and avoided Saima's stare while waiting for the inspector to look up from his notes again.

"I saw you there, both of you." Saima turned to the inspector. "I . . . I can't remember who I saw, so many faces all around . . . but I thought I saw Aalya and Rozeena near . . . near there." She paused to swallow before continuing. "And then the photograph in the newspaper this morning reminded me. I did see both of you."

Rozeena bowed her head in agreement. Those flashing cameras had captured it. They'd placed Rozeena and Aalya in the garden with the rest of the guests.

"I remember searching for Waleed at the party." Saima frowned and turned to Inspector Mirza. "Someone must've seen him leave."

"We're interviewing everyone." He nodded. "We'll know very soon."

Saima moved to the edge of her seat. "He was with that girl, Aalya, for a long time, a very long time. And then, he was on her roof."

Rozeena shook her head. "But she was with me on Haaris's roof. Remember? The photograph shows us—"

"The photographs!" Saima whipped around to the inspector. "What about the ones on Waleed's camera?"

Rozeena froze.

"We're developing the film right now. The camera was damaged, but the film was intact. We'll know soon."

"Yes, yes. It was still in his suit pocket when . . ." Saima got up and began pacing the room between their two sofas. "The film will tell us a lot. It will tell us a lot, won't it? Won't it?" She stopped in front of the inspector. "We'll know who else was up there. We'll know what Waleed was doing on the roof with that Zohair Ahmed.

We'll know how this happened, who did it, and why." Her breath came fast. She began panting and wrapped her arms around her middle, as if in pain.

Rozeena jumped up, but Sweetie reached Saima first and pulled her close. "Yes, yes. All of that. We'll know everything, and the police will find the person who did this." Saima's body tilted into Sweetie's thick trunk, head resting on her breast. "And once they do, we'll see the murderer hang for what he did," Sweetie murmured soothingly, caressing Saima's back. "Won't we, Inspector Sahib? We'll see him hang."

Rozeena fell onto the sofa unable to breathe.

There were photographs. Proof of someone else on the roof. But Aalya would've known if Waleed aimed his camera at her. She would've seen the bright light of the flash even under the light of the moon, wouldn't she?

26

NOW, 2019

The nursery men run to bring chairs and place them near the entrance, by the wall of fanning areca palms.

Rozeena sits down heavily and keeps Zara's hands in hers. Their chairs face each other, knees touching. Pervez stands next to Rozeena holding her purse. Light falls on Zara from the naked bulb overhead, strung from the electrical pole on the street.

"Your parents are on their way." Rozeena searches Zara's bowed face and clothes for violence.

Her cheeks are streaked with dirt, probably from hours of roaming around in rickshaws and walking on the street. But there are no cuts, not even a scratch or the beginnings of bruising. Her hair is still in a ponytail, though messy. She's wearing her pink tunic, crumpled but intact. The slim strap of her black purse still hangs across it.

One of the nursery men brings them two glasses of water, but before Rozeena can say anything, the other nursery worker barks at him to get bottled water, obviously, from the general store behind.

Rozeena wonders who will reach them first—the man with the

bottled water or Zara's parents, who have discarded their car and are sprinting down the main boulevard, according to Pervez's latest telephone conversation with Mansur.

"Maybe you want to talk to your parents on the phone?" Rozeena points to her purse in Pervez's hands. There's a constant buzz coming from her phone. "It must be them calling."

Zara shakes her head.

At least she's coherent. Thank God. Alhamdulillah. Maybe she wants to delay contact. If Rozeena doesn't answer, the parents might think she left her phone in the car. It'll take them a while to reach Mansur and get Pervez's number to contact Zara.

Rozeena settles in to wait, hunched forward, clinging on to Zara's hands, which reciprocate the tight hold. Everything sticks to Rozeena's skin, wisps of hair across her forehead, her shalwar to the backs of her legs and kameez to her chest. She pulls her dopatta off her throat. There's a breeze, but not enough to dry all the moisture. At least the exhaust fumes are replaced by the scent of growth, an overload of greenery surrounds them.

"I didn't plan this, you know." Zara's voice is rough, beat, tired. She doesn't look up from her lap but stays glued to Rozeena with her knees and hands.

"Of course you didn't plan this."

Zara folds over her lap, closing the gap between their heads too. "Now I've made things even worse."

Rozeena's tone is gentle but firm. "What things have you made worse? Tell me."

"They're already all . . . about Fez, and now this."

"Your parents will be so relieved, Zara." She smiles. "No one will be angry at you."

The man returns with two bottles of water, and Zara drinks hungrily while Rozeena pours some on one end of her white dopatta and waits.

"Can I wipe your face a little? It'll feel nice and cool." And, Rozeena thinks, your parents will be less terrified when they see you.

Zara's eyes close as Rozeena wipes the dirt and tears with soaked chiffon. "It's so soft."

"Better?"

The first hint of a smile appears on the girl's face, nodding as she reties her high ponytail. "They didn't hurt me or anything, just like catcalled and stuff. But it was scary, you know?" Her voice trails.

"It could've been much worse." Rozeena winces at the thought.

"Yeah. I guess. But I only went to places I knew, like Sea View, and then I got lost, even with the rickshaw-walla. I couldn't find this place. But I just had to keep going."

"Running?"

Zara frowns. "Maybe?"

This has been the reason behind all of Zara's actions, even if she hasn't known it herself. It's a constant struggle, a push and pull between the version of herself she believes she must be, and the old Zara, that always was. When she can't bear it, she runs.

"You can't keep going like this," Rozeena says. "You were lucky this time." She shakes her head at the thought that being catcalled is considered lucky. "So many things are out of our control."

Zara nods and folds over completely now to rest her clean, cool cheek on their four hands, pressing down on their joined knees. Her torso rises and falls as her breath slows, and then she begins talking.

"That night, Fez snuck out of the house. He'd done that before too, like twice. But nothing bad happened before, so we did it the same way that night, after our parents went up to their bedroom. We turned off the alarm, so Fez could leave. I had to make sure the alarm was back on after he left. I kept my phone by my pillow, so I'd hear his text when he got back." She pauses. "I helped him because it was kind of unfair. All his friends had a driver's license because you can drive at sixteen in Minnesota. But Fez had to wait till he was eighteen because my parents are super strict, like crazy strict." She sucks in her breath and falls silent.

"So, he left the house to drive a car?"

"Oh no." She lifts her head. "He left the house just to drive around in a friend's car. Fez wasn't driving himself. But there was frost that night, even in April. The roads were icy, and the police said the boy who was driving took a turn, skidded, and when he braked, he spun out on the slick road. The car just kept on spinning and spinning until it slammed into an electrical pole, on Fez's side."

Zara rocks back and forth, hands tightening around Rozeena's. She squeezes her eyes shut and her voice cracks.

"At least he didn't suffer. He died on impact."

Rozeena's mouth falls open, and she releases a loud breath, a groan at the words they must've heard as consolation. She turns away and blinks at the dark street behind her, still empty. Zara's parents must've wanted to die on impact too.

"Listen to me." Rozeena tugs on her hands. "There was nothing you could've done."

Zara's chin is buried in her chest. "If I had just—"

"No, you couldn't have," Rozeena says firmly. "Don't you think your parents feel that if they had just been less strict, then maybe Fez wouldn't have been so desperate to sneak out? There are too many if-onlys and maybes. The boy who was driving that night probably feels that if he had just slowed down before turning, or if he hadn't braked in just that way to make the car spin, he wouldn't have lost control. And what about the frost in Minnesota? Whose fault was that?" Rozeena frowns. "Does the ice look white on the black road?"

Zara straightens a bit and shakes her head. "No, it's more like clear ice, you know, transparent. When it's on the road, they call it black ice because of the asphalt color, so—"

"Exactly, so the boy couldn't see it. Whose fault was that?"

Zara blinks, waiting.

"No one's, right? Some things happen because events align in such a way to make them happen." Rozeena sighs heavily, remembering her own past. Sometimes there was a clear guilty party, but . . . "Sometimes, some things just happen. That's all. What you can control now is how you react to that awful, dreadful, tragic thing that happened."

"But that's what I'm doing." She loosens her grip on Rozeena's hands.

"No, Zara. You're trying to be what you think your parents need, but what everyone wants is for you to be yourself, to find your happiness again. You deserve that." Rozeena stops and feels the weight of what she just said. If she'd had this wisdom all those years ago, then maybe that fateful night of Haaris's party wouldn't have happened. Maybe she'd have never asked for his help in growing her clinic, would never have met Saima who'd insisted Haaris invite Rozeena and the neighborhood friends to his ball. "Tell me. What did you feel today, going around on your own in the city?"

"I felt like . . . like me, you know?" Zara's eyes start to water, and everything begins to rush out of her. "Like what you said before at Sea View. Facing the sea with my back to everything, I could see what I really wanted. I mean, I know nothing can be the same again, ever again. But I want to be me again. You know?"

Rozeena smiles and wipes a tear that's about to fall down Zara's cheek. "Yes, I know all too well."

Zara was treading a path Rozeena had already walked. She'd spent so much of her life trying to replace Faysal, in duty and profession. Guilt can make one do that. Every time her parents looked at her, Rozeena believed they saw Faysal—the son, the caretaker, the responsible provider, who should've lived and lived and lived.

Rozeena says the words she wished someone had said to her all those years ago. "You have permission not to be your brother."

Hollering reaches them from down the street. Four or five male voices and Zara's mother all shout Zara's name.

Zara whispers, "It's so hard to always be him."

Rozeena squeezes her hands. "I know. So don't. Let go and be yourself."

They rise together, knees detaching for the first time. But Rozeena keeps a tight grip on Zara's arm, releasing it only when her mother pounces on her, grabbing Zara by the shoulders to examine her face and then flinging her arms around her with cries of relief.

27

THEN, 1964

Two Days After

Rozeena saw the police just as she turned onto Prince Road. What if she was too late?

Sweetie didn't utter a word until her driver came to a complete stop at Rozeena's front gate. After Saima's outburst and subsequent unraveling, Sweetie's broad face had been in various states of grave concern. Now, her mouth unscrewed itself.

"Don't you involve yourself with those neighbors, Rozee. Let the police do their work." She gave a firm nod. "They'll find the murderer, one way or the other."

Rozeena got out of the car and waited for it to turn left and disappear onto the main road. Then she went straight to Zohair's gate, pushed it open, and found Aalya standing stiff and pale under the tamarind tree with Haaris pacing before it.

"ASI Iqbal is on his way," Rozeena said running up to them. "Aalya, you mustn't say—"

"He's coming back?" She raised her eyebrows. "But he just left."

"What? Did he . . . did you talk to him?"

Aalya nodded, eyes darting to the gate. "I said what I was supposed to."

"I entered just as he was leaving," Haaris said, joining them.

Rozeena shook her head, unable to speak.

"What is it? What happened?" Haaris asked.

Rozeena swiped at her forehead, dotted with perspiration even though they stood under the dense shade of the tree. November cool filled the air, but her insides burned, as did their plans to keep Aalya safe. Rozeena recounted what had happened at Saima's.

"She's right." Aalya blinked, as if suddenly recalling. "Waleed was taking photographs." The little remaining color in her cheeks vanished and she stared past Rozeena. "But I can't remember if I was in them. I really didn't see the camera, I think, only some flashes here and there." Lost in thought, she resembled a photograph herself, until she vigorously shook her head. "I said what I said to ASI Iqbal. I can't change it now. I need to go. Ammi is preparing food for Rauf Uncle, and I don't want him to leave without—"

"No, wait." Rozeena raised her palms like a barricade. "We have to think."

"What's there to think about?" Aalya flicked her hair back, blue-black waves cascading over her straight, rigid spine.

"How can you be thinking about food right now?" Rozeena said. "If you're caught lying to the police, if there are photographs of you on the roof, there'll be no question of your involvement. It's all connected." Rozeena wanted to shake her. "Don't you see?"

"Of course I see," Aalya said. "I've always seen that, Rozee. Every choice I make, my family makes, it's all connected to where we came from and where we will go from here." She glanced at Haaris, perhaps worried about divulging too much of her family's past. "But right now, Zohair is in the hospital, and he's hurt. It's a miracle that he survived after . . . after saving me." Her voice turned small. "Right now, I need to care for him and Rauf Uncle."

Rozeena slowly nodded at her friend who was now openly focused on Zohair like she'd never been before. As Aalya hurried away, Haaris kicked the dirt near the tree's roots before dropping onto the fountain ledge.

Rozeena joined him.

This time, they faced the front gate, their backs to the veranda, the roof, and the rotting jasmine buds. And if ASI Iqbal walked through the gate with photographs proving Aalya had been on the roof, they'd have nowhere left to face.

She shivered, the cool spray tingling her back as her mind raced for a solution. "What was that about suicide in the newspaper? Are they really considering it?"

"They are." He stomped his shoes on the grass turn by turn, but the dirt clung. "And I said yes, it could've been. I mean, maybe."

"Why did you say that? And who did you say it to?"

He shrugged. "Everyone knows about Waleed's divorce. So, when Apa's husband asked me about the suicide possibility, I said, it's possible."

Their faces were close.

"Why would Waleed be so upset over the divorce?" she said slowly. "He didn't seem heartbroken or even harmed in any way."

Haaris looked away. "There are rumors, Rozee. Lies, of course, but still."

Her heart quickened. "What rumors? And why didn't you tell me before?"

"What was there to tell?" He didn't meet her eyes. "Kulsoom's family said it was impotence. Most probably a lie."

Of course. That's why Waleed had been in such a hurry to remarry. The sooner he could reproduce, the sooner he could prove them wrong.

And Haaris was right. It was most probably a lie. Impotence was a common reason given by women, though divorce itself was highly uncommon. But impotence not only placed blame on the man, it also preserved the woman's virginity, increasing her chances of remarriage, albeit slightly. Because even Kulsoom, with her social status, parents' wealth, and marriage of only a few months, would suffer for her divorce, for the black mark it placed against her name. No wonder she was being sent abroad. No one knew her there. She could disappear and shed the constant weight of everyone's judgment.

"What was the rumor against Kulsoom?"

Haaris shook his head. "Nothing. Waleed's family didn't say anything against her."

She frowned. "Why not?"

"I don't know, Rozee," he snapped. "Because they're decent people?" He got up and shoved his hands in his trouser pockets before nervously pacing in front of her.

"You don't believe that."

He shook his head. "They probably wanted to stop all the talk. Forget the whole thing and move on, quickly."

That's where Rozeena had entered the picture. How convenient for Saima to have stumbled upon Haaris's suggestion for a new pediatrician just at that exact time. And then from Rozeena, they moved on to beautiful Aalya.

Oh God.

What had Rozeena done?

"It's my fault," Haaris said. "The party, inviting everyone, all of this." He winced at the veranda.

"We need to fix this," she said.

He nodded and sat back down, closer this time. Their thighs touched, pressed into each other.

"We'll fix it together, Rozee."

When he tilted his head to rest it on hers, the warmth of his weight made her ache with love and terror, both.

The next afternoon, Rozeena dropped her mother and Khala at Waleed's family home on the way to her clinic. The gathering for soyem prayers marked the third day after his death. She wasn't attending the event, on Sweetie's orders to avoid any public interaction with Kulsoom.

When Jamal ushered in Rozeena's second appointment that evening, the baby entered first, carried by his ayah.

Then, Kulsoom walked in.

Her eyes widened instantly and swung to the ayah, perhaps as a warning for Rozeena. The ayah wouldn't understand English, but she'd pick up on any extraordinary behavior or tone of speech.

Rozeena kept her smile frozen on her face.

"My sister's son," Kulsoom explained quietly, taking the chair next to the ayah. "She had to be elsewhere, a soyem actually, but her baby's cough was concerning, so I thought I'd bring him here."

There was a fragility in Kulsoom, one that hadn't been there at Waleed's funeral. Rozeena wondered if the police considered Kulsoom's brother and cousins primary suspects.

"I'm glad you came," Rozeena said gently, picking up her stethoscope to examine the child.

The ayah handed him to Kulsoom, but he immediately began whimpering, twisting, and reaching back for his ayah.

"Maybe it's best he stay with her." Kulsoom clutched the purse on her lap as if it were more important than her nephew.

Rozeena finished examining the baby and then asked about his health history. The only information Kulsoom had was his date of birth.

"Well then, everything looks good." Rozeena tickled the child's belly, and he giggled, throwing his head back into his ayah's chest and kicking his legs. "Unless there's something else?"

But Kulsoom got up immediately, suddenly in a rush to leave, mumbling thank you and that she'd been worried for no reason, and her sister will think it so silly of her to come to the pediatrician. The ayah certainly looked interested in this young, divorced aunt who was supervising the baby while the rest of the family attended Waleed's soyem.

Without any reason to delay, Rozeena walked them out into the large hall where Jamal sat at his desk to take payment. The other doctors' patients filled the waiting room. Rozeena watched Kulsoom walk away without a single glance back. But when the ayah had nearly reached the end of the hall, with Kulsoom right behind, Rozeena grabbed a file from Jamal's desk and called out to her, waving the papers in the air.

"Could you please come back for a minute." She offered an apologetic smile. "I forgot some paperwork for the new patient." She nodded at the ayah to sit down where she was. "No need for her and the baby to come all the way back."

This time Kulsoom walked into the clinic quickly, crossed it, and went straight to the window. Rozeena hadn't noticed her hunch before. The bony curve of her spine rose sharp against her sari blouse.

"I wasn't sure if you'd be here today, or at the soyem with everyone else." When Kulsoom turned around, the light from behind made the shadows under her eyes appear darker. "Are you avoiding it too, after your Sweetie Aunty told you about me? I hear she's moving into your house now."

Rozeena pursed her lips to keep her mouth from falling open. Kulsoom knew everything, and if she knew, everyone did. Perhaps that was Sweetie's plan all along.

"Did you come here to meet me without anyone else knowing?"

Nodding, Kulsoom closed the distance between them. "I wanted to explain about the other day. I didn't mean those words about

Waleed deserving it." Her tense fingers squeezed the black purse she clutched in front, draining her nails of blood.

"Of course. I know, and I didn't say anything about it to Sweetie Aunty, or the police." Rozeena couldn't implicate the innocent to save her own. There had to be another way.

"I want you to know, since you have Sweetie Aunty's attention, that my family is completely innocent." Kulsoom wrapped her arms around herself now, so tightly she started to shake. "Please, please don't let Waleed's family do this to us."

Rozeena reached for her arm, but Kulsoom flinched and jerked away.

"I'm sorry." Rozeena raised both hands and took a step back. "You shouldn't worry though. The police are questioning everyone. It doesn't mean they suspect your family. It's what they do."

Kulsoom shook her head. "I know exactly what they do."

"The interviews?"

"No. I mean the help they provide certain people." Kulsoom paused. "Even us, at times. But right now, Waleed's family will use it to find who did this. They'll pay what they have to and make sure someone pays for their son's life."

"You seem very sure."

"I know them very well."

Swallowing deeply, Rozeena offered a solution, though she didn't know if she was being asked for one. "In the newspaper it said the police were considering suicide."

"No. The family will never accept it. Suicide is a sin, isn't it? How can they accept that of Waleed and condemn him for eternity?" She shook her head. "And I don't believe it either, but that's not why I'm here. I need to make sure my brother and—" Crying outside the door grew closer and closer.

"A pen. I need a pen," she whispered.

Rozeena grabbed one from her desk and offered the file in her hand. Kulsoom scribbled a telephone number, dropped the pen on the chair, and reached for the door just as it opened. The ayah walked in with the wailing child and a suspicious glance around the room. But there was nothing to see.

28

THEN, 1964

Four Days After

Haaris burst into Rozeena's front gate the next morning, and stood there frozen, eyes locked on hers. Even from the veranda, Rozeena could see his chest heaving.

"What is it?" she yelled running down the steps. "Is it Zohair? Is he . . . ?"

Haaris said nothing.

She reached him, an ache rising in her chest, ready to erupt. "What is it? Tell me."

"He's paralyzed, Rozee. They say he'll never walk again."

"What? No, no, no." She dropped forward, bracing herself with hands on her knees. "Who told you this? Did you speak to the doctors?"

"It's the injury to his back, his spinal cord. They thought it wasn't as bad, but it's serious. It's permanent." He shook his head over and over. "And Rauf Uncle knew but didn't tell us before, because he had hope, he said. But today at the hospital he told me—"

"You were at the hospital?"

He nodded.

She turned to leave.

He reached for her arm. "No, don't. I don't think they want that. Not yet. Rauf Uncle asked us"—he dropped his hand—"asked me to visit this morning because—"

"Us? You and Aalya? She went with you?"

He sighed. "Yes. You know how Zohair feels about her. And I think it was Aalya's suggestion that he shouldn't have too many visitors right now."

"Not even me?" It had to be a mistake.

"Rozee, it's a terrible, terrible time. Talk to Aalya later, if you want. Right now, I'm simply telling you what she said. She'll stay at the hospital while Rauf Uncle gets some rest. Then, he'll return to spend the night with Zohair." Digging into both temples with the heels of his hands, Haaris made small, tight circles. "I can't believe this is happening. There's nothing else they can do for him. He'll be home soon." Then, frowning, he added, "Is that Sweetie Aunty?"

She was standing on the veranda, summoning Haaris. Rozeena watched as he hurried toward her to convey the same dreadful news. Rozeena saw her mother rise from her chair and drop back down. Haaris moved closer and continued talking, his palms facing upward, his head shaking.

Rozeena turned and ran out the gate.

On the empty, early morning road, she fell back against the boundary wall between her gate and Zohair's. The rough concrete scratched harder and harder through her kameez as she dug herself into it, pushing with her feet against the asphalt. Tears curved over her lips, down her chin.

Zohair's future would be entirely altered now. He'd need all sorts of help and people and . . .

A tiny spark flashed in her mind. She grabbed on to it. There was nothing else. It was the only way she could help now, whether or not her mother agreed.

Wiping her face with her sleeve, she smoothed back her hair and headed next door.

Coughing sounds came from inside Zohair's gate. She paused imagining it was any other morning. Rauf would be at the office, Zohair at the railway station. The only person in the garden would be Ibrahim, tending to its beauty. But when she pushed open the black metal gate, she saw Rauf bent over the line of jasmine bushes along the side boundary wall. A few still lay crushed against the earth, trampled on by spectators the night of the fall. Rauf was picking up the pieces, coaxing them to stay erect.

"I can help, if you'd like." She approached him.

Rauf turned to her, his hands covered in dirt. He'd completed most of the picking up and straightening out. He slapped his hands clean before gesturing at the tray of dishes on the chair by his front door.

"Your mother is already doing so much, sending food regularly." His grateful smile pushed at the lines around his eyes.

Rozeena's throat constricted at his grace, even now. She wanted to say so much to him, beg his forgiveness for being selfish and careless and disregarding her duty—if only she hadn't stopped and lost track of time, lost sight of Aalya.

Instead of confessing her culpability, she blurted, "We're leaving Karachi."

Rauf stood before her, frowning but silent, until her throat opened enough to speak. Without mentioning they didn't have enough money to stay, she told him her mother had finally agreed to live with Shehzad in Lahore.

And then Rozeena lied.

"When we sell the house, Ammi wants Zohair to have our share of the money, for his work, his business idea, and whatever else he needs. In Lahore, Shehzad Uncle will take care of everything, and of course I'll have my work."

She hoped she would. She hadn't thought that part through yet, but it was indisputable in her mind that the money from the sale of the house would go directly to Zohair. She had nothing else of value to give. Now, Rozeena welcomed her mother's decision to leave Karachi. But she'd have to convince her mother to give the money to Zohair.

Rauf shook his head, completely disregarding this option. He patted her shoulder, comforting her as if she were a child. Tears spilled as she closed her eyes.

"But why didn't I know about this, Rozee?" he said, sounding more concerned about the move to Lahore than his own situation. "Why would your mother make this decision? And what do you mean by your share of the house?"

If she told him about the constant repairs in the house, the dying Morris, and her mother's empty bank account, he'd never be persuaded to take the money. So, she answered his other question instead, blinking against wet eyelashes and the bright sky.

"Khala owns half of the house, you know. Remember she bought it with the money her husband gave her after the divorce?"

He frowned, shaking his head. "I don't think so." He opened his mouth to speak, but then shook his head again. "I should sleep now. I need to rest before returning to the hospital."

"Wait, please." She reached for his arm. "Why don't you think so?"

"You should speak to your mother. Ask her. It's not my place."

"Please, Rauf Uncle." She was certain her mother wouldn't tell her whatever it was that he knew.

He sighed. "Your khala's husband gave her a monthly stipend. Nothing more."

"But there must've been more," she insisted. "We've lived and eaten and run the house for all these years."

"Your father's savings—"

223

"No, there was never enough, not for so many years." She shook her head vehemently.

Perhaps Rauf had little strength left for any battles other than Zohair's health and survival. Or maybe he was too sleepy and wasn't thinking clearly. Whatever the reason, he answered her question.

"It came from me. The money came from me, but it's been no burden, Rozee," he added quickly. "None at all."

"From you? But how, and why?" And of course it had been a burden. He couldn't be blind to his own ragged clothing and empty house.

"I've worked here for so many years now," he said. "With my government salary, we have more than enough for our own needs." Smiling, he swept an arm over everything they had and turned to the house, done with his explanation. She followed him, her mind working to comprehend what he'd been doing since her father died. Perhaps he'd been returning a loan, or a favor of some kind. There had to be a reason for Rauf to feed and clothe Rozeena.

"Why, Rauf Uncle? Why have you been paying my mother? What for?"

The question struck him on the back like a whip. He hunched forward and pulled his shoulders up to his ears. His fingers reached for the veranda. He collapsed onto the black-and-white tiles, unable to walk further, and dropped his head into his hands. Rozeena rushed over to sit by him, comfort him, and say sorry for whatever she'd said. But right there in front of her was the spot where Waleed and Zohair had landed, where blood had pooled, and Waleed had died and Zohair had become paralyzed. As she balked at the spot, Rauf twisted around and placed both palms on the blood, washed away now, but forever in their minds.

Sprawled there, forehead to ground, he cried softly.

She reached for him and gently pulled him up. Turning him away from the invisible bodies, she sat down next to him. His legs fell helpless on the grass, his dusty, black shoes erect. He stared at his open palms, lying lifeless on each thigh, begging for alms, or for forgiveness.

In that position, he told Rozeena what he'd been paying her mother for.

29

No one blames Rozeena directly for Zara's secret trip to Sea View and her subsequent disappearance. But Rozeena hasn't heard from anyone since then. There hasn't been a single telephone call from Zara, her parents, or even Haaris.

When the phone finally rings on the morning of the fifth day after Zara's recovery, it's her mother calling to invite Rozeena to dinner the same night.

"My father-in-law arrived in Karachi yesterday," Zara's mother says. "Of course, he's still tired. You know how awful the jet lag can be." Her laugh is stilted. "But before he went to lie down, he asked to see you and your son tonight. He's only here for a short while, so he's in a rush to meet all his old friends."

Rozeena leans back in her dining chair, ignoring her breakfast. "I thought Haaris wasn't coming till later this month."

"Oh yes, that was the plan, but he moved it up because of Zara."

Rozeena waits for an explanation, but none is given. She imagines the scare rushed him over.

"Thank you. I'd love to join you tonight. Mansur might be busy though." She must discover what Haaris has to say before presenting her son to him. "But I'll pass on your thoughtful invitation, of course."

"Actually, I already texted Mansur. My husband had his number from when Mansur texted to introduce himself the day he met Zara at your house. Mansur said he'll pick you up and be here by eight o'clock."

Rozeena's free hand quivers on the table, the pinched skin on the back shaking like an earthquake brewing. She says thank you and ends the conversation, her mind racing for a solution. They must not meet, but she doesn't have much time before tonight. She picks up her tea and gulps it down.

The coughing starts instantly, liquid entering the wrong pipe again.

Tears stream down her face and her chest begins to ache immediately from the hacking. Basheer runs in from the kitchen, pulling out a phone from his kameez pocket, but she raises a shaking hand to stop him from dialing. She's not dying yet. He need not panic. Basheer's thumb slides away from Mansur's number, but he stays by her side. Slowly she quiets down, inhales and exhales fully. She's sweating profusely. Basheer switches on the fan overhead. In the kitchen, the fan whips at full speed, but Rozeena has begun to feel a chill in the mornings, even in August—unless of course she chokes on her breakfast and the coughing leaves her brow slick with perspiration.

This time it happened because her mind was elsewhere.

But over the next several hours, even when calm and collected, she can't manage to find a solution to her problem.

When Mansur arrives at exactly seven forty-five p.m. to pick her up, she can do nothing but proceed with the evening. If not today, it will happen another day. Haaris is here for the first time in fifty-four years. If Mansur is part of the reason, Haaris won't leave without meeting him.

"She has book club," Mansur says, explaining why his wife isn't with him.

But Rozeena knows her daughter-in-law's book club meets on Thursday evenings, not Saturdays. Perhaps Mansur is also afraid of what Haaris has to say, and he'd rather hear it alone.

It's dark when they park outside the house. Zara meets them at the gate. She's smiling, relaxed, as if she's sitting on Rozeena's veranda munching hot, crispy potato samosas. She wonders if Zara has spoken to her parents openly, trying to make sense of the turmoil inside her. Rozeena attempted to dig out some of the truth in those moments before Zara's mother pulled her daughter to her chest, relieved she hadn't disappeared forever, like her son.

But Mansur is Rozeena's main concern today.

She frowns keeping her eyes lowered to her feet, taking small, tentative steps. The smooth, pink stone of the driveway is set in a lovely pattern, but new terrain, and she doesn't want to risk a fall in her low-heeled maroon sandals. She's not a vain woman, but she chose the shoes to match the small maroon paisleys on her gray kameez. It's Haaris, after all.

"If you don't look up, Rozee, you'll walk into a wall."

She draws a breath. His voice is close and clear, teasing. A smile automatically spreads over her face before she raises her head. He's standing alone under the pool of light at the front door. Mansur and Zara must've gone inside already.

Zara's drawing was accurate. Haaris's plume of white hair waves like a tail along his head. Perhaps a moon is appearing at the top. Rozeena can't see. He's retained most of his height and posture. But she wants to tell him his voice doesn't match his face anymore. The long, dark lashes of his youth are gone, maybe lighter, maybe fewer, and his face is fuller, the jawline smudged.

Instead, she says, "You've developed quite a sense of humor in Minnesota."

He smiles back. "Thank you for coming. You look well."

A strong breeze ripples over them. She clutches her black shoulder bag and tilts her head to one side, tucking a gray lock of hair back into her low bun. Her eye catches a blue shimmer in the distance.

"Is that a swimming pool?" It sits between two houses all within one long boundary wall.

He nods. "It's a compound of sorts. Apa lives in the other house, where I'm staying. This one is the guesthouse she keeps for family visiting from Australia, the UK, or America."

The luxury doesn't surprise Rozeena. This would be expected of Haaris's family, a symbol of their continued and growing wealth and success. Rozeena is certain the swimming pool is rarely used by visiting grandchildren who probably have similar ones in their own homes and are terribly bored of it all.

Haaris fills his chest with a deep breath. "I can't get enough of this Karachi air, that strong breeze from the sea. We're so much closer here than before." His voice trails, like he's remembering Prince Road.

She takes the opportunity to notice his perfectly ironed light blue shirt, gray trousers, and neatly laced and polished black shoes—a flash from the past.

Dinner is served and the conversation innocuous, mostly about chicken tikkas and Pakola, which makes an appearance in beautiful and very heavy crystal glasses. Zara says she's trying to have as much as she can before returning to Minnesota.

"You can get it there in some stores, but they're not super close," she explains. "The food and drink is the best part of Karachi." Zara flashes a smile at Rozeena across the table and adds, "Except my internship this year."

Rozeena smiles back, happy that their time together was as important to Zara as it was to her. She pulls a tender, juicy piece of barbecued chicken off the thigh on her plate. Rozeena's mouth waters at the spicy aroma even before the meat hits her tongue. It's quite a treat since she's lessened her meat intake. They say legumes and vegetables are the healthiest, but in truth she'd rather eat chicken tikkas every day.

"To be honest, I have, like, zero interest in gardening, but the internship was the best because I got to meet you." Zara smiles at Rozeena again. "And since Haaris Daada connected us, I just want to say thank you to both of you." Zara swings her head from Haaris, seated next to her, to Rozeena across from him.

"Well, you're most welcome, Zara. It's been the highlight of my summer, really," Rozeena says, feeling proud of the girl's honesty, and warmed by their connection.

Next to Rozeena, Mansur clears his throat. "Yes, it's been wonderful for my mother. But isn't it a coincidence that your Haaris Daada connected another pair at this table?"

Rozeena's eyes lock with Haaris's over the platter of rice. She gulps her saliva and squeezes the fork so tight between her fingers that it flips sideways with a loud clatter onto the delicate china, tossing rice and meat right across her plate.

"Oh. I'm so, so sorry." She leans back to assess the damage and then immediately reaches forward to pick up the rice scattered on the white embroidered tablecloth.

"Please, let it be, really. It's nothing," Zara's mother says from the head of the table. "In fact, I want to thank you also, for all the care and concern you've shown Zara. She's a little like her old self now." Eyes moist, she smiles at her daughter who nods back.

Appreciative murmurs spread across the table. Rozeena retrieves her fork and hopes the topic will change from her spilled food.

It does.

"So, what's the mystery?" Zara says. "Who else did Haaris Daada connect?"

Mansur gives a short laugh. "Well, it's nothing mysterious. I'm adopted, that's all. And your Haaris Daada matched us, mother to son."

30

THEN, 1964

Four Days After

Rozeena had faint memories of the time Rauf spoke about.

She remembered leaving their home on Alipur Road in Delhi in the middle of the night that September 1947. She'd been asleep when she was shaken awake by her mother, her eyes wide, stunned.

Only a few weeks earlier, on August 14, they'd been celebrating independence from the British and the creation of Pakistan. It would be a homeland, a country for the Muslim minority of British India to call their own and have a voice in the government. But they hadn't known then that they'd have to leave their home like this, running for their lives.

They had to leave within the hour.

But they were in the bungalow that had belonged to her father's father, young Rozeena thought. They should be safe.

Kabir had come to warn them of the approaching danger. Rozeena had never seen him at night before. Milk was only delivered in the early morning. She wondered if he always looked frightened after the sun set.

He entered the kitchen door and stood there, helplessly shaking his head as he spoke to her father. Violence had begun immediately after independence, but now mobs were destroying the predominantly Muslim villages on the outskirts of the city. The burnings and killings were out of control and had reached Muslim areas in the city too: Sabzi Mandi, Karol Bagh, and Paharganj.

Her mother rushed around with the servants gathering what valuables and necessities they could think of and packed two suitcases. Thinking back, it was shocking how silently they left their home that night, forever. There should've been more discussion, more packing.

Her father was concerned with only one thing. "Do you trust the tonga-walla, Kabir?"

The horse-driven cart belonged to Kabir's cousin. He used it to pick up and deliver the neighborhood's clothes that he washed, dried, and ironed.

"I trust him. But you must stay hidden between the bundles of clothing."

After Kabir hoisted up Faysal next to her in the tonga, Rozeena reached for Kabir's hand. She'd never held his hand before, or even touched him. But that night it felt all right.

"You have to come with us."

Kabir said there was no time for this, that she needed to get to the Old Fort. She'd be safe from the mobs in the Purana Qila. But she insisted.

"I can't," he said finally. "I have to go back for my family in the village and keep them safe. You go now, and maybe we'll meet there, in Pakistan." His eyes glistened in the moonlight.

At the first jerk of the tonga, Rozeena tightened her grip on his fingers. "But what about Billee?"

He pried off her hand and promised he'd care for their cat, give her a splash of milk every morning, while he was still here.

It wasn't much later that Rozeena got separated from her family in the chaos and violence and fires all around. But Faysal found her. He pushed her toward the house where their parents were headed. It would lead to a safe house behind. He held her by the shoulders and aimed her toward it.

"Run, Rozee, run!"

Without looking back, she ran like she'd never run before.

She was certain he'd catch up and probably beat her by a hundred feet if he wanted. Not only was he two years older, but he'd spent all of his eleven years playing cricket on the street with the neighborhood boys, running forward and backward and sideways all afternoon, ready to catch the ball. That was the advantage of being so close to the ground, their father always said. Faysal was extra swift because he was short, a little extra short.

So Rozeena listened to Faysal, and she ran and saved herself.

But not him.

On that particular night, Faysal hadn't been fast enough, because he'd stopped for her.

At least that's what she always believed. No one had ever spoken about it. There'd been no reason to. Faysal was gone and nothing could bring him back. But now Rauf explained what had really happened when Rozeena's tonga was forced to stop.

In that dark and violent night of shouting and running and attacks with sticks and spears and knives, her brother had died because he'd been mistaken for Zohair.

Rauf had been told to run to the same house Rozeena and her family were headed toward. They'd find refuge there. It belonged to an acquaintance of Rauf and Rozeena's father, who both worked in the same office. But Zohair's mother had been separated from the rest of the family. When Rauf finally caught sight of her, she was across the street, already running toward the safe house where he and Zohair hid.

But Zohair's mother must've spotted Faysal, who was running behind Rozeena to the safe house. And Zohair's mother must've thought the little boy was her son.

Now, sitting on the veranda next to Rozeena, Rauf said he wanted to believe his wife's last emotion was one of elation, extreme joy, and relief at finding her son.

When she reached the little boy, she pounced on top of him to keep him safe, but in doing so, she halted his escape. Before she could scramble up to her feet, the mob reached them, engulfed them. Rauf watched his wife and Faysal disappear underneath pounding legs.

Rozeena had already reached the safe house by then, and her face was pressed into her mother's chest. Instead of seeing what happened, Rozeena felt the shudders of her mother's torso. Seconds later it combined with her father's giant heaves as he wrapped himself around the two of them. Both her parents fell to the ground, sliding against the outside wall of the house, pulling Rozeena down between them too, as they shook crying, groaning. Rozeena didn't know why until she pushed them apart to take a full breath of air.

Faysal was gone, they told her.

Now, from Rauf, Rozeena learned that her parents had seen his wife and Faysal fall to the ground. Men stomped on her back as she shielded who she thought was her son. Then, as the hordes of shouting bodies moved on, someone pulled out a spear from her back, and from Faysal's back too.

Rozeena's face had been smothered in her mother's chest, so she'd seen nothing. But she knew they weren't waiting for Faysal anymore. After that, she remembers only running blindly in the night as the mob turned to the other houses and set them ablaze too. But her small leftover family managed to escape those streets, circling back to the tonga. Like the other Muslims who'd escaped, she and her family were herded into the Purana Qila for their own safety. Tens of thousands of refugees stayed there in squalor, until they could cross the border into Pakistan. Her father always reminded her how lucky they'd been to have only stayed two days in the crowded grounds of the Old Fort, under the open sky and with no proper bathrooms or food or covering.

Rauf explained now that he and Zohair, who still didn't know the truth of his mother's death, also crossed the border at Khokrapar by train, but some weeks later. In Karachi, Rozeena's father asked them to move in next door. An eternal optimist, her father believed they'd survive their combined losses with their joint effort to build new lives in their new country.

"I didn't want to live here next to your family," Rauf said, sitting helplessly on the veranda. "How could I, after what happened with your brother and my wife? But your father said it wasn't anyone's fault." He gave a slow, disbelieving shake of the head. "Can you believe that?"

Rozeena's mother certainly hadn't believed it. Her anger and anguish at seeing Zohair's face made perfect sense to Rozeena now. She squeezed her knees to her chest, her heart pounding in her head, blurring her vision. She'd lived her life with a blindfold tight around her eyes, shrouding the truth of the past and allowing her guilt to dictate her actions and choices in the present.

Rauf explained how he'd supported Rozeena's mother financially for so many years out of guilt for having a living and breathing son while she didn't. It was atonement, of sorts, and he had managed to afford it until her expenses increased.

"And now, Zohair will need help when he comes home." Rauf stood up. "Did you know Abdul is back from the village? Poor man. But I'm grateful he's returned. We need him. Not just for the cooking, you know, but . . . well, many things."

Rozeena squeezed her eyes shut and tightened her grip around her knees. Her head throbbed with the quantity and magnitude of information he'd poured into her.

Rauf pressed her shoulder. "Abdul wanted to see you. I'll tell him you're here."

Her eyes flew open. "No. Don't." She worried about what he would say. "I mean, I'll go to his quarters later and meet him myself."

Rauf nodded and headed to the front door. She held her breath, hoping he wouldn't thank her for the tray of food on the chair again.

It was his food to begin with, bought with his money.

31

If Rozeena didn't get up now, Rauf would find her pasted to the veranda tiles hours later when he emerged to leave for the hospital.

But she didn't know where to go. She felt cut loose from everything, abandoned by all the knowledge she'd held as fact, as truth, about herself and her loved ones.

Finally, her feet led her down the side of the house, the same side she and Aalya had emerged from the night Waleed and Zohair fell to the ground. She reached the back and gazed up at the concrete stairs that first stopped at Aalya's door and then headed all the way up to the roof. Rozeena's eyes watered. The glare of the sun, higher now, blinded her, like how she felt about her unrecognizable past. And what about her future? Everything she'd planned and done had been based on losing Faysal, on her version of losing Faysal, and needing to take his place.

"I was coming to meet you myself," Abdul said from behind.

She spun around, brushing fingers across her eyes and wet cheeks. He stood alone, framed in the door to his quarters. When he smiled at her, she crumpled, whimpering quietly, head bowed to her chest, arms wrapped around herself. He stepped back inside his quarters and emerged with two small wooden chairs and placed them beside her.

Sitting next to Abdul, Rozeena was reminded of National Hospital, where she'd quietly cried with him for Gul. Now, Abdul's presence comforted Rozeena. He understood. His pain was immense and raw.

When Rozeena's crying stopped and her breathing calmed, Abdul shook his head.

"I cannot believe what has happened while I was away. When I was in the village, I was angrier and angrier every day. I wanted to come back quickly, but when I reached here, I learned about Zohair Sahib."

She pressed the heels of her palms into her eye sockets, trying to keep the tears from starting again and then blinked to clear her vision.

"It's awful, terrible. Everything is just . . ." She paused. "But why were you rushing back, Abdul? You should've stayed longer." With Gul.

He scratched his unshaven face. Rozeena had never seen it stubbly like this. She couldn't tell if he hadn't shaved for a couple of days or a full week.

"I am too late now," he said. "Hakim Feroze has closed his shop. I was coming back to confront him, to tell others of his sins, but he ran away the same day my Gul went."

"Hakim Feroze? The new shop there?" She gestured toward the back gate, down the road and to the left, to God Bless.

Abdul nodded. So, Rozeena had been right about the source of Gul's datura.

"But didn't you know he was a fraud? I mean, your friends there, didn't they warn you?"

He shrugged. "No one knew. He was a hakim, and his cost was less. The other doctor there is also a hakim."

You should have come to me, always and only, Rozeena wanted to shout. But now she wasn't seeing patients in her free clinic anymore. She'd closed shop. She'd stopped caring.

"When news spread about my Gul, the people living there in the flats above the shops and in the streets behind, they all went straight to Hakim Feroze. They knew he was giving people datura leaves, even the seeds." Abdul folded his arms across his chest. "Hakim Feroze ran away the same day, they told me. He won't be back." He gave a firm nod.

Abdul's satisfaction was obvious, and she had no desire to diminish it. She resisted the urge to explain that the police should've been called immediately, that scaring off Hakim Feroze wasn't a solution, that now he'd simply set up shop in another innocent neighborhood.

"But now there is more suffering with Zohair Sahib and the other sahib too, the one who died," Abdul continued. He frowned, staring up at the roof. "Falling from there? But how could it happen?"

She couldn't bear to look up again. "I don't know. I just don't know." She shook her head and got up. Abdul fell in step with her as she headed for the back gate. "Zohair should be home soon, and he'll need a lot of help. Rauf Uncle is so grateful that you're back, Abdul. We all are."

Offering a weak smile, she stepped out and then quickly into her own gate next door.

The whiff of sizzling onion reached her from the kitchen, its windows facing the back. From the aroma, she knew Shareef would add ground garlic and ginger to the hot oil next. It would be so easy, too easy, to walk straight through the cloud of familiar, comforting spices and into her home. But she knew it wouldn't be lasting relief. The sense of security would vanish with a breeze, or even a sneeze.

Now that she knew the truth, she needed to feel safe anew. But how? Rozeena turned around and let her feet take her to God Bless.

Short, neat concrete boxes connected to form a row of shops on both sides of the two-lane main street. Some buildings had second stories, small flats with balconies and clotheslines filled with fluttering color. The street had just been swept by city cleaners, like every morning, and it hummed with the early activities of the day. Milk shops and chai stalls were always the first to open. Bittersweet aromas filled the air as she passed by large pots simmering with black tea and lots of milk and sugar.

Across the street the other hakim had propped open his door already, ready for business.

She continued down the street, past the general store where they'd gotten toffees as children, until she reached Hakim Feroze's shop on the left. She checked the flat above. The balcony was bare, no clothesline. The shop's door was locked, but the window shutters were open. He'd run away leaving behind his furniture. A table and chair sat on a gray concrete floor in the center of the square room. A row of cabinets lined the left wall. The only other items were a ceiling fan, two naked bulbs hanging on either side, and a door in the center of the back wall.

Once she managed to find the owner of the shop, Abdul's news was confirmed.

Hakim Feroze was gone.

32

NOW, 2019

Silence falls over the dining table. The quiet humming of the air conditioner is the only sound, until Rozeena exhales loudly.

"Well, I'm sure no one is interested in our past." She pats Mansur's arm and continues smoothing down his crisp, white sleeve from elbow to cuff. "It all happened so long ago. Best to leave it there."

Pulling his arm away, he turns to face her. "But you know how important this is to me. It's essential."

Worry spreads over his entire face. It's just high cholesterol and borderline diabetes, she wants to say. But maybe now he wants to know more. He wants to know whose blood is running through his veins, and not just for his medical history.

"I know how important it is to you, Mansur." She reaches for his arm again. "But after dinner, all right?"

Everyone is studying their food, careful to allow them privacy in this very public setting. Haaris's head hangs the lowest. He's sitting back in his chair not even pretending to eat. He knows it's his fault.

His presence is to blame, as is his silence all these past months. If he'd written back to Mansur with the story Rozeena had recounted, Mansur would've ended his search right then and there.

The story had begun without thought. While rocking newborn Mansur in her arms, she cooed all sorts of things to him, reassuring him with her love, telling him the best day of her life was the day Haaris brought Mansur to her. She knew she had to stop mentioning Haaris as Mansur grew older. Toddlers were able to remember and repeat phrases sooner than people realized. But perhaps Rozeena hadn't stopped soon enough. Or perhaps Khala had answered one of young Mansur's persistent questions after he brought the photograph of the four friends home from Rozeena's clinic. Either way, Mansur knew Haaris was the source, and she was forced to recount the fabricated story of how an anonymous employee at Haaris's family business had left an infant at the main office. There'd been no note or blanket or other items that could help identify his parents. Haaris's office had carried out inquiries of all the employees but had come up with no answers.

For Mansur, the story of his origins had begun and ended with Haaris.

But now, instead of staying gone and leaving Rozeena to carry and suppress the heavy secrets, Haaris has reappeared to complicate things.

"You know what I want to know all about?" Zara's overly chirpy voice springs up, probably trying to change the topic again. "I want to know all about that party," she says to Rozeena. "You never finished telling me what happened at Haaris Daada's Welcome Home Ball."

Haaris's head shoots up, hands grab the edge of the table.

His son leaps to his feet. "What is it? Are you in pain? Is it your chest?"

Mansur pushes back his chair, a loud scrape against the marble floor, and runs around the table. But Haaris's arms lose their tension, and his shoulders relax before Mansur reaches him.

"It's nothing," Haaris says, with a guttural clearing of his throat. "Felt like some food got stuck but was only a feeling." He reaches for his water and drinks the whole glass. "Much better." He even turns his head this way and that, to smile up at the two men standing behind each shoulder.

Rozeena avoids looking at Haaris. She focuses instead on all the other activity—his daughter-in-law who's rushed to get her purse in case they need to go to the hospital, and Zara who's grabbed her grandfather's arm and is caressing it gently now.

"Go, go. Sit back down in your chairs so we can all continue with this wonderful dinner." Haaris waves away his son and Mansur, still hovering behind him.

"Yes, come and sit." Rozeena smiles up at them. "Standing back there, you look like the two angels, one on either shoulder recording good deeds"—tapping her right shoulder—"and bad," tapping her left.

"Oh yes, that's right!" Zara laughs. "So, Haaris Daada, which book has more entries?" She winks, squeezing his arm. "Which shoulder feels heavier to you, the good deed one or the bad deed one?"

He nods slowly. "You have so many questions today, don't you?" Turning to Rozeena, he adds, "What has this internship done to you?"

Rozeena meets his gaze finally, and her tone loses any sign of levity. "You didn't really arrange the internship for actual gardening, did you, Haaris?"

He leans back in his chair and pushes his plate away. He's done. But so is Rozeena. She's done with this charade.

Around them there's still a bustle of activity. A servant is called to gather the dinner plates. Dishes clatter, and Zara's mother suggests they all move to the drawing room for chai and dessert.

But Zara glances from Haaris to Rozeena and back. "The internship was really cool, Haaris Daada. Really. I mean, not all the plants and stuff." Her laugh is brief and self-conscious as her eyes dart to her parents who both nod with encouraging smiles. "That was more of Fez's thing anyway."

Her mother's hand goes to her mouth, but she continues smiling, her eyes glistening.

The room is silent now. The table has been cleared and only the twinkling reflection of the chandelier is left on the tablecloth.

Rozeena is ready to leave, ready to escape this reunion.

Smiling across the table, she tries to make peace before leaving. "Zara asked me about the old days. So, I told her about going to God Bless for toffees, and meeting in Zohair's garden, and then I also mentioned your Welcome Home Ball, and the posh parties at your family home. That's all."

Haaris's shoulders relax a bit more. He nods.

They all move to the drawing room where chai and cake await them. Rozeena wants to skip dessert and leave, but Mansur wants to stay.

The swimming pool, lit by underwater lights, glows through a wall of French doors along the entire length of the drawing room. Rozeena has seen many homes, but once again, Haaris's family is at the top of the pyramid.

"So, I'm leaving in two days with my parents. Change of plans," Zara says. "Haaris Daada will stay for a week more because he's not even over his jet lag yet." She smiles and sits down on the sofa between him and Rozeena. "I wanted to give you this as, like, a gift." She's holding a sketchbook-sized frame, facedown, on her lap.

Mansur and Zara's parents walk over from where they've been

admiring the wall of original art—bright orange calligraphy, silhouettes receding into the desert, fishermen's boats bobbing in the transparent sea.

"I used the photograph you gave me." Zara smiles up at Mansur as she turns over the frame on her lap.

Young Rozeena and Haaris stare up at everyone. Zara has brought the two figures to life in her pencil drawing, and she's brought them closer too. Aalya and Zohair are missing from the middle.

"I didn't have time to do everyone." Zara points to the original photograph on the side table.

"This is remarkable." Rozeena has put on her reading glasses while Haaris's son dashes off to get his.

The figures are center stage with enough of Zohair's garden to make it recognizable but not distracting. The fountain behind them sprouts water overhead, and further back, bougainvillea covers the front boundary wall. The left corner is filled with the trunk and lower branches of the giant tamarind tree. With all that beauty around them, Rozeena and Haaris stand serious and unsmiling.

"Their expressions are exactly the same as in the photograph," Mansur says. "This is amazing, Zara. You know, I've always wondered what the four friends were talking about when this was taken. My mother says—"

"I don't remember." Rozeena speaks quietly, knowing it's a lie. She's lied consistently to Mansur over the years, always to protect him. How much longer can she keep doing this though?

"I made copies of that photograph for all of us before leaving." Haaris too speaks quietly. "The last photograph of us four."

Rozeena is certain he remembers the conversation they had that night. She asked him why he wanted the photograph, and he said he wanted a reminder of old friends, from before. Now she knows it was a premonition of what was to come—a definitive after, one in which the friends would be ripped apart and away, for good.

After admiring Zara's drawing a bit longer, the others saunter out the French doors to relax by the swimming pool. Zara's gift lies in her vacated spot on the sofa.

"You've become very close to my granddaughter," Haaris says, taking off his glasses.

"I think so, yes." Rozeena pauses, but there is no time to waste anymore. She needs to know. "Isn't that why you sent her to me?"

He nods. "Perhaps. I always admired your strength, Rozee." He glances down at their younger selves. "But I also thought we could reconnect over Zara, you and I."

"You don't need an excuse to reconnect. You can always pick up the phone."

His mouth pulls down from the corners. "After all these years of quiet and distance, maybe I did need a reason." He sighs. "It was Fez's accident that made me see that things need fixing."

"Fixing?"

Haaris angles himself to face her. "I need to tell Mansur. I need to tell him the truth."

Her breath catches. "The truth?"

"Where he came from, Rozee. He has a right to know."

Haaris's white, airy hair and dark eyes blur into a swirl before her eyes. She's dizzy with panic and hears only bits more of what he says.

"Must do right . . . not much time left . . . fix as much as we can."

When her vision clears, she realizes she isn't as surprised as she should be. The past has always felt too close to her, and since Zara's arrival, the need to atone has been bubbling up to the surface even more. Maybe her soul is seeking redemption before it leaves her body.

"No." She shakes her head. "Mansur is the only pure thing in all of this. What good could possibly come of telling him?"

"He wants to know, that's why it's important and good. We have to do something right, don't we?"

If penance was meant to hurt, Rozeena couldn't imagine a more painful act than what he was suggesting. It may just kill her. Telling Mansur would mean having the most precious part of her life turn against her. And what would it do to Mansur himself?

"But we promised, Haaris. Don't you remember?" Her voice is desperate, and her trembling hand reaches for him over their younger faces. "Please. Don't."

He keeps his hands glued to his knees, unflinching.

33

THEN, 1964

Five Days After

The next morning, Rozeena startled awake to hammering and pounding. Zohair would be home soon, and laborers were building ramps and widening doors for his wheelchair. From the veranda, she could hear Sweetie on the roof, grunting her displeasure at all the workers next door, calling their efforts amateur and shoddy.

"She thinks she knows everything about carpentry too." Khala scoffed, tilting her head up to catch a glimpse of Sweetie peering into Zohair's house from above. "And the indigestion is making her mood worse."

"Maybe it's because the food here doesn't suit her." Rozeena hoped Sweetie would decide to leave for the sake of her health.

But her mother dismissed the idea, and rightly. The indigestion was most likely caused by all the crunchy bites of green chilies Sweetie took with every morsel of food. Even cardamom tea couldn't neutralize that burn. Though usually this was a problem, today Sweetie's irritable focus on the work next door was an opportunity to slip out the back and see Aalya.

As Rozeena stepped out, she caught Aalya pulling open her own back gate.

"Are you going somewhere?"

Aalya gave a small smile. "Getting a rickshaw so Ammi and I can go to the hospital."

Rozeena still hadn't been asked to visit. "I telephoned last night to talk to you, but Neelum Aunty said you were resting. You'd spent the whole day there."

Aalya nodded. "You heard? About Zohair?" Her voice cracked.

Rozeena reached for her hand, but Aalya stepped back.

"I'm sorry." Rozeena screwed her eyes shut. She wanted it to mean so much more than those two useless words could convey, but she didn't know how.

When she opened her eyes, Aalya was staring blankly past her at the road.

"Maybe I can come with you to the hospital?" Rozeena said.

"It's better that you don't."

"But why?"

"It's not me, Rozee."

"Zohair?" It dawned on her then. "He blames me."

"But he'll understand." Aalya forced a smile. "Soon."

Rozeena reached for the gate, grabbing tightly for support, afraid that he'd never understand. But right now, she couldn't think of herself. She had to focus on the police. They were going to question Zohair any day, and he still hadn't told Haaris what he'd say.

"Does Zohair know about the camera? Does he know you could be—"

"Yes, he knows everything." Aalya hung her head, wringing her hands, making her left sleeve pull tight over something before riding up.

"What's that?" Rozeena fixed her gaze on the threaded jasmine buds, four lines forming a thick pearl bracelet around Aalya's wrist.

Her face softened as she caressed the buds, their floral sweetness filling the space between them.

"I wanted to tell you, Rozee. I wanted to say something, but . . ." She shrugged. "I think I've always known. Zohair has always been good to me, to my parents too. If only I'd let myself see how I felt too, then none of this would have happened." Her face twisted in pain. "I wouldn't have even gone to the party. I should've told my mother that I couldn't do what she wanted and find a wealthy match, even if it meant people might discover the truth about us."

Rozeena grabbed Aalya's hand and held it tightly between her own palms. "It's not your fault. Nothing is. I should've known what you really wanted, and I should've wanted it for you, been on your side, always. We should've found another way to keep your family safe."

"Can you believe that Zohair has always known who we are?" Aalya said. "All the while, Zohair and Rauf Uncle knew the truth, and they too were helping my parents hide it." She stroked the flowers on her wrist. "Rauf Uncle brought the bracelet upstairs for me this morning when he came back from the hospital. He put it on my wrist and said it was from Zohair. He wants an answer, to his proposal."

Rozeena released a long breath. A proposal from Zohair wasn't surprising at all, but the timing, the emotional encumbrance of what he'd done for Aalya, the criminal charges that the police could find against them both, and the guilt Aalya herself felt over what happened—it was all too much.

"Well, there's no rush to decide," Rozeena said quietly. "What did Neelum Aunty say?"

"She's worried, of course, about money and how Zohair won't be able to continue at the railway station now without the use of his legs. She's worried about what people will say watching us go from poor to poorer in front of their eyes because her daughter is marrying someone not worthy of her beautiful face." She turned around and glanced up at her house. "She doesn't know there are bigger things to worry about. When the police—"

"Do you know when they'll question him?"

Aalya shook her head. "Maybe they're doing it right now."

"Haaris is at the hospital, so—"

"I told Zohair to lie about what he did on the roof, Rozee." Her eyes widened, as if surprised by her own instructions.

"And say what?" She wanted him to lie too, to be free. But what lie would he tell?

They inched closer to each other.

"At first, I told him I wanted to tell the truth," Aalya said. "But he insisted I keep to the plan we all agreed on. And what could I say that would protect him now? Who would believe I did that to both of them?"

Rozeena shook her head. "No one."

"So, I begged him to save himself, for me."

"But how?"

Haaris burst into Rozeena's clinic at the end of her hours that evening.

"Have you seen this?" He planted *The Star* on her desk and leaned over to anchor the open pages with his palms.

Their heads nearly met in the middle as Rozeena stared at the photograph.

"Aalya?" Her knees buckled, and she dropped onto her chair, eyes still on the caption.

> *Miss Aalya Ibrahim—resident of the house where Waleed Khan fell to his death. Photograph from deceased Waleed Khan's camera film*

"How could they print this? Isn't it insinuating her involvement, like spreading rumors?"

Haaris nodded and fell into a patient chair. "At least she's on my roof and not her own."

Yes, the photograph was definitely taken at Haaris's party, with other people in the background. But Aalya was clearly the focus. Her thick, black waves fell over her shoulders as she stared off to the right somewhere, her cheeks pushed up by a smile, her smooth neck curving to her throat. She might be looking at her own roof across the street, remembering their childhood spying on these posh parties. Perhaps this was when Waleed approached her and discovered a way to whisk her away.

"He took this without her knowing, didn't he?" The paper crunched in Rozeena's fingers. "How did the newspaper get it?"

Haaris sighed and leaned forward, elbows on his knees. "I think the family must've slipped it to them. They don't want the investigation to rest, and this"—pointing to the photograph—"will cause a sensation."

"Do they know something? Otherwise, why a picture of Aalya? There must be so many other people on that film."

"I stopped at Apa's on the way here. Her husband says they know nothing, other than how much Waleed enjoyed taking pictures of Aalya." He looked down at his shoes. "There are many of her in the film."

"All at your party?" She held her breath waiting for his answer.

"That's what I hear." He looked up. "The other photographs on his film are of my roof, taken from Aalya's. But as far as I know, she's not in them."

Rozeena released a breath, relieved. "But then why flash her face in public like this?"

"Because she's a mystery, a stranger. And the whole situation has turned strange, Rozee. Zohair spoke to the police today, before I got to the hospital." He shook his head. "His story makes no sense. He told the police he doesn't know how it happened, that Waleed must've tripped over something, or slipped and lost his balance. They were there so Waleed could take photographs of the ball from high up. Anyway, Zohair reached out to help him and got pulled over the wall too. But the wall is waist-high, Rozee. How can that happen? No wonder the police don't believe him. And no one else was there to see it happen, no witnesses. Apa's husband says that for the judge to dismiss the case, he has to believe it was an accident." Haaris looked straight at her. "Otherwise, it can be five to twenty-five years in jail, depending on intent and other circumstances."

Her hands turned cold on her desk. This is what Aalya must have meant when she asked Zohair to save himself, to make it seem as if he wasn't the one who pushed Waleed, that it all happened by mistake.

"How can we prove it was an accident?" Rozeena said.

"We can't. And Waleed's family will do everything to prove it wasn't."

"But Zohair fell too. How can they accuse him after what's happened to him?" Her voice became small. "He could've died."

Haaris dropped his head in his hands and said nothing.

"What if it was self-defense?"

Haaris shook his head. "How? There'd have to be evidence of some fight or attack on Zohair's face or body. I mean, other than the fall. And Zohair has already given his story. He refused to even discuss it with me. I think he wanted no possibility of anyone else's involvement."

It made sense now why Aalya hadn't wanted to tell Rozeena the plan earlier.

But Rozeena had made the same decision as soon as the bodies had launched over the boundary wall that night. Her instinct had been to keep Aalya away, safe. The lie had begun then, and now when a witness was needed, it was too late to tell the truth.

And while Rozeena, Haaris, and Aalya were trying to save Zohair, she wondered if they were doing the right thing. Each time the thought bubbled up in her like bitter bile, she pushed it back down. Zohair wasn't to blame, really. When she pictured Waleed and Aalya on the roof, Rozeena gagged from revulsion, from the terror of what could've happened if Zohair hadn't stopped him.

The fall was an accident.

34

THEN, 1964

Seven Days After

Rozeena sat in the murderer's chair. It was surprisingly comfortable—the woven wicker seat taut and wooden arms polished to a shine, like the table before her.

"Why are we meeting Kulsoom there?" Haaris had asked when Rozeena suggested the empty hakim shop sandwiched between the general store and shoe shop in God Bless.

"Where else can we meet? Sweetie Aunty is living in my house, and everyone in your house recognizes Kulsoom, right?"

That had silenced him.

They needed a new place because Kulsoom had refused to return to the clinic. She feared being seen by her acquaintances in the waiting hall and arousing suspicion by borrowing her sister's child again. The last time Kulsoom had been there, all her friends and family had been at Waleed's soyem, the day she'd quickly scribbled a telephone number on a file. Rozeena had forgotten about it, thinking Kulsoom probably wanted to reiterate that her brother and cousins were innocent and that she'd meant nothing by her comment at Waleed's funeral.

But when Haaris burst into Rozeena's clinic with news of Zohair's weak testimony to the police, Rozeena had desperately searched for something, anything. All she could think of was that scribbled number still in her desk drawer, and she'd passed it to Haaris hoping it could be of use.

Now, Rozeena jumped up from Hakim Feroze's abandoned chair and went straight to the window to push open the shutters all the way. She didn't want Kulsoom to drive off thinking Rozeena wasn't here, or the shop was closed. She was propping the door open more fully when Haaris came rushing in, also early for the meeting.

"What is this place?" He frowned, looking around the concrete gray room, and then peering out the door shaking his head. "I wish you weren't a part of this, Rozee. It's not safe."

But she'd insisted on being a part of this, even though she didn't fully understand what it was. Haaris had never wanted these entanglements, asking for favors, applying pressure, and who knows what else. Yet, when she'd asked him to do everything he could for Zohair and Aalya, he'd agreed. For their sake. For her sake. And now they were in this together.

Rozeena was about to ask him if he'd spoken to Kulsoom again when a white car stopped outside the general store next door. A woman stepped out. Very little of her face was recognizable behind the large sunglasses and long, dark hair falling from temple to chest, slicing her cheeks into even thinner slivers. It had to be Kulsoom. No one dressed like that would be found roaming about in God Bless. Kulsoom tugged at the camel-colored shawl wrapped around her lemon sari and headed straight for Hakim Feroze's shop.

Nodding at Rozeena and Haaris, she said, "How did you manage this?" and sat down in the sole chair. When she slid her sunglasses onto her head, pushing back the curtain of hair from her face, she looked exhausted already. "Thank you. No one will recognize me here, surely."

Standing on the other side of the table next to Haaris, Rozeena ran a hand over the untamed waves of her hair and felt like a schoolgirl before the headmistress, though Kulsoom was probably a year or two younger. But Rozeena was in a simple shalwar kameez, not wanting to arouse suspicion or alert Sweetie when she'd slipped out the back gate this morning. She planned on returning before Shareef announced lunch in thirty minutes.

"You said not to meet at the clinic, so Rozeena arranged this." Haaris smiled at them both, like it was a social event.

But it worked to relax Kulsoom. She nodded, and her grip loosened around the black purse on her lap.

"I'm so tired." She spoke looking around the room. "I've wanted Waleed to vanish for so long, since the day we got married, actually. After the divorce, I still needed him to disappear, so I could continue with my life. But even now, I can't seem to move on." She snapped open her purse, took out an envelope, and placed it on the table between them. "I have others, but these will do. I'm certain." Rozeena reached for the envelope, but Kulsoom raised a finger like a schoolteacher. "Not until I'm gone. Please."

At the door, Kulsoom nodded at her driver to bring the car closer.

"Thank you," she said, squeezing Rozeena's hand.

"For what?" Rozeena searched Kulsoom's face but could see nothing behind the sunglasses.

Haaris quickly ushered her toward the car then, worried someone would see, and Rozeena ran back for the envelope to understand what had just transpired.

The first photograph was a close-up, the bust of a pale, stiff Kulsoom, her eyes closed, skin bloodless and naked down to the tops of her breasts. Circular dark purple bruises covered her chest, her shoulders, one cheek.

Waleed's fists?

Rozeena swallowed her revulsion, her sickening fear too.

There were other bruises also, older ones that had turned a mossy green and filthy yellow. She moved to the window for more natural light and noticed a faint ring of discolored skin around Kulsoom's neck.

"What is it, Rozee?" Haaris hurried toward her.

Unable to speak, she handed him the photograph, picked up the envelope from the table and headed straight to the back hallway. She didn't stop until she entered the apartment above and crossed the small, empty room to the balcony overlooking the street. There, with gently bustling God Bless below her, she exhaled and looked through the rest of the photographs.

"Rozee? Rozee! Where are you?" Haaris's voice echoed in the empty spaces below, doors banging, feet stomping. Then from close behind he said, "Whose house is this? What are you doing here?"

"It's nobody's, Haaris," she snapped. "I couldn't stay downstairs. It's too open. Anyone could walk in and see." Eyes wide, she swung around to face him. "Did you see?"

He nodded and took the envelope from her hands. She turned away just as a young woman stepped onto the balcony next door. Catching Rozeena's eye, she smiled hesitantly and then busied herself pulling off fluttering red, orange, and green clothes from the line. Rozeena tried to focus on the activity, her eyes going to the soft cotton fabric each time she heard Haaris flip to another photograph. Kulsoom's legs and thighs were bare and beaten in one. In another, Waleed was off to the side, only a profile visible. Kulsoom was dressed, with her hair in a bouffant, but the loose end of her emerald-green sari was off her shoulder, revealing three deep lines etched onto the top of her right breast. Who would've taken that photograph?

"This one, with Waleed in it, is at Kulsoom's parents' house," Haaris said. "I recognize the place. I've been there many times since we were children. Her brother came back from London earlier this year, so I've been there recently too."

Rozeena stepped away, trying to distance herself from it all, from Haaris's other childhood friends that belonged to his other world, but the balcony was too small.

"I spoke to Kulsoom this morning," he continued. "She called to explain because she trusts me, and because she couldn't do it here, face-to-face, she said. It was because of these photographs, this proof, that Waleed's family kept silent during the divorce. Kulsoom said they even suggested she use the impotence issue as the reason and put all the blame on him. It was in exchange for her family's silence about the truth." He sighed. "And Waleed's family knew impotence would be proven a lie soon enough."

She heaved, leaning over the concrete balcony. "I should never have left Aalya with him."

"How could you know? That was the whole point, remember? Everyone kept it a secret."

Rozeena pressed her palms into her eyes, willing the violence out of her mind. "And now? What are we supposed to do with this secret?"

"Leave it to me."

She turned to him as he slipped the envelope inside his coat pocket.

"Waleed's family will never want this known about him, Rozee, not even now after his death. Certainly not now. The fear of this coming out might even make them accept Zohair's story, maybe."

Blackmail? She turned away again, unable to look Haaris in the eye. It's for Zohair, she told herself. For Zohair. Nothing can bring Waleed back, and he did terrible things to Kulsoom, and to Aalya, and would he have done them to his next wife too?

"Whose house is this?" Haaris said again, and looked around as if someone might appear suddenly.

She let out a breath, grateful for the change of topic.

"It's mine." She turned back to him with a small smile. "Just for a month, for now." She told Haaris her plan for the future, one that was nothing like she'd imagined, but was everything she wanted.

"No one knows yet, and I'll need to set this up before I can shut down my clinic in MPS Chambers."

His brows furrowed. "You're shutting your clinic, and you expect people to come here to that little room downstairs?"

She laughed at the ridiculous suggestion. "Can you imagine? Those ladies, with their bouffants and perfume trails and ayahs tagging along, carrying the little patients, all arriving here in God Bless?" Guiltily, she added, "Even I only pass by here on the way to the clinic. I haven't shopped here since we were children. Mostly, I look down at it from my roof and eat the vegetables and things Shareef gets from here every morning." She paused. "But I'll be living in God Bless now, Haaris, and my patients will be people who live here too."

"You'll live here? Nobody lives in a place like this."

"Not anyone you know, right? Because it's low class and meant for laborers and such. The poor."

He shrugged in acknowledgment of the obvious. "You'll be cutting yourself off from everything. Who's going to come here? You'll be leaving everything behind."

"Not you," she said with a smile.

"Of course not me." His fingers reached for her hand. "But why are you doing this?"

"It's important to me, and it makes me happy. It sounds selfish, but—"

"But you've got a perfectly good life." He waved his other hand over the street below. "You can't live here. Set up the clinic downstairs if you want, do good and all, but you can't move here. What will people say?"

Her body turned rigid. "What people?"

"Well, not me, obviously."

"And Aalya and Zohair?"

He shook his head absently and turned back to staring at the people and shops below.

"Shouldn't it matter which people are doing the talking? If it's people I don't care for, then why should I worry? I have to do what's right," she said quietly, as if to herself. "I can't only do what's expected. There's got to be some balance, you know?"

"But you already have your storeroom clinic to help these people. Isn't that enough?"

She shook her head. It hadn't been enough. "I need to be here. People need doctors, not just hakims, even if they're good hakims." She smiled. "I should thank you. Your referrals paid for this."

But she wouldn't tell him that she needed more, so much more, to be able to keep her family comfortably in Karachi. She knew he'd suggest the easy solution, but she had to do it on her own, not by marriage. That was true independence. She couldn't possibly get entangled in the Shah family expectations that Haaris himself was struggling with.

He tugged on her hand and led her to the bare room inside.

There, his fingers brushed her cheek, pushing strands of hair off her face and settling on her nape. He caressed her up to her hairline and then back down. His other arm wrapped around her waist, and he pressed into her. She shuddered, her eyelids heavy.

His breath warmed her forehead before a tender kiss. "I will always love you, Rozee." She tilted her head back to look up, wondering what he meant, but he continued, "And I want you to be safe, cared for. How is your mother letting you do this, and what about Sweetie Aunty?" He frowned. "You haven't told them yet, have you?"

He was right, but the mention of them reminded Rozeena of the time. They'd have to walk terribly fast to reach home before Sweetie found her missing.

"You didn't tell me," Rozeena said as they neared her gate. "Why is Kulsoom doing this? Why is she helping us, and what was the thank-you for?"

He shrugged. "She needs something."

"What?"

His lips formed a closed, forced smile. "Later, when the work is done." He patted the pocket holding the envelope.

"It must be something big." Her smile quivered slightly.

He nodded but said nothing more.

Dread washed over her. This was exactly why he wanted to run away from his family—the favors, the blackmail, the bribes, and everything that came with it.

Just this once, Haaris, for Zohair and Aalya. Just this once. I promise.

35

NOW, 2019

Zara's mother is in the car too when the driver pulls up to Pepper 'n' Spice.

"She doesn't want me going anywhere alone anymore," Zara says, settling in across the table from Rozeena.

"Well, let's order then, before she's back to pick you up." Rozeena puts on her glasses to read the menu.

"Thanks for inviting me." Zara smiles. "They have the best samosa chaat, you know the one with chana and yogurt and tamarind chutney and all? And they make everything with bottled water. That's why my mom lets me eat here."

Rozeena chuckles. "Your mother and my son sound like the same person." Mansur has limited her outings to certain places too, afraid that another bout of indigestion will be the end of her. "Anyway, I thought we should celebrate the end of your internship."

She smiles, but the ending feels more like a loss. Rozeena will miss her new friend terribly.

After ordering, they settle back to take in the over-chilled, mostly empty restaurant. It's too late for lunch and too early for dinner, so

Rozeena has gotten the best table, right by the wall of windows over-looking the line of trees planted on the road's divider.

"I know Haaris is excited for you to be going home, and I'm sure your grandmother can't wait to see you too. She must be missing you so much." Rozeena is already missing Zara's evening visits.

The waiter brings Zara's Pakola, and she takes long sips through the bobbing straw before shrugging in response. When he returns with Rozeena's tea and two samosa chaats, Zara pulls a purple velvet scrunchie off her wrist and gathers her hair into a ponytail.

"Actually, I don't know my grandmother too much." She pops a spoonful of chaat into her mouth and her eyes close. "Perfect," she mumbles and takes several more bites. "Not even too spicy."

Rozeena smiles, tasting some of her own chaat.

"What do you mean, you don't know your grandmother?" She adjusts herself on the chair. The short back doesn't offer the support she requires now.

"I mean, she was at the funeral and everything." Zara pours some extra chutney on top. "But she moved away before I was born, so we just see her at Thanksgiving and a couple of other weekends a year. She doesn't always visit when my aunt comes up from New Jersey."

Rozeena pushes aside her half-eaten samosa and leans forward, trying to free herself of the chairback that makes her shoulders ache.

"Perhaps New Jersey suits her?"

"Yeah, well Minnesota definitely didn't suit her. At least not with Haaris Daada."

"It sounds like you think it's your grandmother's fault that she stays away."

"I guess it's not fair of me, right? But I'm closer to Haaris Daada. He's always been there, since I was born."

Not wanting her questions to sound like an interrogation, Rozeena sips her chai and tries to change the subject.

"And has Minnesota suited him? Is he happy there?"

Zara nods slowly. "I always thought so."

"And now?" Rozeena holds her breath for the answer.

Zara pulls off her scrunchie and returns it to her wrist. "I don't know. Haaris Daada has been talking on the phone with my grandmother a lot more these past months, because of Fez, I guess. And Haaris Daada is never happy when he hangs up."

"Well, that's understandable." Rozeena's voice turns soft. "Loss brings people closer, but not always in a good way."

"Yeah. Maybe closer isn't too good for them."

Rozeena feels guilty for prying about Haaris and his wife. Apa has always conveyed a happily-ever-after story regarding Haaris in America. Even now, she'd worry about what people would say if they knew Haaris Shah hadn't turned out successful in every area of his life.

"Well, being close to you, Zara, has been absolutely wonderful for me." Her voice quivers, and she purses her lips into a smile, composing herself before continuing. "I never thought I'd make a new friend at my age."

Zara smiles back with a little shake of the head. "Me neither. I mean, I didn't think I'd make a new friend like you."

"You mean, old?" Rozeena laughs. "I'm just as surprised as you are."

The waiter clears their table, and Zara takes out her phone. "I don't have any pics of you," she says. "Can we take some selfies?"

For the best light, they stand facing the wall of windows. Zara takes what seems like a hundred photographs in ten seconds when they see her mother's car pull up to the restaurant. Rozeena raises a hand to say they're on their way.

But she doesn't move.

She's reminded of the first day she met Zara. They stood side by side just like this, watching her parents drive away. Rozeena didn't know then that this young girl would lead Rozeena to rediscover herself. Yes, her life is different now. She has no career, no young grandchildren to need and adore her, but it's still not too late. Rozeena has a lot to give to the world, and a lot to receive from it.

"I'd love to have some of those photos," she says, gesturing at Zara's phone. "You choose which ones to WhatsApp me, all right?"

Zara nods eagerly. "And maybe we can WhatsApp just to, like, talk and stuff?"

"Of course." Rozeena brings a hand to her heart. "I would love that so much." She wants it for herself just as much as for Zara, whose struggle with loss will surely continue.

They reach for each other in an embrace. Zara's voice is tiny, childlike in Rozeena's ear.

"I'll see you next summer?"

"That would be wonderful," Rozeena says before releasing a quiet breath.

She won't make any promises, but she dearly, wholeheartedly hopes to be on this earth next summer. And maybe Zara will surprise her with a drawing of one of their selfies. Rozeena smiles to herself as they sway.

36

THEN, 1964

Seven Days After

Her mother looked surprised to find Rozeena waiting in her bedroom after dinner but said nothing until she'd settled on the stool in front of her dressing table.

"If it's about Shehzad's arrival and my decision—"

"No, it's not that," Rozeena said quickly.

She perched on the edge of her mother's bed and stretched her lips into a smile. Her mother's shoulders relaxed, and she smiled back in the mirror.

Heavy teak furniture lined one side of the room, facing the bed that extended into the center from the other side. A row of windows covered the wall opposite the door, allowing the breeze to push the scent of jasmine all through this wing of the house.

Rozeena remembered complaining to Khala about the overpowering scent. Nauseating, Rozeena had called it once when Khala sat threading jasmine buds into garlands for Rozeena's mother to wrap around her wrists or weave into her bun.

"A woman has to have some jewelry," Khala had snapped. "Even if it is only flowers from her own garden."

Rozeena's guilt had bloomed, the makeshift jewels reminding her of all the jewelry her mother had sold over the years. Now, Rozeena's nose twitched again at the fragrance, thick in the air. Long necklaces of strung flowers, some moist and fresh and some yellowing, hung on closet door handles and even lay in a swirl by her mother's pillow. Rozeena wondered if Khala was threading these jewels for Sweetie too, now that she'd moved in.

Rozeena doubted it.

"Ibrahim's tamarind paste seems to be working on Sweetie," her mother said, sounding relieved.

Rozeena nodded. She couldn't deny the efficacy of the harmless mixture.

"My parents' traditional concoction to settle the stomach," Aalya had said, laughing over the phone after sending over some thick paste made with tamarind, ginger, cumin, and black pepper.

"And why didn't I know about this before?" Rozeena had said, trying to hide her hurt with humor.

Aalya had remained silent, but Rozeena knew it was because she'd been so outspoken against these herbal cures.

"It won't harm Sweetie Aunty at all, Rozee. Trust me. I've been raised on all these odd mixtures." Aalya had laughed again. "And now you know absolutely everything about me."

For that, Rozeena was grateful.

Sweetie had spooned a big, thick dollop of the paste onto her plate. Clearly, she was willing to try anything to stop the twisting and burning in her gut. And surprisingly it had worked. The entire household was relieved at the improvement of Sweetie's digestion and resulting mood. Today she felt well enough to leave after lunch and visit her parents.

Rozeena's mother unraveled the last string of jasmine encircling her smooth, full bun and dropped the flowers onto her dressing table before joining Rozeena on the bed.

She reached for her mother's hand and took a deep breath. "Rauf Uncle told me about his wife, and about Faysal too."

Her mother's grip tightened, and her eyes squeezed shut, deep frowns filling her forehead.

Rozeena shut her eyes too, visualizing the details Rauf had recounted, the stampede, the fire. But in seconds, Rozeena's eyes flew open hearing her mother's short, quick gasps. She shook with quiet crying, her mouth and eyebrows twisted in agony, eyes pressed shut but streaming unending tears. Rozeena pulled her mother close and held her. They cried into each other's shoulders, cheeks, chests. Finally, Rozeena quieted and found herself somehow resting in her mother's lap, on the soft folds of her lilac sari—a mother consoling her child.

"And then some years later, we lost your father," she said, smoothing the hair off Rozeena's temple and forehead. "Shehzad immediately offered to take care of us, but I said no, because your father had a plan for you." She smiled down at Rozeena.

"So, you sold your jewelry instead." Rozeena caressed the single gold bangle on her mother's wrist.

"Yes, the other jewelry and then these too. When these became fewer and fewer, Rauf started to notice. He said I should keep the last one, at least, to give to you someday. I refused his money, over and over again, Rozee, until he convinced me. He insisted their needs were few, and their lives wouldn't suffer for it. But they have suffered, and their needs after the accident will be tremendous." She paused. "But Rauf always had this guilt inside him, for what happened to Faysal." With a sigh, she added, "It was hard for me not to . . . not to resent . . ."

"And I believed it was my duty to take care of you," Rozeena said. "Since Faysal was gone, I was the one who had to keep us here, in Karachi, in this house. And I tried, I—"

"What are you saying? That was never your duty."

"I know. Now, I know." She rose from her mother's lap, replenished and clear-eyed. "Can I take out the attaché case?" She bit her lip.

Her mother nodded and wrapped her arms around herself, bracing herself for what she was about to see.

The attaché case had crossed the border with them in 1947, the border Faysal had never crossed. Rozeena pulled it out from under the bed now, so light, it slid out easily against the smooth mustard and green tiles. Scratches had softened the brown leather, and the corners and edges were worn. Black marks dotted the metal locks on either side of the handle. Placing the case on the bed between them, she rubbed at the locks a bit, but Karachi's humidity had been aging them for years now. She popped them open.

Other than a checkbook and some bank papers, it contained a slim, brown envelope. It looked fresh, new. Her mother must've been replacing the shroud. Rozeena slid out the small black-and-white photograph and held it in her palm between them.

"We didn't take many photographs in those days." Her mother caressed Faysal's face. "And that night when I was packing in a rush, I thought we'd be back. Of course we'd be back to get the rest." She frowned, peering closely at Faysal's face. "Has he faded, Rozee?" Her voice rose with panic. "What have I done? Have I ruined him?"

"No, not at all. He's not fading, Ammi," Rozeena said quickly. "This is what photographs looked like then." She smiled down at the blurred outlines and melding features of a brother she hardly knew. "Cameras these days take sharper photographs, that's all." She passed Faysal to her mother and watched as she cradled him in her joint palms, like a prayer.

"I understand now what Abba meant about independence," Rozeena said. "Why we fought for it. We sacrificed so much for it." Her mother nodded at the picture of her son as Rozeena continued. "Abba spoke of independence from the British but also that he wanted it for me, personally, didn't he? I thought it was because I was taking Faysal's place, the man of the house and all." She smiled, making light of it though she'd clung to that belief since she was nine years old.

"Of course not." Her mother looked up and blinked, confused. "You're our Rozee."

"I know that now, and I have a plan, for me."

Rozeena explained about her clinic in God Bless and watched her mother's eyebrows ride up her forehead.

"But it'll take time to set up." Rozeena braced herself for the next statement. "And when we sell this house, we'll return Rauf Uncle's money."

Her mother nodded, relieved. She wanted it too. She was in perfect agreement about the money, and Rozeena felt a giant burden lifted off her.

"But I won't be able to afford a house like this, Ammi. I'm not worried about what everyone, the whole of Karachi, thinks. I only care about what you think, and what Shehzad Uncle thinks too," she quickly added, knowing her mother's attachment to her brother was important. They had such little family left.

Her mother said nothing until she'd carefully slid Faysal back into the envelope and clicked the attaché case shut. She then cupped the single bangle on her wrist and, squeezing the sides of her hand, pulled it this way and that until it finally came off.

"I don't want it." Rozeena leaned back, waving away the offering. "I won't sell it, Ammi, and I don't need the money."

Her mother laughed softly. "Silly Rozee. It's not to sell." She took Rozeena's hand and slid the bangle onto her wrist. "Why wait for your marriage? Let's celebrate this, your new path, your independence, just like your father and I both wanted."

A lump lodged in Rozeena's throat, gratitude and relief filling her. With her head bent low to hide her welling tears, she tucked the attaché case back under the bed before straightening.

"What will you say to Sweetie Aunty?" she asked. If Sweetie approved of the plan, Shehzad would too.

Her mother frowned, and then said slowly, "As long as her standing in society isn't hurt, she'll accept your decision."

37

THEN, 1964

Ten Days After

There was an unnerving calm surrounding Sweetie within days of Rozeena's talk with her mother.

Rozeena's unease grew when Aalya and her family arrived for Shehzad's welcome dinner, and Sweetie actually rose from her seat with an admiring smile, instead of being appalled by the odd neighbors.

Aalya was cause for concern too.

She looked beautiful, but her clothes were more appropriate for a wedding rather than a family dinner. Her shimmering silver and pink sari matched the flush of her cheeks. Thick bracelets of jasmine buds encircled both wrists, and strings of the same, like fat pearls, crisscrossed over the thick, dark braid down her back.

"These are your father's, aren't they?" Khala said, nodding as she inspected the buds. They were nearly double the average size. "He has magic in his hands."

While the elders greeted each other, Rozeena moved closer to Aalya. "Why are you so dressed up? What's the—"

But before she could finish the sentence, a round of congratulations erupted in the room. There was surprised laughter and hugs, and Aalya was pulled away and embraced by all the women, turn by turn. Shehzad slapped Ibrahim's back and joined the tight circle around Aalya. Neelum suddenly appeared in front of Rozeena carrying a box of ladoo. She broke off a piece and stuffed the sweet treat into Rozeena's already open mouth.

"Your sister is engaged today," Neelum said, breaking off another piece. "Here, have some more." Her eyes glistened, the smile turning into pursed lips to contain herself. She seemed to have accepted it wholeheartedly, perhaps out of gratitude for Zohair's life.

Smiling back, Rozeena hugged Neelum tightly, mostly to hide her own hurt that Aalya announced her decision publicly without first telling Rozeena.

Dinner was served immediately, and the conversation turned to the seating. With a belly that hung over his belt, Shehzad required the most space, so he sat at the end of the table, opposite Rozeena's mother. Sweetie was on Shehzad's right and Ibrahim on his left. Aalya tucked in her chair between Sweetie and Khala.

"So, tell us. What does this Zohair do for a living?" Sweetie said, spooning polao onto her plate, making sure to dig out pieces of tender goat meat from underneath the rice before passing the platter to Shehzad. "Do we know him?"

Neelum shifted in her seat next to Rozeena, and everyone studied their food intently until Rozeena's mother spoke.

"We've known Zohair since Partition. He's like a son." She smiled at Aalya, who still hadn't met Rozeena's eyes across the table. "Unfortunately, he's been in an accident, a very bad one. But he'll be home soon. Isn't that right?"

Aalya nodded, and Sweetie immediately followed up with questions about the accident.

Until she knew.

Her fork clattered onto the plate. She fell back in her chair. "You mean he's the Zohair who fell off the roof with Waleed? Zohair from next door?" With a deep frown, she blinked at Aalya. "Why on earth would you marry an invalid?"

Silence fell over the table as pink rose from Aalya's throat and spread across her cheeks. She kept her eyes steady on her plate of rice, as if the question hadn't been directed at her. Finally, Sweetie's gaze went past her to Rozeena's mother at the head of the table.

"Did you say he's like a son to you?"

Her mother's hand lay firm and flat on the white embroidered tablecloth. "Since Partition. Since he lost his mother the same night we lost Faysal." She spoke clearly, loudly, and without any hesitation.

Shareef entered with fresh roti, offering an excuse for a pause in conversation while he determined which guest required more bread. Shehzad raised an index finger but quickly lowered it when Sweetie tapped her fork on her empty side plate. Shareef deposited the steam-filled roti, puffed up like a balloon from the open flame.

"Sad," Sweetie said, stabbing the roti with a fork to release the steam. It snaked up as the balloon collapsed into a flat disc. "Waleed is gone too." Her bosom heaved and dropped with a sigh. "And apparently he tripped or slipped and fell over the boundary wall."

Aalya finally looked up and locked eyes with Rozeena, who tried to keep her voice calm.

"Is that what the police are saying, their conclusion?" she asked Sweetie.

"Yes, and Waleed's family has accepted it." Sweetie nodded, adding no critical remarks. She wouldn't pursue it further as long as her business relationship with the family remained intact and unharmed.

"When did this happen? It wasn't in the newspaper." Rozeena frowned.

"It'll be in *Dawn* tomorrow morning." Sweetie had all the information.

Rozeena's mother shook her head. "Such a terrible, terrible tragedy. One child lost and the other—"

"An invalid for life." Sweetie's eyes flicked toward Aalya before continuing. "Our Rozeena here has made an unusual choice for her future as well." She spoke between big bites as she told everyone what Rozeena's mother had divulged the previous evening. "Moving to that place, can you imagine? I think only laborers live there."

Aalya's eyes pulsed. Rozeena hadn't told her yet. She'd kept a secret too. Meanwhile, Aalya's parents made appropriate comments of surprise followed by genuine pleasure that Rozeena wouldn't be leaving for Lahore now.

"If your khala weren't moving there with you, this would be completely unacceptable," Sweetie said. "You do understand, don't you?"

Before Rozeena could answer, Aalya blurted, "But if you're staying in Karachi, why leave this house? Your house?"

Rozeena swallowed. "We have to sell it." And return the money to Zohair and Rauf, she wanted to add. Would Aalya and Zohair ever forgive Rozeena's family for taking and taking and taking, if they knew?

"But why? You can work in God Bless and stay here."

"It's too expensive, Aalya," Rozeena said quickly. "You know that. We've had the sewage pipe burst and the car problems, and we need so many other repairs constantly." She hadn't planned on telling Aalya in this way, in front of everyone.

"And now there's no need for you to spend on the house at all." Sweetie pushed away her empty plate and leaned back. "Because I'm buying it."

"Yes," Rozeena said. "It's staying in the family and—" But her mother's hand flew to squeeze her arm tight.

"No, no." Sweetie waved her large, thick hand. "Not staying in the family. We're having it demolished, the whole house. Didn't you know?"

"What?" Rozeena's head swung to her mother. "What?"

"What does it matter?" Her mother tightened her hold. "It's a house, a building. That's all."

"But why didn't you tell me?" And turning to Sweetie, Rozeena added, "Why would you do this?"

Sweetie's satiated face and Shehzad's bowed head indicated that this had been the condition. This was what Sweetie was getting for allowing Rozeena to taint the family's image by lowering her address, her neighborhood, her status.

She remembered now, Sweetie's reaction to the commercial buildings, universities, and other structures that had cropped up in the area behind Prince Road. The two of them had been up on the roof when Sweetie had warned Rozeena of the odd neighbors and the rumors about Rozeena that had to stop before they harmed Sweetie herself. That day, she must've hit upon the idea of grabbing up property here for development while prices were low.

"It's nothing, Rozee." Her mother patted her arm over and over again.

Rozeena disagreed. Her lips quivered with anger.

"Yes, it's nothing at all." Aalya jumped up from her chair and rushed around to her side. "Are you done with dinner?" Without waiting for a reply, she grabbed Rozeena's arm and led her across the drawing room and out the double doors onto the veranda.

Aalya held on to Rozeena's waist as they faced the moonlit garden and the front gate, the gate Rozeena had entered with her father and mother just weeks after losing Faysal. Here, her father had said they'd build their future. Here, Rozeena would grow to be independent. And now because of her independent, selfish choices, the house would be destroyed.

She dropped onto her knees, onto the hard black-and-white tiles. Bending over, she placed her hands flat before her and let the winter cold of the ground seep through her fingertips, her palms, her forearms. But still, hot shame grew in her chest, her throat. She bent over to touch her forehead to the cool tiles, but Aalya yanked at her arm, pulling it over her shoulders and hoisting Rozeena off the ground.

"Why didn't you tell me?" Aalya led her to the chairs laid out in a semicircle facing the garden.

Rozeena refused to sit. It was easier not to face Aalya but to be held by her instead. They remained shoulder to shoulder, practically cheek to cheek.

"I know. I know," Aalya said. "I didn't tell you either, about saying yes to Zohair. But you knew I would." She sighed. "Are we being selfish, Rozee, you and I?"

Rozeena took several deep breaths to calm herself. They'd both tried so hard to fulfill their responsibilities. She reminded herself that they were still doing so, only differently, in their own ways—letting go of some things, holding on to others.

"No. We're not selfish."

Rozeena would let go of the house. It had served its purpose. If this was Sweetie's condition, Rozeena would accept it. What did it matter if the house stood or not when she wouldn't be living in it anyway?

"I won't be far. And God Bless isn't all that bad." Her voice sounded lighter, even to herself.

Aalya's face lit up. "It's a new start, for both of us, isn't it?" She bit her lip. "We have a plan too, Rozee."

"You and Zohair?"

"Yes, but it's my plan," she said, with a wide smile. "My and my parents' plan."

The doors behind them swung open, and everyone stepped onto the veranda. Rozeena pushed back her shoulders, lifted her chin, and presented a smile especially for her mother whose relief was visible.

But Shehzad ducked past Rozeena and went straight for the chair at the far end of the semicircle. Before sitting down, he angled it so his back was toward everyone else.

"Shehzad Uncle?" Rozeena called.

He didn't respond, and a brand-new shiver ran down her spine.

There was something more. There was something worse coming from Sweetie.

38

NOW, 2019

How do you fight this traffic every day, Rozee?"

She laughs at Haaris's state in the back seat of her car. With one hand, he grips the handle above the door. The other arm is straight out in front, holding on to Pervez's headrest. Every once in a while, Haaris slams his foot on an imaginary brake and veers away from vehicles too close to his window.

"Why do they drive so close?" He shakes his head. "Six lanes of cars on four-lane roads."

"Don't they have cars and trucks and buses in Minnesota?" She smiles. "Anyway, we're nearly sixteen million in Karachi, so yes, it gets a bit busy."

They stop at a traffic signal, and he exhales. "It's unrecognizable."

His face is glued to the window now, the high-rises and the endless buildings, the packed expressways between circular overpasses and broad underpasses. They've left their bubble and are far from their spacious homes with tree-lined, relatively empty roads, far from residential areas interspersed with fancy restaurants and quaint shops selling imported cheese.

"Can we stop at God Bless first?" He turns to her. "Is it still there?"

Rozeena nods. His questions are childlike, so inconsistent with the folds of skin around his eyes and that white plume. She's offered to take him around Karachi this morning, but it's a weekday and traffic will be worse in that part of the city, the old part now. But Haaris wants to revisit it. He'll be gone in three days, back to Minnesota. She hopes this drive will satisfy him, fill him enough to make him forget his other desires, such as talking to Mansur.

When they get out of the car in God Bless, Haaris doesn't know which way to look.

"I haven't been here in years, in decades, myself," Rozeena says.

Pervez waits at the curb, while they squint against the near-noon sun trying to recognize the area. She steps back into the doorway of a tailor shop. At least there's a strong breeze in the shade. They have no idea where they are.

"It's grown beyond the little main street it used to be."

"It looks like it's eaten up all the neighboring homes," Haaris says.

"That's what happens, doesn't it? Commercial areas expand, changing the neighborhood." She peers down the street. "God Bless is practically part of downtown now."

The width of the street is still the same but filled with exhaust fumes and honking unlike before. It doesn't look like it's been swept in days. After a while, they recognize some of the old, squat buildings sandwiched between modern blocks of shops. But they still can't determine where Rozeena's clinic would've been.

"It's probably been razed to the ground," Haaris says, shaking his head.

"It's progress. Nothing to mourn. As countries go, we're still very young, just in our seventies. It's like children having to adjust to their suddenly taller, longer limbs." She smiles at her clever comparison. "A growth spurt."

He pulls out a white handkerchief from his trouser pocket. Not many men carry one nowadays. Mopping August humidity off his face and neck, he nods.

"Yes, but it wasn't even a peaceful childhood for Pakistan, what with Russia invading Afghanistan and millions of refugees pouring in over the mountains."

"What were we supposed to do? Say no?" She shakes her head. "Your America must feel so safe, sitting far and pretty from the rest of the world. Here, if nations want to reach the warm sea, our sea, they wage wars." She starts walking toward the corner down the road. "Maybe the old milk shop is still there."

He falls into step. "All I'm saying is that it's a shame it happened. The invasion, the wars that came from it, they all changed the course of the country."

They reach the end of the street and the end of Rozeena's patience. She's tired of politics and of the same mistakes being made, over and over again.

"No milk shop here," she says, and they head back to the car and its dry, cool air-conditioning.

Her nape is slick. Sitting in the back seat, she dabs it with a tissue that immediately shreds into pieces. Haaris reaches over and picks off white specks from the back of her neck. She turns to him, and his fingers grow still. She remembers too. Right here in God Bless, he touched her like this, in the empty flat above her clinic. He caressed her nape and told her he'd always love her.

He'd known then what was going to happen. But she hadn't.

She reaches up and behind for his hand now and holds it between her own. "It feels like a lifetime ago, doesn't it?" With a couple of affectionate pats, she lets him go.

His hand drops onto his lap, palm up, and she sees a flash of her seashells resting there, his offerings, his gifts for her from Clifton Beach. He never did complete her collection. She glances up at him and sees his smile has faded, like her own.

They arrive at Prince Road within minutes. The road itself is much the same, preserved because it's so short and not a throughway to anywhere. Haaris gets out and stands in the middle, hands on his hips, rotating in place slowly. Rozeena stares at the spot where her gate used to be. It's a white metal gate now.

"When did your mother move back from Lahore, Rozee?"

She feels Haaris's hand, heavy on her shoulder, as she stares up at the place where her house used to be. Her mother's departure still hurts Rozeena's heart, and he knows it, but it's a dull ache now, a memory of pain.

It happened the night of Shehzad's welcome dinner, with newly engaged Aalya and her family there too. After dinner, when they all moved out onto the veranda, Sweetie revealed her second condition. As a decent and respectable widow should do, Rozeena's mother would move to Lahore and live with Shehzad instead of moving to that godforsaken neighborhood with Rozeena.

She remembers pleading with her mother later that night.

"Stay. Please. You don't have to go. If Sweetie Aunty is letting me stay, then you can too."

"What Sweetie considers acceptable for you is different from what she demands of me," her mother said. "If Sweetie wants this, I must agree. Otherwise, your life here will never be your own, Rozee."

"What will she do if you don't listen, drag me out of God Bless?"

But Rozeena knew before her mother had to say the words. "They're powerful people. If she doesn't want you to have a clinic, you won't."

"It took some years," she says to Haaris now. "Ammi visited us in God Bless off and on from Lahore, but after Mansur came . . ." She shook her head remembering Sweetie's horror at the news of a new-born in unmarried Rozeena's household. "Ammi's move was delayed a little longer. Even when I had enough money for a more respectable address, it wasn't until I married that my status normalized, to a certain extent." She ends with a smile.

Haaris laughs, knowing full well that Sweetie wouldn't have considered Javaid, the animal doctor, an ideal match. But it was respectable enough, and at least Sweetie knew Javaid's family.

"I was so lucky to have him." Rozeena's smile widens as she thinks of Javaid. "He never cared about what people said, you know? He loved Mansur like his own, even before we discovered I couldn't have children myself. And he knew I had given up my mother to her weak brother, so I could follow my path in God Bless. He waited until I was solidly on my own feet. Only then would I marry him."

Haaris is so still she wonders if he's even listening, or perhaps he doesn't like hearing about how good her husband had been.

"You're facing the wrong way, Haaris. These flats are where my house used to be, remember? And Zohair and Aalya's too. Don't you want to see your own house?"

"It's all gone," Haaris says slowly. "All the green is gone."

"Of course. People in this neighborhood can't afford to give up land for jasmine bushes and grass, and certainly not for three-tiered fountains."

The flats are a dusty sand color. Children's voices rise over the boundary wall. She remembers there was a small courtyard between the two blocks of flats, each building four stories high. She'd seen the new construction after Sweetie's company completed the project. Later, they'd built a third block of flats in place of Aalya and Zohair's house.

Rozeena and Haaris start a careful walk down the road now, pointing out new buildings in place of old homes and trying to guess where those families moved to and what they're doing.

"None of them would've guessed you'd have clinics all over the city one day." Haaris shakes his head, impressed.

"None of us knew what our futures would be, did we?" She keeps her head down, careful to watch her step.

"And no one would've thought I'd be a maali."

She stops, surprised at this mention of his green thumb, as Zara calls it, and looks up at Haaris's face, lit with an open smile, a silent chuckle.

"You didn't know, did you? Apa has never considered it respectable, even though my landscaping company has grown quite large over the years, spanning forty-eight states now."

"Your Apa told everyone here that you were doing extremely well taking care of family business in America. We didn't know what you were actually doing."

"She was right, in the beginning. I did start with the family business. Gardening was just a hobby. But it also felt like a connection to here, to all of us and Zohair's garden too." They're standing at the end of the short road now, and he turns around as if to face the ghosts of their childhood homes. "And to you, Rozee. Remember that first morning after I returned from Liverpool? I went looking for you and found you right there, outside your gate."

"You remember that?"

"I remember everything." He turns to her. "I remember how things could've been different."

She's silent. What is there to say now, at the end of their lives?

He falls in step with her as they head back. When they reach his old house, she stops. "Aren't you curious to see what they've done inside?"

It's one of the few original homes still standing, painted a stark white now. The twin tamarind trees in the back are long gone and replaced by a parking lot with its own black metal gate to one side of the boundary wall. A sign on Haaris's original gatepost reads KRT COMPANIES.

Haaris glances at the house, all the way up to the roof, before turning away. "I want to fix what I can before I die, Rozee." He looks her straight in the eye. "That's why I need to tell Mansur the truth. I need to make my hell a little less painful, maybe."

There it is, what she's been dreading.

He gestures to the white BMW turning onto the street from the main road. Apa's driver is meeting him here for some other visits today.

"I leave in three days, and I'd like a meeting with Mansur."

She takes a deep breath. "Do you remember how shocked you were the other day, when you thought I'd told Zara about your Welcome Home Ball? You were terrified I'd told her everything."

"I'm ashamed of it. How can I not be? But of course you wouldn't have told her."

"I wouldn't ever tell anyone. Our lives took a sharp turn after Waleed." She hasn't said his name out loud in decades. "And now you want to turn everything upside down, again? I don't understand, Haaris. Why would you want to hurt Mansur?"

"It's about doing the right thing, this time at least." His hair lifts with a breeze giving him even more height over her.

"No. It's not the right thing to do for Mansur. Telling him where he came from isn't like coming here to the old neighborhood." She lifts her chin. "It's not like coming back to Karachi after half a century, walking around staring at a couple of buildings, commenting on how it's all so different now, a little run-down and much more congested, but nostalgic just the same." She shakes her head. "Telling Mansur will hurt him so much that . . ." She has to squeeze her eyes shut for a moment before continuing ahead to her car.

"But it's the right thing to do."

"For who? Just yourself." She reaches her car. "You want to atone before it's too late, that's all."

He shakes his head. "Not only that. Mansur wants to know. He's been emailing—"

She raises a shaking hand to silence him. Her breath comes fast. "Yes, you told me already." Her words are clipped now, between clenched teeth. "But a little bit of medical history is not worth discovering whose biological son you are." She rocks on her feet with the effort it takes to utter these words. "I will not talk of this further."

She gets into her car, but before Pervez can shut the door, Haaris grabs hold of it and lowers his face to hers in the back seat.

"I want this to be our decision, like the ones we made before. That's why I'm here." He softens his voice to a whisper. "After Fez died, I knew I had to respond to Mansur's emails, but not without seeing you first. I want you to want this too. Let's fix what we can, together."

He straightens then and steps back to allow the car door to close.

She blinks at him through the window but says nothing, terrified that if she doesn't agree to the meeting between Mansur and Haaris, he'll simply email her son with the information.

39

THEN, 1965

Three Months After

The windows were fewer in Rozeena's God Bless flat, and the ceiling was lower than in her old house. In God Bless, the fan had to whip at full speed in March.

"Maybe it's good that Ammi is in Lahore." Rozeena dragged a chair across the concrete gray to join Khala on the balcony after dinner. "At least she's more comfortable there."

"Why do you say that?" Khala snapped. "What more do you need? We have everything here."

Khala slid the drying clothes to one side of the line so both of them had a view of the street. Everything was shut, dark and quiet except for the laughter of children in the flat next door.

"And Dawood says it's peaceful here," Khala said.

He'd been one of their constant visitors from the old life, as Rozeena referred to it. She imagined he was comfortable here because he was used to his mother choosing the odd path, and because he only visited at night when the noise was less.

But Khala was right that they lacked for nothing, even though they'd sold the house and car. Rozeena's clinic was growing, and their needs were not many. She'd asked the sign maker two stores down to paint the board above her clinic, DR. ROZEENA MASOOD, in big, bright red letters. In return, she was pediatrician to his three young children. These were her new neighbors, on the main street and in the web of streets behind. They'd accepted her and Khala as a novelty, not firmly belonging to this place, but here for now, offering a necessary service at an affordable price. Even the hakim across the street had visited to welcome her.

"When Ammi comes in July, maybe she'll stay."

"If Sweetie lets her stay, that is," Khala snorted.

Leaning back in the chair she'd brought from the old veranda, Rozeena sought out Aalya's house down the street and across the way. They met regularly, but Rozeena had to visit them on Prince Road since the stairs to this flat made it difficult for Zohair.

She sighed with relief thinking of Zohair. He was a free man, living in his own home. She'd gotten what she'd asked for.

The day after Sweetie made the announcement about the police closing the investigation, Rozeena had run down and grabbed the *Dawn* at the front gate. Sweetie's news had been correct. The article was on the front page, bottom left. Waleed's death had been deemed an accident. The lack of bruising, cuts, or other evidence of an altercation had also contributed to the decision. With the paper rolled tight in her fist, she'd run across the street to Haaris, wanting confirmation that the police themselves, alone, had come to accept the slipping and tripping and falling story.

But of course they hadn't. Kulsoom's photographs had done the job.

Zohair was safe. That's what mattered.

She blinked at the dark building in the distance and pictured Zohair's garden, another one of the few constants in Rozeena's life—the fountain, the tamarind tree, and pink bougainvillea arching above the gate. A baby kangi palm had been added too. Haaris had brought it from his house. He said he would've given one to Rozeena too, but she didn't have a garden anymore. Her old house was long gone, demolished.

A car crawled up the street toward them now—Haaris or Dawood. Who else would be driving on a street where every store was shut and no one owned a car? As it neared, she recognized it, and the date was right too.

She jumped up. "He's here. Are we ready?"

Khala heaved herself off the chair with a grunt. "No one would believe you're a pediatrician. Why are you so worried?"

Rozeena released a quivering breath. "I'm not worried. It's a huge responsibility, that's all."

"Yes, it is, and we're ready." Khala offered a rare smile before adding, "Go now. Go bring them upstairs. What are you waiting for?"

Rozeena met Haaris on the street and walked him up slowly, carefully opening doors and telling him to watch his step, pointing out the higher threshold, the turn in the hallway.

"I have nieces and nephews, you know? I have some practice," he said with a smile. "I won't drop him."

Him. A boy. Rozeena pursed her lips to contain a sudden rush within, unable to comprehend her extreme emotions for this tiny stranger.

Inside the small main room, Khala had propped open the doors to the balcony to let in a breeze. Rozeena quickly walked ahead and settled herself on one end of the only sofa.

"Here, bring him to me," she said, extending her arms out.

The baby was perfect.

She wanted to unwrap him and check each part of him, certain he'd be even more perfect than she could imagine, but she sensed both Haaris and Khala staring down at her. They hadn't moved from where they stood in front, eyes steady on the woman and child, mother and son. Were they thinking she'd made a mistake? That she should've found some other, more conventional family to take the baby?

No.

"Welcome to your home, Mansur," she said softly, rocking him so his eyes closed again. She touched the tip of his nose, his chin, his forehead. His hair was full, a shocking black.

Haaris pulled out some documents from his trouser pocket and read out the information, time of birth, baby's weight. "And of course you can have the name put on the birth certificate." He paused. "Why Mansur?"

Without taking her eyes off the baby, Rozeena said, "It means victorious."

She thought perhaps he was already victorious by coming to her instead of being delivered to an orphanage. Her chest tightened. No, there were no winners here, only survivors, like his mother, Kulsoom.

Rozeena marveled at how Kulsoom had managed to hide the pregnancy from Waleed's family, and from everyone else too. Even Rozeena had missed the signs, the chronic fatigue, the blossoming abdomen. But the divorce and Waleed's accident had easily explained away Kulsoom's dark circles, and winter shawls with purses held tight to one's stomach managed to hide a lot as well. In the final three months Kulsoom hadn't been spotted by anyone anywhere, and now she'd delivered her son in secret. Her family obviously had some well-trusted doctor friends.

"His name is Mansur, so he may overcome all his difficulties, all the challenges," Rozeena said, like his mother had done, rightly or wrongly. Rozeena would not judge her.

"I don't want my child to go to an orphanage," Kulsoom had said to Rozeena over the phone after they met in God Bless, perhaps because she'd been unable to say those words face-to-face. "It has to be a family like mine, like yours. That's what I want in return for giving up those photographs." For saving Zohair, for blackmailing Waleed's family into silence. "Find him a good home, and make sure he never learns who his parents were. I don't want him to ever wonder what Waleed did to me."

Rozeena didn't ask what that meant. She didn't want to know if Waleed had beaten his wife and forced her to submit. And she didn't want to know if Mansur was the result. Looking down at him now, all she felt was intense love for this being who was the only completely blameless one in all these happenings.

"Mansur is a good name," Khala said. "I don't know what your parents were thinking when they named you. With a name like Rozeena, of course you'd be destined to bring home the rozee, the daily wages, for the rest of your life."

Rozeena laughed as she patted the seat next to her. She saw right through Khala's criticism to the pride she felt for Rozeena's work, for her decision to remain in Karachi, and now for accepting Mansur. Her mother and Khala both knew he was Kulsoom's child, but that was all they knew. And Rozeena hoped Mansur himself would always remain untouched by everything that had preceded his existence.

As she passed him to Khala's eager arms, he didn't feel like penance or like atonement. He didn't feel like something she owed Kulsoom or anyone else.

Mansur was pure.

"Does Kulsoom know he's here?"

Haaris shook his head, still standing before her, refusing to sit. "She said she didn't want to know where he went. She'd never imagine you'd keep him yourself."

And she'd never discover it by chance either, now that Rozeena had exited from the society where Kulsoom lived.

"But she trusts you to keep your promise, Rozee."

She nodded. Of course she would. This was the only good that had come from all they'd done.

She walked downstairs with Haaris. His driver stood by the car holding the door open. There was no one else on the road, not even at the milk shop on the corner, the one with the longest line in the morning. Each time Rozeena passed by it she was grateful the sour smell was far enough so it couldn't invade her clinic. She much preferred the general store next door with its mix of spices, soaps, and daals. These were scents of home that eased her panic when she was reminded, a hundred times a day, how little of her old life remained. But then she'd remind herself of what her parents had done, left everything behind and crossed the border into Pakistan, and that without Faysal. Their little leftover family had survived, found sustenance and even new family on Prince Road.

And she'd found Haaris.

He stood there before her in his white shirt with the rolled-up sleeves. The breeze was strong outside. Her loose hair crisscrossed over her face while he glanced up at the sign and then down at her.

"What is it, Haaris?"

He shook his head, frowning. He stared at his polished shoes for so long she thought he'd fallen asleep, until he spoke. "I'm leaving, Rozee."

"Leaving?"

He looked up then. "I'm leaving Pakistan."

"What?" She pushed strands of hair off her face. "For how long? For more studying?"

He shook his head. "Because of everything." He jutted his chin toward Prince Road.

"But everything is settled now."

"Settled?" He lowered his voice. "Is that what you think?"

"What are you saying?" she whispered back, afraid Khala would hear from the balcony.

He shook his head and kept on shaking it at the ground until finally he stilled and looked up. "Let's go inside."

She flipped on the ceiling fan and lights in her clinic, and they sat down on the waiting room chairs against the wall.

"I have one more obligation to Kulsoom, for those photographs." He spoke so softly against the fan's noise that she had to lean in.

He closed his eyes, his forehead creased in pain.

"What is it, Haaris?" Her heart beat loudly in her ears.

"Kulsoom and I . . . we have to . . . we have to marry."

"What? What are you saying, Haaris?"

His eyes flew open and overflowed, spilling tears down both cheeks.

"No, Haaris. No. Why are you saying this?" Her voice trembled.

Looking down, he slammed his forehead with both hands, once, twice. "Because it's true. It's true, Rozee, and I agreed to it. I promised her, for the photographs. She wouldn't do it otherwise. I did it for you, and—"

"For me?" She jumped up and grabbed his shoulders. "Look at me! Look at me!"

He lifted his head and looked at her with defeat. She pulled him to her chest. "You just have to say no, Haaris." He tightened his arms around her middle, vibrating with the tension. "You don't have to do it anymore. Zohair is safe. It's done. Settled."

Her front soaked with his tears until finally, his breathing slowed down, relaxed. It would be all right, she thought. He'd say no to Kulsoom and take back the promise.

Keeping one arm around her, he pulled over a chair and lowered her onto it, so they faced each other.

"Zohair isn't safe yet." Haaris's voice was stronger now. "Kulsoom's family can deny the photographs, take back the truth. I told her about us, Rozee, and Kulsoom agreed easily not to marry. But her parents say they will take it all back, deny everything, if we don't do it."

"But I took her baby. I kept my promise. Why do they want more?"

"It's their solution to her divorce, a respectable way out, and away."

"Yes, but—"

"You told me to use whatever I got from Kulsoom, anything and everything, for Aalya's sake, you said. For their sake."

Her eyes twitched, stinging, but she kept her grip tight on Haaris's hands, shaking him, refusing to agree.

"You have to stay here with me. You have to, for me. For us."

"But Zohair . . ."

She fell over their hands, crying from deep inside. "No, no, no." She wailed and pleaded.

His head shuddered over hers, moving to meet her cheeks with his, her lips with his, her tears with his until they were holding each other exhausted and broken.

The next day, Haaris and Kulsoom married.

By the end of the week, they left the country.

A week later, Zohair left too.

From her seat next to Aalya, Rozeena scanned his drawing room, filled now with furniture and lamps and even a carpet.

"Won't Zohair wonder where all the money suddenly came from?" Rozeena had asked Rauf when he'd first filled it up and then had the whole house, top to bottom, painted a fresh, bright white before the wedding a couple of months ago.

Rauf had smiled. "I told him it's from the sale of some old property."

Rozeena couldn't bear to think of the anger and hurt Zohair would've felt if he'd discovered where the money came from. She'd been terrified of losing him.

But ultimately, she did lose Zohair.

The fan whipped overhead sending the sweet scent of burning

incense sticks to all corners. Even though the windows were open, heat radiated from the number of people filling every chair and every inch of white sheets covering the floor. Rozeena swiped at her damp upper lip with the back of her free hand. The other held Aalya's fingers, limp and clammy cold.

Aalya had been told to sit on the main sofa since she was the closest family, Zohair's widow.

Aalya's mother sat on her other side, and outside in the garden, poor Rauf prayed with the men for his son's soul before they all left for the graveyard.

Rozeena shut her eyes and shook her head in disbelief for the hundredth time since last night. The telephone had rung in her God Bless flat. Slowly, taking deep breaths after every few words, Ibrahim had recounted the news of his son-in-law. Zohair's wheelchair had been hit by a bus on the main road, at the end of their short Prince Road.

Zohair had been on his usual route to the nearby market. He'd been waiting to cross the road when the bus driver lost control of his vehicle and drove right into Zohair. An unfortunate and unforeseeable mechanical fault, they said.

How could this have happened, she kept asking herself now.

But accidents do happen, however tragic, however devastating.

40

NOW, 2019

It isn't by accident that Rozeena has waited for Haaris's last day in Karachi to arrange the meeting.

As she leads him in from the foyer, Haaris stops in the drawing room, at the windows facing her garden. "Your kangi palm there." He points. "Zara told me it's related to the one in our old house."

"That's right. It's a descendant of the one you gave Ibrahim Uncle for Zohair's garden."

She smiles at the plant before moving ahead.

"I thought we could have chai at the dining table. It looks like it might rain finally, so the veranda won't work." The table is set for three. Haaris sits to her right. "Who else have you been visiting here these past few days? You haven't been in touch with Aalya, have you?"

He shakes his head. "The last time I spoke to Aalya was the day after Zohair died," he says quietly. "I called from London after Apa passed on the news to me. Apa said our parents should sell the house and move away as soon as possible. So many deaths in the neighborhood was a bad sign." He pauses. "And what about you? Are you still in touch with Aalya?"

"Not quite. You know she moved to Nairobi six months after Zohair passed?"

Haaris nods.

Aalya's new marriage, arranged quickly by her parents, had been to a widower with two young children. Within a few years, Aalya had two children of her own. The family of six then moved from Nairobi to Dubai, and ultimately three generations of them settled in Toronto.

"She never answered my last few letters." Rozeena doesn't add that she sent them decades ago. Since then, she's only heard of Aalya through friends of friends. Lately, there's been little news, or perhaps Rozeena has not remembered to ask. Her throat constricts at the sudden thought. "She may not even be here anymore."

"You were like sisters, and now you don't even know if she's alive."

It's not a question or an accusation, so Rozeena lets the statement go unanswered. She's lived long enough to know that love manifests in different ways. Aalya sounded happier when she wasn't reminded of the past, and Rozeena embodied that past.

"I used to check the stores, the herbal medicine and newfangled ones, you know?" A slow smile appears on Haaris's face. "I was certain I'd see Zolya one day. I wanted to see it."

She nods. It had been Aalya's idea, the one she'd hinted at when she told Rozeena about her engagement to Zohair.

Zolya would've been established with Ibrahim's family recipes, combining herbs and regular kitchen spices to alleviate basic, everyday ailments. Aalya's father had kept those practices hidden for years, like his ancestry of serving masters, whether in the kitchen or in the garden. After Zohair's accident when both families, upstairs and downstairs, had nearly lost everything, Aalya and her parents decided to embrace it all. Zolya, from Zohair + Aalya, would be born from the secrets, the lies, and the rubble.

"It was the perfect big idea Zohair had been looking for, and they had the perfect logo," Haaris says now.

Rozeena remembers the bold and black text of Zolya clearly, with the green feather-like tamarind leaf underlining it. They would've started on a small scale, using the money Rozeena's mother returned to Zohair's father. Ibrahim grew the plants himself, so the ingredients would be affordable and of the best quality. They'd start by preparing mixtures and selling them from the house. Slowly, they'd expand Zolya, and perhaps one day people would've found the cures in stores outside Pakistan as well.

"It would've been a huge success. The world is hungry now for all these natural remedies," Haaris continues. "You can find turmeric and—"

"Don't, Haaris. What's the point?" Zolya died with Zohair.

A car honks at the gate, silencing him further. He pulls his back straight and places both hands on the white embroidered tablecloth.

They watch Mansur enter the foyer. "The artwork looks fantastic," he says, walking up to Rozeena to give her a kiss before shaking hands with Haaris.

She's hung Zara's framed drawing above the sideboard, and the old 1964 photograph sits below. Neither picture looks appealing to Rozeena right now. One is a fading memory she wants to tuck away in a drawer, the other a ghostly reminder of Haaris's reemergence.

Tea is served immediately to give everyone something to do. Basheer serves samosas with tamarind chutney, pound cake, cubed mangoes, deep fried pakoras to go with the rainy season, and more. Mansur is eager to please, polite as usual. But he's fidgeting today. He stirs his tea too long, especially since there's no sugar in it, and rambles on about the old times as if he knows anything.

Finally, he says, "Haaris Uncle, what can you tell me about my origins?"

Perspiration dots Haaris's forehead even though the air-conditioning is set on high, pulsing out cool air overhead. Slowly, he leans back in his chair.

"Unfortunately, I don't know any more than your mother, Mansur. It's just how things were done in those days. Not many records and such."

Mansur asks a few more questions, trying to find a way to the truth.

Rozeena keeps her eyes lowered, hovering just below the faces around her. Fingers tightly interlaced on her lap, shoulders tense and up at her ears, she braces herself for any unexpected revelations.

When there's quiet all around, and Haaris has revealed absolutely nothing, Rozeena releases her rigid fingers and looks up. Mansur is slumped back in his chair, disappointed but not wholly surprised. Haaris stares over Mansur's head at Zara's drawing, nodding like he knew that particular day had been the beginning of the end for them.

"I should go," he says. "My flight is tonight, and I have a lot of packing . . . also Apa . . . some things to get done."

His disjointed words worry Rozeena but not enough to ask him to stay longer. She doesn't want him to change his mind about what he hasn't revealed. She walks him out, telling her son to remain at the table.

Halfway down the driveway, Haaris stops. His mouth dips on the ends, like his shoulders, tired.

"I fought with Kulsoom for this, for permission to tell her son where he came from. But I won't fight you, Rozee." His eyes fill instantly and spill tears over the folds and the lines. "I never said sorry to you. I should've worked harder. I should've looked harder for another solution. For you. For us."

His words take her breath away. She blinks through continuous tears of her own, like they've been collecting for years. "I should've said sorry too, Haaris. I made you do all those things, the ones you never wanted to do, the ones you always ran away from."

They nod, unable to look away from each other. She sees the same brown eyes of years ago, shrouded now by loose skin. And she sees sadness in those eyes, the sadness captured in the photograph on her sideboard and then replicated in the drawing above.

It frightens her, like he foresees the end of something else now.

He reaches for her shoulder and squeezes, pressing down with his weight, adding to the heaviness of August's humidity around them.

"I won't make this decision without you. You're his mother, Rozee."

Her face crumples, lips quivering. "Yes, I am his mother."

Haaris leaves then, and she knows they'll never meet again. She watches his car vanish down the road before going back inside. From the foyer, she sees Mansur pour himself another cup of tea and check his phone.

Yes, she's his mother, and Mansur is her son.

But he's also a whole, complete being in himself. She's done her job, brought him up, loved and cared for him with her entire being. Now he belongs to himself and the earth and the skies.

She waits until he's done scrolling through whatever he sees on his screen. Then, she wipes her hands one by one on her kameez. Her face feels as damp as her palms. She releases a long, shaky breath and enters the room.

Author's Note

Like Rozeena's family, both my parents' families crossed the border into Pakistan at the time of Partition. After celebrating independence, they joined the millions of people who migrated, who were displaced, who ran and became refugees. But historical facts and numbers, however horrific the scale, don't convey the true human impact, the life-altering consequences, and the trauma that ripples through generations.

It's the personal stories that speak to us.

Under the Tamarind Tree grew from my desire to learn more about my parents' lives in their youth and about their families' struggles during and after Partition.

Like many characters in the novel, there are those in my family who never speak of the past. During my research and writing, I finally came to learn about some of their experiences, and many of those emotional truths are explored and reflected in the book.

As I was researching the book's historical setting through sources such as newspaper archives, documentaries, and works by historians and journalists, I came across the Oral History Project of the Citizens Archive of Pakistan, as well as the 1947 Partition Archive. Both these organizations record and preserve oral histories of the survivors of Partition. It's been seventy-five years now, and every year there are fewer survivors left. Keeping their stories alive is essential and valuable work that's being conducted by these and other organizations and individuals worldwide.

Acknowledgments

This story grew from an idea into a complete book with the help of many people. Thank you to my agent, Giles Milburn, for seeing the potential in my first few chapters and going on this journey with me. His belief in the book, and in my abilities, pushed me through numerous edit letters and cross-Atlantic Zoom discussions, and with his guidance, I found the story I was hoping to tell.

Thank you to Tara Singh Carlson for being the best editor I could have, for championing this book and bringing it into the world. After our very first telephone conversation, I knew that Tara *got* my book, and it was the most wonderful feeling. I also worked closely with Ashley Di Dio during the editorial process and am so grateful for her razor-sharp insight, brainstorming sessions, and kindness.

To the fabulous people at Putnam, thank you for all the work and effort you put into this book: Anthony Ramondo and Sanny Chiu for the brilliant cover design that I can't stop staring at; Tiffany Estreicher and Laura Corless for the most elegant layout; Madeline Hopkins for such thorough copyedits; and the entire production team, including Emily Mileham, Maija Baldauf, Marie Finamore, and Erin Byrne. Thank you to my publicist, Katie McKee, marketers Shina Patel and Emily Leopold, and also to everyone in sales and distribution who supported *Under the Tamarind Tree*.

My gratitude to Aftab Nabi, former Inspector General of Police, Sindh, and Director General, National Police Bureau, for our conversations about police procedures in Karachi. Thank you to Mehmood Alam Abbasi, Advocate High Court, for his help in understanding the Pakistan Penal Code and for answering my many questions about crime and the law.

To my fellow Madeleine Milburn mentees, Ronali Collings, Sophie Jo, Avione Lee, Francesca Robbins, and Sophia Spiers, I couldn't imagine navigating this mentorship, and everything it's led to, without you. Thank you for the continuous support and for embracing me in every way.

My gratitude to the Loft Literary Center in Minneapolis, where I was fortunate enough to attend numerous craft and critique classes. A special thank-you to Mary Carroll Moore, whose class not only taught me the importance of structure at the scene level but also introduced me to the best writing group ever: Kathleen West, Stacy Swearingen, and Maureen Fischer. I'm so grateful for their gentle and supremely insightful comments that inspired me to keep writing and revising. This book wouldn't exist—not even a chapter—if it weren't for them.

Thank you to Nina Hamza for her abundant wisdom and affection that has sustained me through the ups and downs of publishing, and life, over the years. If we really are long-lost twins, Nina is definitely the better one.

Thank you to my husband's family for always encouraging my never-ending love of learning, which has ultimately led to this book, albeit in a winding way. I'm grateful for all the support and love over the years.

Acknowledgments

To my beloved parents, thank you for everything. I can't even begin to make a list. I appreciate it all, including the many stories you told us growing up—even though I grumbled, saying I'd already heard story #346, while Murad listened patiently and politely. And Murad, your unwavering faith in me since the day I was born has been a precious, powerful gift. I used to laugh it off as simply a sign of an older brother's affection, but now I know your belief in me has made all the difference. Thank you, and I love you.

My darling Ali and Noor, I'm so lucky and blessed to be your ammi. Thank you for all that you've taught me and continue to teach me. I'm humbled, and I'm grateful for every second with you. And dearest Aamer, this book wouldn't even be a seed of an idea without you. Thank you for our life together, for brightening up my world every time I see you, and for being my best friend. I love you, all of you.